WHISTLERS OF THE DARK

TALES FROM THE DARK PAST BOOK 4

HELEN SUSAN SWIFT

PRELUDE

KINGSMOSS PRIORY, SCOTLAND, AUTUMN, 1252 AD.

THE BELL RANG FOR MATINS, with the harsh clamour sounding from the small, squat bell tower across the dark mists that clung to the low damp-lands of the Kings Moss.

The monks rose from their hard beds, some eager, most groggy with sleep, and made their way to the chapel on its inch, the raised island within the Moss.

Brother Matthew shivered, pulled his hood over his head, remembered the dry heat of Outremer, and said a short prayer for strength in this northern chill. A raised timber causeway connected the monk's dormitory to the chapel, with a rudimentary handrail to prevent the monks from slipping into the treacherous peat moss on either side.

"What a place to build a holy site," Brother Simon grumbled.

"God is here as much as anywhere." Brother Matthew tried to sound convincing as the raw cold bit through his woollen habit. He remembered the labour in constructing that causeway, with the monks hewing the wood by hand and carrying it from the Sidlaw Hills' forests to this lonely place. Brother

1

Matthew knew that a long-gone king had founded a religious site here but wished his Grace had chosen a more salubrious spot, away from the miasmic moss and the steep slopes of the hills.

Now the monks filed across the causeway, their sandals slapping on the greasy timber and each man huddled in his black habit. Brother Matthew looked back over the procession, twelve Benedictine monks, which was the entire complement at this small establishment. They moved in silence under the soft rain, for it always seemed to rain here, which was one reason it was the most unpopular of all the Benedictine sites in Scotland. Brother Matthew slipped on the already-green slimed planks, recovered, and smiled. For a moment, his thoughts drifted away to his previous life, and the girl who had not waited for him.

Adelina had been beautiful, with wide blue eyes and a straight nose, and her hair! Her hair would cascade from her head in soft golden curls, scented with birch-water. Brother Matthew shook his head, chasing the memory away. When he returned from Outremer, she was already married to another knight, taking Matthew's joy with him. That life was gone, and women were no longer important in this life of sacrifice, prayer, and work.

An owl hooted from the hills that overlooked the chapel, beyond the black peat of the moss. Another owl answered, and then a low, undulating whistle that Brother Matthew could not identify.

"What kind of bird makes that sound?" he mused, pulled his hood tighter around his head and tried to think of more spiritual matters.

That low, undulating whistle sounded again, vaguely irritating. Brother Matthew could not judge from where it came, which was unusual, for before he took Holy Orders, he had been a Crusader and was well-versed in seeking out potential danger. Not that there was any danger here, in one of God's religious communities.

Brother Matthew thought he heard Brother Paul chanting as he walked and felt glad when he saw the chapel loom ahead, a sanctuary from the cold. The site was ancient, with a Celtic church founded here many years before the Benedictines arrived. It was the Celtic Church that the old King had founded, nearly two-and-a-half centuries ago. Brother Matthew touched the birthmark on his cheek, the mark that people had always ridiculed until he took Holy Orders and joined the Church. The Benedictine monks accepted him for what he was, not for how he looked. And the Benedictines would not replace him with another, unlike the faithless Adelina.

The brothers filed into the small, stone-built chapel, with the tolling of the bell drowning out the rustle of clothing and scuff and shuffle of sandals on the stone-flagged floor.

Only when the bell stopped did the service begin, with the elderly prior taking the lead and the sonorous Latin words echoing from the chapel's austere stones. Brother Matthew tried to concentrate, but his mind slipped away elsewhere, to a land more colourful than grey Scotland, and a place where men and women danced and sang together. He knew it was not the East, where he had seen hard fighting, but somewhere even brighter.

He shook his head, fighting the images that had been so prevalent recently. The Chapel was no place to allow his mind to drift to musicians and dancing, particularly as half the dancers were women, some very shapely and with infinite promise in their eyes. Brother Matthew saw Adelina among the dancers, all alone and with her hands stretched towards him.

"Adelina!" Matthew said, yearning to hold her white hands.

"Brother Matthew!" He heard Brother Paul say his name,

yet moved away, with the lure of Adelina and the dancers too strong to ignore.

The brothers watched him, with some attempting to prevent his leaving and the prior stopping his sermon in mid-sentence. Ignoring them all, Brother Matthew walked out of the chapel. He saw the land ahead, bathed in a soft green light, with a host of people waiting for him with open arms, smiling as they played musical instruments.

"Join us!" the musicians invited without saying a single word. "Come and join us!"

The monks were behind him, their voices harsh in comparison to the whistles of the musicians. "Brother Matthew! The moss! Be careful of the moss!"

"It's all right! We'll look after you!" The young blonde woman stood in front of the musicians, beckoning him over. "Come to me, my love."

Brother Matthew smiled. "Adelina! It's you! You married somebody else when I was out East! You said my birthmark made me ugly." He touched his face.

"It was all a mistake," Adelina said. "I don't mind your birthmark at all. I've been waiting here for you! Come and join us."

Leaving the Causeway, Brother Mathew stepped towards Adelina, laughing, with Adelina's acceptance cancelling out all his vows.

"Look!" Brother Paul shouted from the causeway. "Look who has come to visit us! It is the Holy Father himself! That's who Brother Matthew saw."

"You're right," the prior said. "Imagine the Holy Father coming all this way. We must greet him. Follow me, brothers."

With the prior in the lead, the brothers left the causeway and strode into the moss, shouting out their welcomes. Within five minutes the chapel was empty, with only the wind left to toll the bell. Eventually that, too, eased, and silence descended, broken only by the gentle hiss of rain on the surrounding moss. A single sandal floated on the peaty surface, a reminder of the men who had once worshipped here, and somebody whistled, the undulating sound lonely in that deserted place.

CHAPTER 1

THE BLACK YETT, FORFARSHIRE, SCOTLAND, SEPTEMBER 1899

"Steady, lass!" The driver of the dogcart soothed his horse as it pulled to the right. "She's always skittish here," the driver explained to me. "She doesn't like passing the old graveyard."

We had reached a crossroads, where the Black Yett of Sidlaw, the main road, eased off towards Perth along the foot of the Sidlaw Hills. Our much narrower track headed north, up a pass between two green heights. The driver's old graveyard was tucked behind a moss-furred dry-stane dyke, with a scattering of gravestones at different angles, as if each was trying to escape the bondage of the soil.

"Why is that?" I asked. "Graveyards and such places don't normally frighten horses."

"This one does," the driver said. "Something scared her here a whiley back, and she's never been happy here since."

"The graveyard doesn't look well-kept." I glanced over the wall with little interest.

"No." the driver shook his head. He climbed off his perch to settle the horse, speaking gently, and lowering the beast's head. "Easy lass, I'll lead you. Steady, now."

I remained in the back of the cart as the driver walked us past the graveyard, with its single yew tree dark green and the grass rank over the humps of neglected graves.

"Why is it so unkempt?" I asked.

"It's a suicides' graveyard," the driver said shortly. He said no more until we were a hundred yards beyond the place, and he gave his horse a final caress and resumed his seat.

"Are there many suicides around here?" I asked as a smirr of rain slithered from the hills to wash some of the journey's dust from us.

"Too many," the driver said. "It can be ill land to farm." He flicked the reins on the rump of his horse, and we moved slightly faster. The iron-shod wheels of the cart ground on the unmade road, deepening the grooves made by a thousand previous vehicles over ten centuries of use. People had inhabited this land for millennia, I knew. I could feel the history pressing in on me; I could hear the whispering voices of the long-dead and sense the slow tide of passing years.

To my northern eyes, the land was not ill-favoured. Grass and heather covered the hills, making excellent sheep country, with parks, or fields, where cattle grazed or lay together.

A colourful gypsy wagon passed us, with the driver lifting a hand in acknowledgement and a gaggle of tousle-headed children running behind. When they waved to me, I smiled and waved back.

"Aye, only tinkers and gypsies use this road," my driver said. "Them and men who can't afford to farm decent soil." He shook his head. "We'd be better off without these tinker vagrants."

I said nothing to that, being a bit of a vagrant myself. I watched the caravan lurch around a bend and heard the high-pitched barking of the dogs.

The hills rose on either side; not the craggy granite of my

previous home, but softly smooth, specked with the white forms of hardy, black-faced sheep and redolent with patches of heather. I thought them friendly heights and hoped I had left my bitter memories behind me.

"Aye, it's a dreich day." The driver misinterpreted my thoughts, as people often do.

I nodded agreement. "It's all of that," I said, for the grey drift of rain obscured the sky and dulled the colours of the landscape. I did not mind that, for to me, rain is only another aspect of nature, and without rain, nothing would grow. I was still thinking of that lonely cemetery with the forlorn graves of men and women who lost their strength to live. I could understand them, and what had driven away all the attraction of life.

A whaup called, its cry one of the most melancholic of all bird sounds, and I saw it rise from the grass to my left. With its long, down-curving beak, the whaup was the centre of fear from the superstitious. I watched the hill-bird fly into the rain and knew the crunch of our wheels had frightened it.

"Only a whaup," the driver said over his shoulder. "You've naething to fear from a whaup."

"Aye," I returned. "They've never done me any harm." It was not the birds and beasts of the fields that frightened me; I thought and prayed again that I had left my tormentors behind in the North Country.

"Please, God, let them stay up there. Don't let them follow me to this southern land of Strathmore."

We turned around the spur of a hill, with an outcrop of heather nodding to the sky. The signboard creaked against its iron rings, wind-bucked this way and that as the driver pulled to a halt.

"There you are, Miss." He gave me a sideways look. "It's a gey lonely place this."

I nodded my agreement as I surveyed the surroundings. "Aye, it's all of that."

The driver shook his head. "Are you sure you want off here, now, lassie? I could take you back in a trice."

"I have a position at the farm," I said.

"Aye, well, maybe the reputation is exaggerated." The driver seemed reluctant to let me off his cart.

"I've accepted the position," I said, clambering down onto the track. "I'm sure it will be fine."

"If you think so, Miss," the driver said. "It's a fair bit walk for you." He handed me my case, his fatherly eyes concerned.

"I'm used to walking." I favoured him with a smile and paid him with the scrapings of my purse.

"Well, good luck to you, Miss." The driver cracked his reins over the rump of the horse and turned it in the road-end. He lifted a hand in farewell, opened his mouth to say something, changed his mind and pulled slowly away.

I watched the dogcart jolting on the uneven road and turned my head towards the farm. The path was barely wide enough for a cart, with flat fields stretching on either side to the hills' sweeping slopes. The name hung from a gallows-shaped cross-post at the track's side, still creaking slightly in the biting wind.

Kingsinch, it proclaimed, and yet I never saw anything less like the road to royalty in my life. I did not know which king had been unfortunate enough to venture to this farmtoun in the back of beyond, nor why he should come here.

I shrugged, king or commoner, it made no difference to me. I was here to work, not to speculate on long-forgotten royalty. Let the dead keep the dead.

From the road-end, the track seemed to disappear into the hills, with no sign of a farm-steading. I shrugged, prepared for a long walk. I lifted my bag and stepped onto the track. I say track, but it was more like a causeway, raised slightly above the fields of stubble, and seemed to sway as I walked. Shrugging off the illusion, I put my best foot foremost and stepped out for Kingsinch, with my boots sinking into the cart-ruts of the track and the wind scouring my face.

In one of the fields or parks, as we called them, a lone horseman was ploughing, with reins wrapped around his wrist and his two-horse Clydesdale team moving slowly. A trick of the wind sent the mesmeric hiss of the plough through rich soil to me, with the soft padding of the hooves on the dirt and the horseman's muttered encouragement to his horses.

The horseman noticed me, lifted a hand in salute, and continued with his work. I waved in reply and trudged on, descending a long slope into the lower ground, with moisture gleaming from the newly turned earth and fail-dykes – dykes of turf rather than stone – separating the fields. A few hundred yards later, the track took a decided loop, with a post thrust into the ground on the left side. A lantern hung from the post, swinging madly in the increasing wind. After the dog-leg bend, the track descended steeply, yet managed to retain its height relative to the surrounding fields. I nodded, working out the lie of the land. The fields occupied a drained moss, a boggy moor, with the track built above it.

After a mile, I noticed a battered ruin of a building, or a rickle of a biggin, as we would call it in the north, crouching on a heather-knowe not far off the track. At one time it might have been important, but now it was tumbledown and forlorn with neglect, despite the stone roof that would hold out the rain. I stopped for a moment, wondering what it was and if it was related to the mysterious king who had passed this way. Perhaps it was the wind, easing from the surrounding hills, but I thought I heard somebody whistling at that building. The sound was not unpleasant, but I stopped to listen with the fear growing inside me.

"Oh, God no," I said to myself. "Don't let it happen again. Don't let it happen here as well."

I sighed with relief as a man appeared from behind the old ruin, whistling to three large black mastiffs. He gave me a glower, turned his shoulder, and stalked away, with the dogs at his heels. I moved on, with the farm steading now in sight amidst a group of gnarled trees.

I stopped to take stock of the farmtoun of Kingsinch, where I was to spend the next period of my life. The steading rose from the surrounding fields, like a mediaeval castle within its moat, yet the buildings were blunt, nearly ugly in their uncompromising functionality. Bare stone walls under sloped slate roofs, with small windows with white painted frames. The steading stood four-square against the weather, giving nothing away.

If buildings could speak, these would say, "Here I am, and damn you," to the wind and rain. I could sense Kingsinch's personality as dour, as it glowered at a pitiless world.

"Well?" the woman who stood at the front door was dark-haired, about thirty-five and not ill-looking. She viewed me with disfavour. "Are you coming, or are you going to dawdle there all day?"

I hurried forward. "I am Ellen Luath," I introduced myself. "The new kitchen maid."

"Aye." The woman did not move as she eyed me up and down. "I guessed that."

"Are you Mrs Lunan?" I asked.

"Aye." Mrs Lunan spoke as if she grudged every word she had to release from her taut mouth. She might have been attractive if she smiled more, and men would undoubtedly have found her shape desirable.

"May I come in?"

Mrs Lunan shifted to the side, allowing me a grudging passage.

The farm-kitchen was as austere as the exterior of the building. A plain deal table and four wooden chairs stood on a floor of stone slabs, with a black range in one wall and a wooden worktop stretched along another. A large sink occupied half the third wall. An array of pots, pans, griddles, and other kitchen necessities hung above the worktop, gleaming in the light of the range fire. There was nothing else, no hint of refinement or comfort.

I had seen a lot worse.

"This is where you'll work," Mrs Lunan said. "You'll also help with the milking, and mucking out the byre, and feeding the bothy-lads, and washing, and anything else I require you for."

I nodded and replied, "Yes, Mrs Lunan," for I had expected no less. A kitchen-maid's life was likened to servitude with no hope of reprieve unless a fortunate marriage intervened and damned little reprieve even then.

"You'll sleep in there." Mrs Lunan jerked her thumb towards a door that led from the kitchen. "Second door on the right. You'll share with Agnes."

"Yes, Mrs Lunan," I said again.

"Well, what are you standing around for? Can't you see the floor needs scrubbing? Get on with it!"

Welcome to Kingsinch.

I got on with it. Depositing my bag and coat on one of the chairs, I fetched a pail, filled it from the pump outside, hitched up my skirt and knelt on the floor. Mrs Lunan threw a scrubbing-brush and a cake of hard green soap to me, watched for a minute, grunted disapprovingly, and stalked away to spread joy to another part of the steading.

I was never averse to hard work, so soon had the floor as clean as it had ever been, with the stone slabs gleaming and the cracks between free of any loose grains or other matter. Of course, I knew that scrubbing was as thankless a task as any woman's work, for as soon as the farmer, Mr Lunan, came in from the parks, his boots would spread mud everywhere.

"What are you dawdling for?" Mrs Lunan asked. "There are cows to be milked. They've been bellowing these past ten minutes!"

I was not long back from the byre when I heard Mr Lunan's heavy footsteps, and withdrew to the furthest corner of the kitchen, out of his way. Mr Lunan flung the door open and stormed inside. As I suspected, he was the man I had seen near the old ruin.

"And who might you be?" Mr Lunan was older than his wife, maybe in his mid-fifties, with a salt-and-pepper moustache that a walrus may have envied.

"Ellen Luath," I said. "I'm the new kitchen-maid." I held his eye, noting the shadows behind the iron.

"Are you now?" Mr Lunan said, nodding. "Have you seen the mistress?"

"I have, Mr Lunan," I said.

"Aye." He nodded again. "You're not very tall, are you?"

"No, Mr Lunan," I said. I had always been conscious of my lack of height, although I made up for it with a boldness of temper that stood me in good stead.

"You don't look old enough to stand the work of Kingsinch. How old are you?" Mr Lunan asked next.

"Older than I look," I said, for I was not willing to divulge my supposed age to him or any man.

"Above twelve then," Mr Lunan said, in what may have been an attempt at humour.

"Above twelve," I confirmed, "and a few years more."

Mr Lunan nodded again, with a glint of humour in his eyes that showed he appreciated my reply. "Spunky, are you? You might need that here. The bothy-boys can be a handful."

"I have two hands," I said, "one for the bothy-boys and one for myself."

"Is that so?" Mr Lunan slumped on a chair. "Well Ellen Luath, tea would be a good idea."

I bustled to make Mr Lunan a mug of tea, hot and black, with two spoons of sugar, which he stirred with a deliberate motion and his gaze never straying from me. "You have scrubbed the floor," he said.

"I have."

"Better finish your work, then." Mr Lunan nodded to the mud he had brought from the fields. "Mrs Lunan does not like a job half-done."

After the scrubbing, Mrs Lunan had me make brose – simple oatmeal and boiling water - for the young horsemen who ploughed the fields and did most of the work, skilled and unskilled about the farm.

"There are three horsemen and a halflin in the bothy. Take the brose into them," Mrs Lunan said as she watched me stir the oatmeal into the hot water. Brose was the staple food of the horsemen, the bothy-boys, in any farm steading. "And don't linger."

I knew that some horsemen could be quite rough, wild young men who boasted of their exploits to their colleagues, so I was prepared for a baptism of fire when I entered the bothy that housed the crew. A bothy was only the name for the building where the horsemen lived; it could be any sort of place deemed suitable to hold several young, unmarried men. In the case of Kingsinch, it was a long room directly above a barn.

I tapped on the door. "Kitchen maid," I warned, for I had

no desire to surprise the men when they may be changing their clothes.

After a few seconds, a voice sounded. "Come awa' in!"

When I pushed the door open, I stepped into a room with two skylights and a plentiful supply of fresh air from missing slates. Four solid beds stretched along the wall, with a battered table and chairs in the centre of the room, and a fireplace at the further gable. I took in the sparse furnishings with a glance and gave more attention to the four occupants of the room.

One man was older, maybe in his early thirties, a long-faced, dark-haired loon with a ready smile. He stood by the fire, watching everything I did. The second man was younger, in his mid-twenties, with serious brown eyes that studied me. He sat on a bed, taking off his boots. A third man lay on the bed. He was auburn-haired, freckled, and grinned to me, raising a hand in welcome. The fourth person was only a boy with haunted eyes.

I knew without asking what their positions were in the farmtoun, as we northerners termed places such as this. The oldest man was the first horseman, the head man of the bothy crew. From the first horseman, the others were ranked in descending order to the boy, who was the halflin, or the orra loon. The halflin was learning how to be a man, performing the menial, thankless tasks.

"Feeding time, lads," I said, laying my tray on the table.

"You're new," the first horseman said. He stepped towards me, smiling. "I'm Dougie."

"I'm Ellen," I told him, aware his man's eyes were assessing me from the crown of my head to my boots and back, lingering around my hips and breasts.

"I'm Andrew," the serious-faced man said, "and the freckled fellow is Jim. The halflin is Peter."

I smiled at them all in turn. When Jim smiled back, his

freckles merged into a solid mass of orange-brown. Lifting a trump, a Jew's harp, to his mouth, he strummed a short tune, drumming one of his feet against the wall. The halflin, Peter glanced at my face and looked away in nervous confusion. I guessed his age at fifteen, although he was tall.

"Here's your brose," I said. "I brought some oatcakes as well. And some cheese if you want it."

The men looked at me in approval. Jim was first to the table, "we don't usually get oatcakes on a Monday," he said.

"It's a special treat," I said, "as I am new." I wondered if Mrs Lunan would mind me plundering her pantry and shrugged. It was a small matter, and food was there to be eaten.

"You can stay as long as you like if you bring oatcakes and cheese," Jim said. He stroked a hand over his smooth chin and sighed. "I'll have to shave after I've eaten."

Dougie looked at me and laughed. "Long after you've eaten, Jim. Maybe six months after!" He rubbed a rough hand over Jim's jaw. "You've got a long way to go before you're even half a man!"

I said nothing, aware that Jim had spoken for my benefit, testing me out, boasting of his maturity, despite his lack of years. Dougie eyed me, assessing my suitability for whatever purpose he had in mind.

"You're not from around here." Dougie spun a chair, so the back was towards me. He straddled his legs across it, facing me, trying to look tough.

"I am not," I agreed.

"We don't get many strangers in Kingsinch," Dougie continued.

"Why is that?" I asked.

When Dougie's smile widened, I knew he had hoped for the question. "People are scared to come to this steading," he said.

"Oh? Why?"

Dougie leaned closer to me. "The bogles might get them."

I did not flinch. "The bogles won't get me," I said, "and neither will the horsemen, so don't think it."

"That's you told, Dougie," Andrew spoke around his Jew's harp. "She's put you in your place."

"There's time yet." Dougie settled back in his chair with his eyes promising much and his body ready to follow. "Kingsinch is a lonely place in the long nights of winter, and a woman can seek a man's solace when the bogles are out."

"Not this woman," I told him bluntly, "and if you put your solace near me, I'll chop it off."

Andrew laughed openly at that, while Jim smiled, and young Peter looked uncomfortable. Dougie's scowl deepened, and I knew he and I could not be friends. Men such as Dougie need to be in charge; they do not like a woman to best them in anything.

I stood up and gathered the empty crockery. "Just you remember that, Douglas Mitchell." I had no intention of allowing another man to intimidate me.

I felt Dougie's dislike as I left the bothy.

CHAPTER 2

"You must be Ellen," the present kitchen maid said. Plump, pretty and pregnant, she wore her dark hair piled on top of her head. Three inches taller than I was, she greeted me with a smile. "I'm Agnes. Have you had the tour of the steading, yet?"

"Not yet," I said, already prepared to like this woman although it was far too early to consider friendship.

"We'll go out in a few moments," Agnes said. "Don't let Mrs Lunan worry you. She criticises everybody. I think it's because she's Mr Lunan's second wife and younger than he is, so has to prove herself."

I nodded. I was not concerned about a carping woman, for I had faced much worse in my time. "Thank you," I said, hoping the words suited the occasion.

"Come on, then," Agnes said. "We don't get much free time here, so we'll go now before it gets too dark." She hesitated, "Make a long arm, Ellen, and fetch down that light," she pointed to a battered brass lantern that hung from a hook on the wall, "and be quiet near the steading. Mr Lunan disapproves of us going out after dark."

"Why is that?" I asked, stretching for the lantern. I shook it, hearing the whale-oil slosh inside, and checked the wick was in place.

In reply, Agnes indicated her belly. "Maybe that's why," she said and laughed. "It's all right, we're getting married soon anyway."

I smiled, although I was unconcerned if Agnes and her lover should get married or not. The idea of making something moral after the event seemed somehow hypocritical. "Congratulations," I said. "Who's your intended?"

"Andrew," Agnes said. "Andrew Ferguson, the second horseman. You would meet him in the bothy."

"The man with the serious eyes," I said.

"Serious eyes, yes, that's my Andrew," Agnes agreed at once. "Better put your coat on, Ellen; it's cold out there. Come on." Scratching a match, she applied it to the wick of the lantern and opened the door. We negotiated the kitchen and stepped outside, where a snell wind from the hills flapped the coats around our legs and nipped our noses.

"We're north-facing," Agnes explained, "and the hills attract the cold."

It was dusk, not yet full dark, and the hills were soft edged against the night. "You already know the bothy where the boys are," Agnes said, pointing to the long stone barn. I heard rough male voices and a burst of singing, with words unsuitable for delicate ears.

"It's sometimes better not to listen to their songs," Agnes said.

I laughed. "I've heard worse," I said.

The dark was gathering, creeping into the steading from the surrounding fields, carrying noises I tried to identify. I heard the creaking of a gate, the distant lowing of cattle, the brush of wind through the trees, and, further out, the bleating of sheep. They were all natural sounds. I did not hear the sound I feared the most.

"Over here." Agnes led me to a pair of barns. "This is where we store the winter fodder and next year's seed. The byre – well, you'll know that already. That's where we milk the cattle beasts."

I nodded. I had already had a stint of milking with the cows warm, friendly bodies around me.

Agnes pointed to the sprig of rowan above the byre door. "Mr Lunan insists we keep that there. He gets all upset if the wind blows it away."

"Why?" I asked. "What's it for?"

Agnes screwed up her face. "It's to keep away witches, I think. That will be one of your duties, ensuring the rowan is always there."

I nodded, hiding my smile. "Maybe one of the boy's should do that," I said. "It's right high."

Agnes laughed. "Yes, you're not the tallest of girls, are you?" She patted her swollen belly. "I'm not one for climbing up ladders in my condition. I had to ask one of the boys. Andy did it for me, but maybe Jim will help, or the halflin. If you ask in the right way, they'll oblige."

"That Dougie may oblige too much," I said.

Agnes laughed again and patted her belly again. "Andrew already has!"

We walked on, with the wind increasing, rattling an open door, howling from the eaves of the farmhouse. A bat fluttered past, its wings brushing my hair. The darkness had gathered now, so the hill-ridge had merged with the night.

"You see that building there?" Agnes nodded to what looked like a ruin. It was a tumbledown thick-walled place with a low blue-slate roof. A twisted rowan tree grew outside the low doorway, nearly stripped of leaves.

"I see it," I said. The door was heavily barred, with two padlocks holding the bolts in place.

"We don't go there," Agnes said. "Not even Mrs Lunan ever goes in there."

"Why not?" I asked, insatiably curious. "What's inside?"

"We don't know, and we don't ask," Agnes said. "Mr Lunan says the building is dangerous. Oh, God!"

"What's wrong?" I asked, wondering if her baby had decided on a premature entrance.

Agnes pushed me back into the doorway of a barn and closed the shutter of the lantern, plunging us into darkness. "Hush! Here's Mr Lunan!"

"Why?" I began until Agnes clamped a hand over my mouth.

I stood still, crowded into the shadows as Mr Lunan walked past, with three black mastiffs at his heels and a shotgun held under his left arm. The dogs stopped, lifted their heads, and sniffed the air. I felt Agnes stiffen beside me as her hand slid into mine.

The leading dog bayed, once, and the others followed, with the noise echoing from the cold stone buildings. Mr Lunan stopped.

"What's that, boys?" His voice grated, like gravel under a farm gate. He peered into the darkness and lifted his voice. "Who's there? Show yourself, or I'll loose the dogs on you!"

Agnes cringed into me, her hand squeezing mine.

Mr Lunan took one step closer. "I know you're there! Is that you, Jock? By the living Christ, you'd better not be poaching on my land!"

"No, Mr Lunan," Agnes spoke in a small voice. "It's us! Agnes and Ellen."

"What the hell are you doing there?" Mr Lunan asked. "Come out of that! Show yourselves!"

I was first to move, stepping into Mr Lunan's line of vision, with Agnes slightly behind me. "It's just us, Mr Lunan," I explained. "Agnes was kindly showing me around the steading."

"Was she now?" Mr Lunan eyed us both as his dogs set up a horrendous din of barking. "I don't like my girls walking about after dark. We're a long way from anywhere here, and Heather Jock is in the vicinity." I was unsure if Mr Lunan was giving us a lecture or looking after us.

"I don't know who Heather Jock is," I said.

"You don't want to," Mr Lunan said. "He's a poacher, vagabond and a thief; a dangerous man." He snarled at his dogs as they tried to surge forward, "Get back! Damn you! Can't you see its only two wee lassies?"

"We'll get back to the house now, Mr Lunan," Agnes said.

"You do that," Mr Lunan said with his eyes deep in shadow.

Agnes edged past the dogs, keeping as far from their slavering jaws as she could. I was less afraid, for I could sense no harm in the mastiffs. The leading dog sniffed at me and would have leapt forward if Mr Lunan had not grabbed the scruff of its neck and hauled it back. "Keep still, damn you! What's got into you?"

Agnes and I lifted our skirts and ran back to the farmhouse, slamming our room door shut and collapsing on the bed. I could not help giggling, and Agnes joined in, stuffing a hand in her mouth to control herself.

"I thought these dogs were going to tear us to bits," Agnes said.

"Who is this Heather Jock that Mr Lunan is looking for?" I asked.

Agnes shrugged took off her coat and began to remove her shoes. "I've never met him; I've only heard the name. Mr

Lunan patrols the toun every night with the dogs so Jock must be quite a lad."

We brought water from the pump and washed in our room to get ready for bed. I hoped I could sleep that night. Even more, I hoped I had left the whistling behind me, this time. Most of all, I hoped to carve out a normal life for myself, although normality was a disappointingly elusive aspect in my life.

I woke without knowing where I was. The whistling was in my ears, undulating, low and insistent as if somebody was calling me. I opened my eyes, peering into the unfamiliar dark. I recognised nothing, not the shape of the furniture, the square of lesser dark that marked the window or the form of the woman who shared my bed. It took me a few moments to organise my mind and remember I was at Kingsinch.

The whistling continued, easing into the room, sliding into my head until it pushed away everything else. I put my hands over my ears and rolled onto my side, trying to block out the sound.

"Go away," I said. "Go away!"

I knew it would not go away. It never did. That whistling followed me wherever I was, haunting my nights, tormenting me with its insistent call.

"No," I said. "I'm not coming! You can't have me!"

"Ellen?" Agnes sat up beside me. "Ellen? Are you all right?"

I shook my head. "Can you hear that?" I asked.

"Hear what?" Agnes looked at me, scratching a match to light the candle. Her hair, so tidy yesterday, was a mess and her eyes were bleary with sleep.

"That whistling sound." I knew Agnes would not hear anything. Nobody was aware of the whistling except me, and sometimes I was not even sure that I heard it. I already wished I had not mentioned it; I had spoken through tiredness, without thought of the possible consequences.

"No; I only hear the wind," Agnes said. "Go back to sleep." She lay back down, leaving me alone with my fears. I was always alone with my fears. I had been alone with my fears most of my life and did not expect that ever to change.

The whistling was louder now, louder than I had ever known it. I felt as if it was right outside the house. I did not know who, or what caused it. I only knew it followed me wherever I went, sometimes leaving me for a few months or years, but always returning. It had found me in Kingsinch faster than ever before.

"Go to sleep," Agnes mumbled.

I lay on my side and pulled the covers over my head. The whistling continued, seeping through the walls, through the gaps in the ill-fitting window, to circle the room, summoning me.

"It's all right." Agnes sensed my distress. "You're in a strange house, that's all. You'll soon get used to it." Turning towards me, she held me close, cuddling me like the mother I never knew, or the sister I always wanted. I lay there, slowly quieting down in Agnes's arms, with the new life inside her stirring against me.

I slept then, with the strangest of images forming inside my head. I could see the baby within Agnes, and knew it would be a boy, with dark hair like its mother and the same serious eyes as his father. I knew that yet did not know how I knew. I slept with that knowledge and woke only once, to see the friendly light from a cottage high on the hill opposite.

Agnes had told me the cottage belonged to Charlie Fleming, who worked a pendicle – a small skelp of land – on the hill. I fixed my eye on that, knowing, somehow, that as long as Charlie was secure in his pendicle, I was safe on the low ground far beneath. I trusted in that light as seamen trust in the Pole Star.

I had lived with apprehension and fear most of my life so that wherever I was, I prepared for my next move. My previous attempts to put down roots had failed. Now, as Charlie Fleming's light flickered on the hill, I fastened my eyes on that solitary beacon.

"Please, God," I prayed, "help me find peace."

So far in my life, God had seldom answered my prayers. Perhaps this time he would. Maybe I could live a humdrum, everyday life, rather than remain a stoorey-foot, a nomad with the dust of the road on my shoes.

Oh, please, God, answer my prayers.

"You two." Mrs Lunan scowled across to Agnes and me. "I heard you were abroad last night."

"Yes, Mrs Lunan," Agnes admitted at once.

"Well, you won't be out tonight," Mrs Lunan said. "Not tonight of all nights."

"Why not tonight?" I asked.

"There's an initiation," Mrs Lunan said, looking me up and down. "When that happens, we leave the boys alone."

"Ah." I nodded without understanding. "What sort of initiation?"

"Our third horseman is learning the Horseman's Word,"

I nodded again. I had heard about the Horseman's Word, a semi-magical concept that gave the horsemen power over horses and women. Glancing at Agnes's very pregnant condition, I wondered if the Word worked.

"Don't forget!" Mrs Lunan left our room after a very pointed look at me.

"I've never seen an initiation," Agnes said. "What do you think?" Her eyes were bright with mischief. "Are we going to watch?"

"I'd love to," I said.

Agnes nodded. "Are you sure you're game?"

"If you are," I said. "I've always wondered what happens at initiations."

"We'll have to be very quiet," Agnes said. "If Mr Lunan catches us..." She did not complete her sentence.

"Let's make sure that he doesn't," I said.

"Mrs Lunan is worse," Agnes said. "She's a tyrant."

I nodded, although I had met much worse than Mrs Lunan.

We did not know where the initiation was taking place, so left our room in the early evening and waited in the steading's dark shadows. I heard an outburst of hilarity from the bothy and then the door opened, a rectangle of yellow light against the dark of the night. One by one, the men came out, with Peter at the back, until Dougie pushed him back inside the bothy.

"This is a night for men," Dougie said. "Children cannae come."

"I'm not a child," Peter complained.

"Get back inside," Dougie said, spun the boy around, and landed a solid kick on his rump. "And stay inside."

I could not make out Peter's reply, although I doubted it was polite.

Dougie slammed the door shut, laughed, and led the way through the tangle of buildings that made up the steading. Agnes and I followed at a distance, keeping to the shadows, ensuring our feet made no noise on the ground and trying to hear what the bothy-boys were saying.

"They're going to the Muckle Barn," Agnes said.

By that time, I knew where the Muckle Barn was, and nodded.

"We'll go to the hayloft, above," Agnes said.

As the men stopped to tease the third horseman, Agnes and I slipped ahead, to enter the Muckle Barn – the largest barn in Kingsinch - and climb the ladders to the hayloft. From there, we would have an excellent view of everything that was happening below, while being invisible to the horsemen. As somebody had left the skylight open, I hastened to close it, first peering into the surrounding darkness.

"Somebody else is coming." I pointed to the swinging pinpricks of light that indicated men carrying lanterns along the track. Further back, I saw a brighter glow from the fixed light on its lonely post.

"Horsemen from other farms," Agnes said. "Come to help the initiation."

"Tell me," I said, "why is there a lantern at the bend of the track."

"In case it rains," Agnes said. "The fields can flood in the autumn rains, and if that happens, we get cut off. The path is the only way in and out, and sometimes the floodwater covers that too."

"So, the lantern keeps people on the path," I said.

"That's right. Dougie sends Peter the halflin out to light the lantern."

"Lucky Peter," I said.

Agnes laughed. "Peter doesn't mind," she said. "He thinks it makes him look like a man." She shook her head. "These young lads are desperate to become men."

The horsemen filed into the Muckle Barn, all wearing broad flat caps and their voices low growls in the gloom. There was an expectant air as the men gathered around, perhaps a dozen strong, with ages from their late teens to mature, be-whiskered men in their thirties. In keeping with their profession, they were lean, fit men without an ounce of spare fat, hard-featured, weather-beaten, with a laconic turn of phrase rather than a gift for rhetoric. I have always been able to sense the atmosphere, and here there was a taste of excitement, even a sexual tension that worried me a little, although Agnes was happy enough.

"The men won't like us to see this sort of thing," Agnes whispered.

"All the better for us, then," I said, although the actions of men were not a mystery to me.

Agnes smiled across to me and settled her belly more comfortably on the straw-streaked planks.

"Is Mr Lunan not coming?" I asked.

"No," Agnes whispered. "This is only for horsemen. Nobody else is allowed, not even the farmer." She smiled again. "It's all very secretive."

I smiled back, for nothing binds women together than sharing a secret, especially a secret about men.

Dougie gave an order, and two of the younger men lit lanterns, which gave smoky light to the centre of the barn while darkening the shadows in the corner. I wondered how often horsemen had performed this ceremony in this place and how old it was.

"Isn't this exciting?" Agnes asked. "Like a secret society!"

The horsemen formed a circle, with a bottle of whisky passed around from hand to hand. Each man took a swig, wiped his mouth, and passed it on before sitting on a hay-bale. Dougie settled on a large saddle perched on a bale, so he was higher than the others. I could not see Andrew or Jim. The barn reeked of tobacco smoke from half a dozen pipes.

"Bring in the candidate!" Dougie announced in a big voice.

Agnes nudged me with a sharp elbow to ensure I was paying attention. After a moment's delay, Andrew came in with another man, both leading a blindfolded Jim.

"Take him to the centre of the sacred circle!" Dougie ordered.

Andrew and the second man led Jim to the middle of the watching horsemen, and left him there, blindfolded and undoubtedly nervous.

"Who are you, candidate?" Dougie asked.

"Jim Blair," Jim said.

"Speak clearly!" Dougie was enjoying his power. "What is your full name?"

"I am James Walter Blair!" Jim nearly shouted.

"James Walter Blair, are you ready to be initiated into the Sacred Society of horsemen?"

"I am!" Jim said, pulling his shoulders back and standing to attention.

"Let us see you, James Walter Blair!" Dougie ordered.

Even from my perch, I could sense Jim's confusion. "You can see me," he said.

"Let us see all of you," Dougie ordered. "Strip!"

I sensed amusement from the horsemen. They were enjoying humiliating Jim, as they had all been humiliated during their initiation.

"Isn't this fun?" Agnes whispered.

"Not for Jim." I felt sympathy for Jim. I knew far too well how it felt to be the butt of others' vindictive humour.

I had a memory of cowering in the orphanage dormitory as the other waifs sneered at me and Miss Deas ordered me to wash my sodden bedclothes by hand in cold water.

"She's wet the bed again, the dirty little teuchter!"

"Dirty little teuchter!" the orphans repeated.

*"She'll have to wash her bedclothes, the dirty little teuchter!"
Miss Deas said.*

"Dirty little teuchter!"

*"Take them off and wash them!" Miss Deas ordered as the
orphans mocked me with forced laughter. I never knew if they
intended to hurt, or if they were as scared as I was. I only knew I
felt like dying as I stripped naked in front of everybody.*

"Dirty little teuchter! Dirty little teuchter!"

I shook away the memory. I had too many of that kind.

As the crowd watched in silent amusement, Jim stripped
off his clothes to stand stark naked in the centre of the circle,
both hands covering his genitals. Many of the horsemen made
crude comments that had Agnes stuffing her fingers in her
mouth to stifle her giggles. I noted that Andrew looked slightly
uncomfortable and did not join in the ridicule.

"Kneel before the senior horseman!" Dougie ordered, and
Jim knelt on the cobbled floor, still with his hands folded in
front of him.

"Repeat the tender of the Horseman's Oath!" Dougie
ordered.

I listened intently, for only horsemen knew such things,
and Andrew, Jim's mentor, must have taught Jim what to say.

"Here, conceal, never reveal; neither write nor dite nor
recite not cut nor carve nor write in sand," Jim said the words
clearly, without hesitation. They meant nothing to me.

Dougie had a broad grin on his face as he asked a series of
technical questions about horses, ploughing and ploughs, few of
which I understood. Jim, still blindfolded, answered them all
without hesitation.

"He's not freckled all over." Agnes was examining Jim with
great interest. If she had binoculars, I swear she would have

focussed on his most intimate areas. "Only on his face and arms." She suppressed a giggle. "His other parts are normal." Agnes gave me a sharp dig with her elbow. "What do you think of him, Ellen? Is he tasty enough for you?"

"He's all right," I said. Naked men did not interest me any more than naked women did. I could see Jim without his clothes on, and that was all; I had no sexual feelings one way or another.

"Oh, he's better than all right. Look at his doup; wouldn't you like to grab hold of that?" Agnes went into even more intimate details as Jim continued to answer Dougie's questions. From time to time, another horseman would fire a question, but Jim coped well.

"Now," Dougie said when he tired of being the question master, "you seem to be adequately versed in the primary aspects of horsemanship. Tell me the penalties for breaking your oath."

The circle of watchful, flat-bonneted, caustic men listened as Jim intoned a litany of terrible penalties. They nodded when Jim ending with, "and in failing may my body be quartered in four parts with a horseman's knife and buried in the sea, or may I be torn to pieces by wild horses."

The horsemen grunted approval as Dougie continued. "Are you ready to meet Auld Horsie, the king of the horsemen, and learn the Horseman's Word?"

"I am," Jim said although I heard the quiver in his voice.

I knew that the Horseman's Word was supposed to be a secret password into the Society of Horsemen, the word that gave the men power over horses and women. Some said the Word was why there were so many pregnant women and illegitimate babies in rural Scotland. I did not know; I only knew that all the young lads dreamed of the day they entered the Society and gained the Word and the power.

"First you must endure the corridor of pain," Dougie said, "to see if you are worthy of the honour!"

I had not heard of this tradition before and wondered if Dougie had added such a refinement of cruelty himself. When I looked at Agnes, she pulled a face and shrugged.

The horsemen formed a human corridor, with Dougie ordering them to remove their belts.

"Andy!" Dougie snapped. "Bring the candidate to the entrance of the corridor. Horsemen! Ensure the candidate remembers his ordeal! Test his endurance to see if he's fit to be a horseman!"

I could not watch as Andrew led Jim to the entrance of the gauntlet, murmured in his ear and gave him a gentle push. Dougie had taken his stance and swung his doubled leather belt with gusto. The other horsemen copied, swinging their belts at Jim's pale body. I only wondered at the cruelty that co-existed with genuine kindness among Scottish farmers, remembered similar instances in my life and hoped Dougie's ordeal would not last long.

"Oh, that will sting!" Agnes whispered and then watched avidly with her right hand in her mouth. I did not know if she enjoyed the spectacle or was fascinated by Jim's torment. I only knew I wished myself elsewhere.

After forcing Jim on three journeys through the gauntlet, Dougie tired of the game. "Lights off!" he ordered sharply, and the horsemen doused every lantern. I could not understand why Dougie should want the lanterns out, as Jim was blindfolded. When Agnes gasped at the sudden darkness, I reached for her hand, squeezed it, and she replied in kind.

Silence filled the Muckle Barn, except for the horsemen's subdued breathing and a sound like feet dragging through the straw-covered floor. I waited, feeling the tension rise. Something was wrong. I could feel that something had entered the barn that was beyond Dougie's sadistic pleasure.

"Lights on!" Dougie said again.

I heard the scratching of matches and saw the small glow of flames, before the lantern-light spread out from a single central point.

"What in God's name?" I muttered, and even the hard-bitten horsemen gasped in surprise.

The lights blazed around what I can only describe as a *thing* in near-human shape. About five foot five inches in height, it stood on the ground with an amazingly devilish face carved into it, with pointed ears, narrow red eyes, a sharp nose, and a mouth curved in a smile, except for the row of sharp teeth.

I looked away. Somewhere in my past, buried under a host of bitter memories, I had seen something like that before. The face may have been carved in wood, but the features were familiar if exaggerated. I found myself squeezing Agnes's hand so hard that she gasped in pain.

"Now!" Dougie stood behind the wooden figure. He extended a long staff, covered in rough, hairy hide and with some animal's paw at the end, complete with hooked claws. "James Walter Blair! If you think yourself fit to become a horse-man, come and shake Auld Horsie's paw!"

Naked as a baby, blindfolded and welted by a dozen belts, Jim stepped forward with his hand extended.

Dougie thrust the hairy paw forward until Jim grasped it, then closed the claws on Jim's hand. Only then did he duck behind Jim and rip off the blindfold.

After more than an hour of darkness, subjected to rigorous questioning and a beating, Jim suddenly saw the hideous grinning face glaring at him as he held the rough, hooked paw. I was not surprised when he let out a yell of shock and dropped the paw, backing away from the carved figure.

The horsemen's laughter was tinged with what I thought was relief, and they all chanted in unison:

"Here's to them that work horses.
Bad luck to them that is cruel
Let perseverance be their guide,
And nature be their rule."

Jim grinned around them, only then rubbing at his backside, which had been the horsemen's belts' primary target. On his pale skin, the heavy leather had left broad red welts. Many of the men laughed again, not unkindly.

"Rub away, Jim, lad, we all know what it feels like."

"Aye, we've all been there," Andrew said. "You can get some lassie to kiss it better, but not my Agnes!"

I heard Agnes suck in her breath at Andrew's remark.

"Is that it?" Jim asked. "When do I get the Horseman's Word?"

"You get it now," Andrew said and leaned closer. "The Word that gives you power over horses and women," he said, and whispered something in Jim's ear.

Some trick of the acoustics carried the words to me – "both in one".

"Is that it?" Jim sounded disappointed. Perhaps he had expected a magic phrase in mediaeval Latin.

"That's it." Dougie produced a pencil and a scrap of paper. "Here, write it down in case you forget."

Jim reached for the pencil, held it between finger and thumb and flicked it at Dougie. "Here, conceal, never reveal; neither write nor dite nor recite not cut nor carve nor write in sand," he repeated his earlier words. "You'll not catch me out, Douglas Mitchell!"

The watching horsemen roared with laughter, and one clapped Jim on the back. "Well done, Jim! You passed the final test."

As the evening descended into a vast consumption of whisky, and the still naked Jim drank with the rest, I looked at the hideously carved wooden object.

That thing worried me. I knew I had seen its likeness before, but I could not think where? I knew it did not belong in the Muckle Barn, nor in Kingsinch.

"Agnes," I started, but Agnes's gaze had not strayed from Jim's naked body. I knew there was no point in asking her anything.

"Where are you going?" Agnes asked.

"Back to bed," I said.

"Don't you want to watch the men?"

I shook my head. I wanted to get far away from that carved wooden object as quickly as possible. The evil within it disturbed me.

CHAPTER 3

THAT FACE HAUNTED MY DREAMS. I was aware of Agnes tumbling into bed at my side and knew she wanted to talk about the initiation, and about Jim, but my mind was elsewhere.

I could see that carved face with the slightly almond-shaped eyes and the pointed ears whenever I closed my eyes. Yet the face was not made of wood. It was alive and looking down at me. I knew it was talking or trying to communicate, although I did not understand the words. It was hideous, emanating an ancient evil, and I wondered if it was connected to the whistling.

I lay in my hard bed, with the compressed straw mattress barely rustling under me and faint moonlight trickling through the bars on the window. The darkness surrounded me, suffocating, pressing down upon me like a solid weight, so dense that I felt I could cut it up if the attendants had not manacled me the bed.

Tears filled my eyes and trickled onto the mattress. There was no pillow; lunatic girls did not have such luxuries, and the single coarse grey blanket was insufficient to fend off the cold.

Even here, I could hear the whistling. It surrounded me, seemingly coming from the air itself, so I could not escape, wherever I went.

"Go away," I pleaded, twisting on my bed. "Leave me alone." I could not speak loudly in case I woke Miss Horne, the woman who ran the institution. I was scared of Miss Horne, and with reason.

The whistling continued, relentless, never-ending, penetrating every thought. A shaft of moonshine seeped between the window-bars to light the far wall, showing the bare, white-washed plaster. I stared at that light, holding onto it as a sign of hope. Was that God showing me mercy?

I could hear my breathing, harsh in the room, and then something blocked the light. I gasped and turned my head toward the window.

The face was peering in at me. It was hideous, with almond-shaped eyes, a slit for a mouth and small, slightly pointed ears. I stared, too petrified to scream as the thing at the window pressed against the bars. It extended its arms through the glass-less window, reaching towards me, and opened its mouth in a ghastly grin. When I saw the row of small, pointed teeth, I found my voice and screamed. I screamed and screamed until Miss Horne jerked open the door and charged inside.

After that, I had other reasons to scream apart from the face at the window.

"Where did that figure come from?" I asked Agnes the morning after Jim's initiation.

"Which figure," Agnes asked. "Oh, you mean Auld Horsie?" She grinned. "I think the bothy boys made it a long time ago. You'd better ask Dougie; he'll know."

"Dougie and I are not the best of friends," I said.

Agnes shook her head. "That's a shame. Dougie's the first horseman. You'd better keep in with him. He's all right if you don't mind his wandering hands." She smiled, "you'll find that if you let his hands wander where they will, he can be quite useful. That's the trick with Dougie." She looked down at herself and sighed. "Mind you; he's been less keen on me since I fell pregnant."

I had no intention of keeping in with Dougie or allowing his hands to wander anywhere near me, so the mystery of Auld Horsie would have to remain unsolved. Part of me wished to revisit the Muckle Barn to see the figure again, while another part warned me to keep well clear. There was something bad there, some old evil, and the terrible memory from my past worried me. Had that only been a dream? Or was it genuine? Until last night, I had forgotten that occurrence; I must have buried it along with so many other unpleasant memories.

I heard the shout when I was in the byre, milking the cattle. It was not a roar of pain, nor a greeting to a friend; instead, it was a shout of surprise. My inquisitive nature made me wonder what had happened, so I listened intently for any other noise. When the cow I was milking sensed my distraction and stirred under my hands, I calmed her down with soft words and emptied her udders before striding to the entrance to the byre.

My other cows complained when I left, so I soothed them with a promise to return.

"It's all right, ladies," I said. "I won't be long." I liked my cattle; they were warm, inoffensive creatures, large, slow, and affectionate.

The byre was at the edge of the steading, handily placed to receive the cattle from the fields, and that meant I had an open view over the farmland to the north. At this time of year, the horsemen were busily ploughing in the stubble left from the year's grain crop, each man with his two-horse plough.

Andrew was two fields away, near to the old ruin, staring at something on the ground and gesticulating to Jim and Dougie, both of whom had left their teams to hurry towards him. As a newcomer to the farm, I knew better than to interfere. I only watched and listened, trying to catch the men's conversation as the wind drifted snatches towards me.

"It's a skeleton," Andrew said.

"What kind of a skeleton?" Jim asked, vaulting over the intervening dyke as if it were nothing. He seemed none the worse for his ordeal of a few nights' ago.

"A man, I think," Andrew said, and then I saw Mrs Lunan striding from the farmhouse, and I returned to my charge. Whatever Andrew had discovered, the farm's work had to continue, we had to milk the cows, and everything else must wait. If Andrew had unearthed a skeleton, then there was nothing I could do to help, and my curiosity would have to remain unsatisfied. All the same, I wondered about the incident until midday, when I brought the men their midday meal and asked what had happened.

Andrew looked up from his oatcake and cheese. "It was an old skeleton," he said, "probably somebody who stumbled into the Moss before it was drained." He shook his head. "I told Mr Lunan, and he'll tell the police, I suppose."

Young Peter had hurried across from the steading to join us in the fields, for he attached himself to the men whenever he could. "Maybe Heather Jock murdered somebody and buried him in the field," he said, hopefully.

Andrew shook his head. "It was an old body. I was deep-ploughing, so the bones were well underground."

"Maybe Heather Jock buried him deep." Peter held onto his theory, with a child's love of drama and gore.

Dougie shook his head. "Ah, Heather Jock, the man who ate the boiled ham raw. No, it will be Old Hangie," he said, looking at me and hoping to shock.

I asked the expected question. "Who was Old Hangie?"

Dougie smiled. "About a hundred and fifty years ago, before the King's Moss was properly drained, Kingsinch was even more isolated than now." Dougie had a deep voice and a captivating way of telling a story so that all the men stopped to listen. "Nobody wanted to live here, because the moss was dangerous, and there were stories of strange things happening."

"What strange things?" I asked as my curiosity overcame my dislike of Dougie.

Dougie glanced at the horsemen before he replied. When his smile dropped a little, I wondered if that was part of his act, or if he was hiding the truth behind the banal exterior. "Kingsinch can be an unchancy place," Dougie said and continued with his story.

"About 1600, Kingsinch suited one man very well. That man was Old Hangie, the executioner of Strathmore. He was the fellow who had to hang the local murderers and thieves and whip the transgressors through the streets. He was not well-liked, as you can imagine, Ellen." Dougie looked directly at me.

"I can imagine," I agreed. Dougie did have attractive eyes, I allowed. I could nearly understand how some women fell under his spell.

Dougie smiled once more. "What made it worse was that Old Hangie enjoyed his job. He sang a little song as he hanged folk and laughed as he laid on the lash."

"Not a nice fellow," I said.

"No," Dougie agreed. "Then one day, the court condemned a child, a little boy, for stealing food for its mother. The Strathmore people were in an uproar, demanding that the authorities free the boy, but the judge was a local landowner, to whom possessions were more important than human life. Anyway, Old Hangie had the job of executing the child. He sang as the fastened the noose around the greeting boy's neck and continued to sing as the boy slowly strangled."

I pictured the scene, already hating the landowner and the laughing, singing hangman. Was it my imagination, or could I hear a drift of song now, rising from the drained Moss, where the fields stretched before us?

"After the hanging, it was the hangman's prerogative to take the executed man's clothes, to sell them for profit. Old Hangie stripped the bairn and left the child at the foot of the gallows. The poor bairn was stark to the world for the sake of a few pennies. Then Old Hangie came home to Kingsinch, singing his little song." Dougie paused for dramatic effect. "And he was never seen again."

"What happened to him?" Peter asked.

Dougie pointed to the skeleton that lay, white and lonely, in the lee of the dyke. "Maybe that's him there. We don't know." He lowered his voice to a whisper. "Some say that the Sidh came down from the hills and took him away in judgement for his sins. Others say that the Lord sent a great bolt of lightning that frizzled him."

The Sidh? I held onto the word without asking questions.

"What do you think happened, Dougie?" Peter asked.

Dougie smiled knowingly. "I think Old Hangie was a drunken fool who wandered into the Moss and drowned." He nodded to the skeleton. "Like that one there."

"Perhaps so," Jim said, "but who took away his ribs?"

I had not noticed that two of the skeleton's ribs were missing until Jim pointed it out. "How strange," I said.

"Kingsinch is a strange place," Dougie deepened his voice in an attempt to intimidate me.

"And with some strange people," I said, knowing that none of them was as strange as I was.

Although Peter laughed at my words, I still heard the music drift across the fields, and I wondered if the skeleton had belonged to Auld Hangie, and who had taken his ribs, and why.

Somehow, I knew that everything tied together, and soon I would find the answer to the questions that had plagued me all my life. I shivered then as if somebody had walked across my grave, and I wondered if I wanted to know the truth. Perhaps I was better to remain in ignorance.

But who or what were the Sidh?

CHAPTER 4

WE DID NOT OFTEN HAVE the opportunity to leave Kingsinch, so I grabbed the chance when Mrs Lunan wanted supplies.

"Coupar Angus?" I said. "I'll go."

Mrs Lunan nodded. "I'd send Agnes normally, but in her condition." Mrs Lunan shook her head. "I'd prefer not to."

I agreed. Agnes was well on in pregnancy and might give birth any day. It was better to keep her near the farm steading.

"Dougie can drive the cart," Mrs Lunan said. "He knows what to do. You've to buy a hundredweight of flour, half a hundredweight of sugar and the rest on this list." She handed me a folded piece of paper before asking: "you can read, can't you?"

"Yes," I said.

The orphanage had hammered reading, writing and arithmetic into us with the aid of a stout leather belt. I remembered Miss Dea's voice now as she leaned towards me, with her thick glasses magnifying her cold blue eyes and enhancing her glint of malicious pleasure as she announced my fate. "You misspelt three words, Ellen no-family. That will mean six strokes for you. Bend over my desk and lift your skirt!"

"You can read. Good." Mrs Lunan dropped her voice. "You might have to help Dougie. I don't think he was ever very academic, however good he is with the plough-team or the binder."

"I will," I said. Dougie would not like me helping him, but he would have to swallow his pride. Sometimes, a man's vanity was the principal cause of his downfall. I had little time for pride. My life had quickly eroded any false images of self-importance. I was nothing, less than nothing, and would never amount to more.

Miss Deas had emphasised that with thorough efficiency.

"You are orphans," Miss Deas told us every morning as we sat on the hard wooden chairs with our backs straight and our arms folded. "Nobody wants you. If it were not for the kindness of this orphanage, you would be starving on the streets. I hope you are grateful."

Miss Deas proved the orphanage's kindness with the barbed lash of her tongue and the leather lash of her belt. We responded with subdued hatred and subtle acts of defiance. Sometimes the orphanage's kindness proved too much for the fortunate inmates and children ran away, to be dragged back and half-killed in front of us all.

On two occasions, orphans showed their gratitude by relieving the institution of their cost by ending their lives. One boy threw himself from the roof. One girl found a kitchen knife and sliced her wrists.

I continued to exist, with my self-respect long gone, no hope for the future and only the incessant whistling to mark me from the other unwanted.

"Are you ready, Ellen?"

Miraculously, there was a break in the clouds as Dougie took the reins and we rolled slowly away from Kingsinch.

Dougie was an excellent driver, negotiating the track without a problem.

"Did you know this road is built on bales of straw?" he asked, puffing out smoke on either side of his stubby pipe with every word.

"No." I sat slightly beside him on the driving seat, enjoying the movement and the feel of the wind in my face.

"Aye." Dougie negotiated the dog-leg bend without stopping, watching me through the corner of his eyes. He was a handsome man, I allowed, tall and lithe, with clear brown eyes and neatly trimmed side-whiskers. I could understand why women would find him attractive. "This was all bogland – the King's Moss they called it – and over the last hundred years or so, a succession of farmers drained it. Now it's good growing land, but soft, ill to plough after heavy rain. The old-time monks, or whatever they were, built a causeway to the chapel there," Dougie nodded to the old ruin. "That was fine in fair weather."

"And?" I urged as Dougie stopped talking to examine one of the fields.

"And? Oh, aye. I was looking at the furrows there. Jim's made them crooked at the head; that's not good." Dougie shook his head. "Aye, the road. The old monks built wooden causeways, and then the rains came. The ground flooded and cut off the inches, Chapel and Kings. So old man Lunan built up the road with bales of straw. The straw makes a foundation and floats on the water when it rains." Dougie grinned at me. "He's cleverer than he looks, is old man Lunan. Despite his obsessions."

"His obsessions?" I probed further.

"You must have noticed." Dougie inched closer to me on the seat so that I could feel his body heat even through my coat.

"He patrols the steading every night with his dogs, and doesnae allow us into some of the buildings."

"Aye, I said, looking ahead as we neared the road-end, where the farm-track joined the public road. "I noticed that all right."

Dougie eased us onto the public road, flicked the reins and increased the speed of the cart. "We'll be on the Black Yett soon, and then it's hey-ho for Coupar Angus."

"Why is it called the Black Yett?"

Dougie laughed, happy to share his knowledge. "It's the only tarmacked road in the area," he explained. "So, it's black compared to the rough farm roads, and a yett is a gate, so it's the black gate to the Sidlaw farms."

I nodded. The explanation was mundane, somehow. I had expected tales of derring-do from the middle-ages, rather than a flat story about a made-up road. I settled down, enjoying the ride.

Coupar Angus is a pleasant little market town, with narrow streets and a long history. It was busy that day, with men and women, carts and wagons on the roads and more bustle than I had seen for quite some time.

Buying the supplies was easy. I just read the list and the storekeeper produced the goods, which Dougie then carried to the cart. While young Peter would have taken the opportunity to display his strength in carrying the heavy sacks, Dougie threw them around without thought, which was more impressive.

"Is that us ready to head back?" I was quite disappointed that our trip was so short. I found that I enjoyed the crowds, and for once, nobody gave me a second look. I was only another kitchen-maid visiting the town, nothing special and nothing to be sneered at.

"Wait." Dougie held up his hand. "Wait for the army."

I had been aware of the heart-stirring thrill of the bagpipes without thinking of the significance. Now I sat on the cart beside Dougie as the soldiers passed. Three pipers lead them, marching with a fine swagger and a slow swing of their kilts. An officer followed, sitting proudly on a glossy brown charger, and then a sergeant and hundreds of khaki-clad men with dark green kilts around their hips and a red hackle bright on their bonnets.

"See the red hackle?" Dougie asked. "That's the Black Watch, the Royal Highland Regiment."

"What are they doing?"

"They're off to South Africa to fight the Boers," Dougie said.

"Why?"

I watched the soldiers march past, every man wearing a neat khaki uniform, every man with a long bayonet at his belt and every man with a rifle over his shoulder. Mostly young, some no more than boys, they moved as one at the command of their officers, a mobile killing machine without thought or seeming emotion.

"Why?" Dougie stared at me. "We're at war with the Boers."

The Black Watch's boots rose and fell in unison, like a multi-booted spider, crashing to the ground at the same time, a body of men trained to fight and kill.

I had never heard of the Boers and had no idea who they were. "Why?" I asked again. "Why are Scotsmen fighting in Africa?"

I closed my eyes as a sudden image came to be. I saw some of these young, brave, determined men lying broken on an open plain, with a series of low ridges in front. I heard the harsh rattle of musketry and the high screams of the wounded. I smelled the raw blood soaking into the hard ground and saw the pride broken as men cowered for shelter where there was none to be had. As I watched the soldiers march past, I could sense the black corbies hovering over them, choosing the slain, the wounded and the maimed.

I did not want this image. I wanted to be normal.

"The Black Watch is fighting for the Empire." Dougie struggled to explain the concept to me. "The Boers have declared war on Queen Victoria and the British Empire."

I was going to ask "why?" again but changed my mind. I knew I would not understand the answer and doubted that Dougie knew the full facts. I knew that he was expert in farming but took little interest in international politics. In Dougie's mind, the Boers were the enemy and must be defeated; he required no more thought.

"If I weren't a horsemen, I'd have joined the Army." Dougie looked sideways at me, trying to gauge my interest.

"Would you?" I led him on, wondering what tale he would spin.

"Oh, yes," Dougie said. "Could you not see me in uniform, leading a charge against the Zulus or the Russians?"

I avoided Dougie's eyes. I had met men like him before, boasting to girls how strong and brave they would be if only things were different. "I can see you on the rough edge of Mr Lunan's tongue if we don't get back soon." I brought him back to reality.

Puffing at his pipe, Dougie cracked the reins over the horse's rump, and we ambled out of Coupar Angus. The horse seemed to know the way, for it needed no directions as it headed home. Dougie lifted a hand in acknowledgement to half a dozen men in the town, for the farming community was tight knit, with men knowing each other by name or reputation.

As Dougie drove, he sang a military song to prove his soldiering credentials.

"Wha saw the Forty-second?
Wha saw the Forty-twa?
Wha saw the bare-ersed buggers,
Coming frae the Ashanti war?"

Dougie looked sideways at me to check if I was offended by his coarse language.

"The Forty-second is the old name for the Black Watch," he explained helpfully.

"Ah." I nodded without interest.

The image of these soldiers marching to fight a war against an enemy they had never seen stayed in my head as Dougie drove us through the autumn countryside. The weather remained dry, with breaks in the cloud allowing bright sunshine to seep onto us, zebra-striping the Black Yett with alternate bands of light and dark. My head was clear, with not a whistle to be heard, so I enjoyed the movement and peace. Yet, as we drove, Dougie glanced across to me, with his eyes roving the length of my body. I guessed what was coming when he pulled off the road into a farm track and stopped in the shadow of a copse of trees.

"I've never met a woman quite like you," Dougie said, leaning back in the driving seat and spreading his legs.

"I'm nothing special," I said.

"I think you are very special," Dougie said, trying to charm me with his smile.

I felt nothing, neither like nor dislike. I was not attracted to any man or any boy, and Dougie was no different. I regarded him coldly as if he mattered rather less than one of the cows I milked, or Mr Lunan's dogs.

"Could we drive on, now?" I kept all emotion from my voice. "There is nothing of interest here."

"Oh, I think there is something of great interest here," Dougie said.

I deliberately looked around the surrounding woodland. "Trees," I said. "We have both seen trees before."

"I meant you." Dougie leaned back and produced his stubby pipe from his pocket. He smiled at me as he filled the bowl with tobacco. "You are the most interesting lass I have ever met."

"You can't have met very many, then," I told him. "We'd better be getting on, Douglas Mitchell. I have work to do."

"There are other things in life besides work," Dougie said, smiling to me. He was a handsome fellow, I admitted, tall enough and strong as a lifetime of physical labour could make him.

I shifted back slightly. "Douglas," I put an edge to my voice, "I am not interested in you. Please drive me back to Kingsinch."

"Only a kiss?" Dougie asked.

"If you come any closer," I said, "I will slap you hard."

I knew other methods of dealing with too-forward men like Douglas Mitchell, but he would be unable to drive us back if I used them. However, I clenched my fist ready for the under-handed blow that would damage more than his pride and felt the blade of the gutting knife that rested up my sleeve.

"Well, we don't want that, do we?" Dougie knew when to withdraw. Sliding back to his side of the seat, he flicked the reins, and we moved off again. Although he hummed a little song to himself and assumed a nonchalant air, I knew I had not made a friend in Dougie.

I shivered as Mr Snodgrass's face returned to me, with his mouth open as he panted with undisguised lust. I did not know men, then, and I had no defence. I looked at the drab late-autumn countryside and hoped my tears would not betray me.

CHAPTER 5

I WAS MAKING the kitchen fire when Mr Lunan came in. He slumped on a chair without taking off his boots and held his head in his hands for a moment.

"What's the matter, Davie?" Mrs Lunan sat at his side, instantly concerned. "Whatever it is, it can be cured."

"They're back," Mr Lunan said. He looked up. "After all this time hunting them, now they're back, Lizzie."

I concentrated on my task, trying to appear invisible so the Lunans would continue to talk. I am not a perfect woman, and one of my faults is inquisitiveness. I must know everything that goes on around me. That fault might be because of my uncertain childhood, or just natural nosiness.

"Who is back?" Mrs Lunan leaned closer to her husband. "Who's back, Davie?"

I had seldom seen a man so shaken as Mr Lunan sat on his chair. His hands trembled as he gripped the table. "They are, Lizzie." He lowered his voice to a whisper." "The Sidh."

What? That was the second time I'd heard that name. I

tried to listen, but made my inquisitiveness too apparent, for Mrs Lunan glowered at me.

"Ellen!" Mrs Lunan's voice was sharp when she addressed me. "Leave the room! It's time you attended to the cows."

"Yes, Mrs Lunan." I left without argument, and lingered beside the kitchen window, trying to hear the conversation.

"Look," Mr Lunan said. "Look what I found in the infield."

I could not see what Mr Lunan deposited on the table, but I knew it was small as he had carried it in his fist.

"That might have been there for years," Mrs Lunan said. "Maybe hundreds of years."

"No," Mr Lunan said. "It was on the surface, in a plough furrow."

"That explains it then," Mrs Lunan said. "The plough has brought it up."

"A skeleton with missing ribs, and now elf-shot," Mr Lunan said. "It's too much of a coincidence."

Elf-shot? I asked myself. What was that? I had never heard the term before. I tried to listen more, but at that point, I saw Dougie and hurried away to the byre to milk the cows. The conversation had intrigued me, although I did not know the subject. I resolved to investigate further whenever I could, but another matter took precedence later that day.

"Did you hear the news?" Agnes spoke in a hushed whisper, as befitted the possessor of great scandal.

"No," I said. "What's happened?" I expected some tale of amorous misbehaviour, perhaps of Dougie having seduced a servant from another toun, or Jim having found a sweetheart, only to discover she had a husband and three children.

"It was at the suicide graveyard," Agnes said as if that explained everything.

"What was at the suicide's graveyard?" I asked.

We were alone in the kitchen, scrubbing, cleaning, and making the unending brose for the boys. Mrs Lunan was absent for once, which gave Agnes and I the opportunity to exchange scandal. Or rather, it allowed Agnes a chance, for I was too new in Kingsinch for anybody to tell me anything. Stoorey-foots are always the last to know.

"Somebody dug up a grave," Agnes said with her eyes wide and her mouth dripping with drama. "They dug up Mr Anderson's grave and," she lowered her voice even further, "they mutilated Mr Anderson's body."

I had not expected to hear that; nor had I known Mr Anderson. "Mutilated?" I repeated. "What did they do?"

"They took away his ribs" Agnes said. "They cut them out and left his body in the open for the corbies."

"Did you know Mr Anderson?" I asked.

I wondered who the mysterious 'they' might be who cut out Mr Anderson's ribs, and if they were related to whoever had removed the ribs from the skeleton that Andrew had unearthed.

"Aye," Agnes said. "A'body kent auld Wullie Anderson. He was a character, and a half was Wullie. He farmed over by King's Seat until the prices dropped and he couldnae take any more."

"What happened?"

"He drowned himself," Agnes said. "He lay in his own horse-trough and drowned himself."

I pictured the scene, with the old man – I imagined him to be old although I had never met him – struggling for years against the poor soil on a hill farm. He was alone, with nobody to share his burden and the pressures of a failing hairst –

harvest - and mounting debt. I could sense his growing despair, and the final decision to commit suicide. I could see him sitting in an old stone horse-trough, with the water rippling against his chest, and then closing his eyes and lying back. It took courage to drown oneself, I knew, but a long succession of hard times could drain one, I also knew.

"Poor old soul," I said. "What a lonely way to die, and then to be disturbed in his grave."

Agnes looked at me, with the drama's excitement fading from her eyes as she comprehended the tragedy. I thought, then, that Agnes was a good woman, and Andrew was a lucky man.

Naturally, such an event as desecrating a grave became the talk of Kingsinch.

"It must have been Heather Jock," Jim Blair said, placing his feet on my newly scrubbed table to prove his manhood. "He's always been a terrible man."

"Why would Heather Jock do that?" I swept Jim's feet aside.

"Out of pure devilment," Andrew said.

Dougie was uncharacteristically silent as he concentrated on his brose. "It wasnae Jock," he said at last.

I looked at him. "Who else would it be?"

"I don't know," he said, "but it wasnae Jock."

The room fell silent save for the scrape of spoons on plates.

"It was them," Peter said. "The Sidh."

That was the third time I had heard that name used in the farm steading, and I expected a storm of ridicule from the horsemen to the halflin. I was wrong. There was an uncomfortable silence, and then Jim spoke quietly.

"You don't say that Peter. They don't like it." He took out his Jew's harp and strummed a few notes in an attempt to appear nonchalant.

Fool that I was, I broke in. "Who doesn't like it?" I already guessed the answer, but I wanted proof. I desperately wanted somebody to acknowledge what was happening here.

The silence descended again, even longer and more profound than before. The bothy-boys looked at each other with even the ordinarily loquacious Dougie appearing to be tongue-tied.

"*They* don't," Peter eventually said with a sidelong glance at Jim.

Andrew looked up from his brose. "It's an old superstition," he said. "It's not worth thinking about, Ellen." He gave a quick, false smile.

I wondered what sort of superstition could cause these muscular, fit young men to sit in uncomfortable silence. Whatever it was, they believed in it. I needed to learn more about these Sidh. Somehow, I knew this old superstition was connected to the Whistlers who had made my life a misery.

"Somebody saw Heather Jock last week." Andrew changed the subject. "He was at the poaching again, up Meigle way."

"He's braw at the poaching," Dougie said, "but he's no grave-robber."

I looked from man to man, with even the perennially cheerful Jim looking serious and Peter trying to appear manly and tough, while his eyes darted away from mine.

"You'd best get away now, Ellen." Andrew rose from the table. "I'll see you back to the farmhouse."

I laughed at that. "It's only a few steps," I said, secretly glad of the company. Whatever had scared these men, I did not want to meet it in the darkness of the farm steading.

"Aye, I ken fine where the farmhouse is," Andrew said. "But it's best if you don't go alone. Not tonight."

The night was still as we left the bothy, with a hint of frost in the air, so our breath clouded around our faces, and our footsteps echoed from the stark stone walls.

"What are you all afraid of?" I asked when we were alone.

"Nothing and nobody," Andrew said. "I'm just making sure, that's all." Yet he walked slowly and peered around each corner of the buildings as we moved towards the farmhouse. I noticed he clenched his fists as well, something I never expected from the placid Andrew.

"Is it the Sidh?" I asked quietly.

When Andrew did not answer, I was quiet for a few moments, listening to the sounds of the steading. The dogs were giving sonorous tongue, while the cattle were lowing loudly, although I had already milked them.

"The beasts are unsettled," I said.

"Aye," Andrew said no more. He hurried me to the farmhouse door. "In you go," he said. "I wouldnae leave again tonight, Ellen, and make sure Agnes stays indoors."

I nodded. "I'll do that. What is it, Andrew? Is it the Sidh?"

Again, Andrew avoided my question. "It's nothing and nobody," he repeated, glancing over his shoulder. "Nothing and nobody."

The kitchen fire glowed a friendly red as I walked to the bedroom.

"I see young Peter's not lighting the lantern tonight." Agnes was at the window, peering into the dark.

I joined her. "Neither he is."

We saw Mr Lunan striding along the track with his shotgun under his arm and his dogs bounding around him. He carried a lantern, with the light bouncing in front of him, an elliptical yellow glow that one minute revealed the uneven path, and the next gleamed across the furrowed perfection of ploughed fields.

"That's unusual," Agnes said. "I've never known Mr Lunan to go himself."

"It must be because of that grave business," I said.

"That'll be it," Agnes agreed. "The dogs are busy."

Even with the fitful light of Mr Lunan's bobbing lantern, we could see that the dogs were agitated. The usually walked at Mr Lunan's heel, but tonight they wandered around the path and explored the parks, sniffing the ground and occasionally barking to the crescent-moon.

"Something's bothered them," I said. "Maybe Heather Jock is around." I waited for Agnes's response.

"Maybe he is," Agnes said. "Maybe we'd best get to sleep." She closed our bedroom door and placed the only chair under the handle. "Just in case," she said with the shadows in her eyes negating her nervous smile.

The police came around the next day, asking questions about the grave-robbing. My bothy-boys were all out at the ploughing, turning over last season's stubble left from the hairst. I was cleaning out the henhouse and seeing what eggs I could gather but walked over to the farm when the police pulled up in a smart gig.

"The lads are busy," Mr Lunan said to the uniformed police sergeant. "You can see them at lowsing time."

"I'll see them now," Sergeant Milne said, "or I'll run you in for obstructing the police in the course of their duty."

The horsemen were as reluctant to see Sergeant Milne as Mr Lunan had been to send for them. They slouched in one at a time, spreading mud over my newly scrubbed floor, and slumped onto the chairs, glowering at this figure of uniformed authority.

"What is it, officer?" Dougie asked. "I've got half a field to plough yet."

Sergeant Milne was used to such disinclination to co-operate and asked his questions as if the horsemen were eager to help.

"Do you know anything of the violation of Mr Anderson's grave?"

"No." The horsemen gave the same short reply, with Dougie adding a few obscene comments that Sergeant Milne chose to ignore.

"Where were you on the night it occurred?"

"What night was that?"

"Thursday, we think."

"Here," the horsemen replied.

"Do you have any witnesses?"

"We were all here; we don't leave the toun except sometimes on Saturday night or Sunday if we go to the kirk."

In my time at Kingsinch, I had never seen the horsemen even mentioning the church, but I did my smile and began to clean up the mud on the floor. Such an activity gave me an excuse to stay and listen while appearing busy if Mrs Lunan appeared.

"Where is Heather Jock?" Sergeant Milne threw in the question, surprising everybody.

"I heard he was around Meigle way," Dougie said, as the rest of us just looked blank.

"Thank you." Having asked the question that mattered, Sergeant Milne snapped shut his little black notebook and strode to the door.

"It wasnae Heather Jock," Dougie said.

Sergeant Milne turned around. "Who was it then, if not Jock?"

Dougie lifted his chin. "It must have been somebody else."

"Some people," Jim said, producing his Jew's harp and strumming a tune. "Or something. Maybe a dog; dogs like to chew bones, Sergeant. Look for a dog with a smile on its face."

Sergeant Milne lowered his notebook. "Desecrating a grave is no laughing matter," he said. "If I find that you lads have done this is a joke, I'll have you inside Perth jail before you can say cheese."

"Cheese," Jim said, holding the policeman's gaze. "And it wasnae us, Sergeant. What the hell would we want to dig up auld Wullie Anderson for? And cutting out his ribs?" He shook his head. "That's queer, that's what it is. Even the tinks wouldnae do that."

Sergeant Milne put his notebook away. "Maybe not, but my money's on Heather Jock. In Meigle, is he? I'll get off that way now."

"And the best of luck to you," Dougie said. once the sergeant had left the room. "You've as much chance of catching Jock as I have of being crowned King of Scotland."

"Is Heather Jock so good at avoiding capture?" I looked up from my position on the floor.

Dougie threw me a smile. "Jock could walk across a muddy field without leaving footprints," he said. "He could track Jesus Christ through the heavenly clouds, call down birds from the trees and guddle trout from the Tay while standing talking to the keeper."

"He's the bane of all the farmers in Strathmore." Mrs Lunan had been listening from the kitchen door. "He's notorious from Scone to the Brothock Burn and the day the polis clap him in jail is the day the farmers will celebrate with wild shouts and laughter."

"That's a day that will never see the dawn," Dougie said.

I raised my eyebrows and said nothing, fighting the dread that gnawed at my insides. Somehow, I knew that we had not seen the last of Heather Jock. I looked at Dougie with new eyes.

I did not like him and thought he was a womanising boaster, yet he had spoken up for the absent Heather Jock. I favoured him with a nod, to which he responded with an elaborate wink.

Dougie Mitchell had more loyalty and goodness than I had suspected. Yet that was immaterial compared to the fear of the mysterious Sidh that tore at me.

CHAPTER 6

"THE WORD WORKS," Jim announced to the bothy-boys, giving me a sideways look that might have been of triumph, or an invitation. A Cheshire cat in a dairy full of cream could not conjure up a more generous grin than Jim wore as he sat, legs extended, at the bothy table.

I smiled and said nothing, expecting the bothy-boys to tease me. I knew there was no harm in Jim, for all his boasting and big talk. He was barely a man yet, and I could control him, as I could handle most men with an ounce of decency in them. I remembered him during his initiation and smiled again. It was hard to be nervous of a man one had seen with no trousers on, rubbing at his glowing bottom.

Andrew gave a small laugh. "It works with the horses," he said. "The Word combined with the knowledge."

"It's no' the horses I am talking about," Jim said. "It's the women. The Word gave me power over women, as well."

I thought it was better if I left then. It's not a woman's place to listen when men talk about such things, lest they become inflamed with passion, or we burst into laughter, which is more likely. However, I found an excuse to linger a little, for curiosity has always plagued me.

"Oh?" Dougie leaned back in his chair and thrust his thumbs behind his braces. "Try it with Ellen there."

"If you try it with me, Jim," I said, "I'll give you such a belt that you'll see stars." I lifted my ladle in warning, although in truth it was Dougie I was threatening, and not young Jim.

"It's all right, Ellen," Jim said. "I am not after you. I have a girl, and I only want one at a time." He clattered the spoon into his plate. "At first, anyway. Maybe later if I have the inclination."

"That would be best," I said, solemnly. "One girl at a time is sufficient."

"Who is she?" Dougie asked, as innocent as a cat sharpening its claws outside a mouse-hole. "Who is this lucky girl?"

"Her name is Brenda," Jim said smugly. "And she is the best girl in the world."

"Brenda?" Dougie shook his head. "I don't know anybody called Brenda, and I know every girl between Invergowrie and the Angus Glens."

Jim smiled across to Dougie. "You don't know Brenda," he said.

"Where did you meet her?" Dougie asked. "If she exists."

"On the braeside," Jim said.

"On the braeside? Like a stray sheep?" Dougie scoffed. "You'll have to do better than that, Jimbo, my lad. Bonnie lassies don't wander over the braes; they parade in the towns, waiting for a rich lord or a handsome first horseman to look at them."

I left the table, shaking my head and smiling. I did not go far, but stood outside the door, listening. In such a closed community as a farm steading, any morsel of gossip was worthy of being gleaned. I would relate the conversation to Agnes later, and we would lick it clean of every scrap of meaning and innuendo. We would leave it only when we had exhausted the subject and satisfied ourselves that we knew more about this Brenda than Jim did.

"Brenda is no stray sheep," Jim said. She is the most beautiful girl I have ever seen."

"Charlie Fleming has not got a daughter," Dougie continued. "So, who is this hill-wandering Brenda?"

"That's for me to know and you to find out," Jim said.

"When are you meeting her again?" Andrew asked with a smile in his eye.

"Saturday evening, after we're lowsed," Jim said.

"Up on the braeside, again?" Andrew asked.

"Yes," Jim said.

"Where?"

"If I tell you, then you'll come and mock me," Jim said.

"It's a queer lassie that prefers the braes to the town," Dougie said. "I've never heard the like of that afore."

I listened as they argued for a while, but despite Dougie's pleading, cajoling, and threatening, Jim did not disclose where he was meeting Brenda except "up on the braeside."

It was not until the following Monday morning that Jim granted us details of his second tryst to the mysterious Brenda.

"I met her again," Jim said without disguising his smile.

"I saw you, Jim, my lad," Dougie said with an air of triumph.

"You saw me? Where did you see me?"

"I saw you and your lass," Dougie said. "Kissing and cuddling as if you were engaged to marry." He gave a sudden frown. "You've not, have you? You've not got her in the family way?"

Andrew looked up with a smile, as Peter made silly noises, and Jim denied he had done such a thing.

"And not only that," Dougie said, "you were at the Pictish House."

Andrew's smile vanished as if somebody had erased it with a damp cloth. "That's not a good place to meet," he said quietly.

"Don't listen to him," Dougie said. "Anywhere is a good place to meet a lassie."

"Not at the Pictish House," Andrew said. "You must have heard the stories."

"There are too many stories around here," Jim said. "It's all superstition and nonsense, tales old grannies tell to frighten the bairns."

"What stories?" I asked, always anxious to learn more.

There was silence for a few moments, and then Andrew told me that people had seen strange at the Pictish House. "Even sensible folk see things there," Andrew said, "and then cannot say what they saw. They see creatures like us, like men and women, but not men and women."

"That doesn't make any sense," I said, resolving to visit the Pictish House whenever I had spare time. I knew I might be walking into danger, but after a lifetime of running and hiding, I wanted to discover what was happening. I was tired of being the quarry; I wanted to be the hunter.

"What is sense?" Andrew asked with a philosophical shrug of his shoulders. "When we live in a country where some men own hundreds of thousands of acres and live in a city, and others, like us, toil all God's hours to scratch a bare living, what is sense?"

"That's communist talk," Dougie said. "I'll not have any of that in this bothy."

Andrew closed his mouth. As first horseman, Dougie had the final say.

I wanted to hear Andrew talk more communism but had not got the time. My affairs did not include theoretical politics.

I was more concerned with the Whistlers, and perhaps the Pictish House. Somewhere at the back of my mind, I thought there could be a connection.

When Agnes and I had exhausted every possible meaning from Jim's meetings with the perfect Brenda, I broached another subject with her.

"Where does Mr Lunan go every night?" I asked.

"Nobody knows," Agnes said, "except maybe Mrs Lunan. He goes off with the dogs, sometimes up the braeside, and other times just around the fields."

I nodded. "Has nobody ever followed him?"

"And risk losing their position, and getting a bad reference?" Agnes shook her head. "No. You know how hard it is to find a position now, or nobody would be at Kingsinch."

"It's not that bad here," I said. "Mrs Lunan's a bit sharp, but I've worked for worse."

"There are other things," Agnes said. "Surely you've picked up on the atmosphere, and the mysteries."

I nodded. "You mean the skeletons and Mr Lunan's night-time excursions?"

"Aye," Agnes said. "The skeletons and Mr Lunan's walks. Then there is the old chapel, always kept locked and bolted, and that ruined building with the padlock." She shook her head. "I've never known a place with so many mysteries."

"Have you ever heard strange noises here?" I asked.

Agnes screwed up her face. "No, unless you mean from the bothy-boys."

I joined in her laughter. "They're strange enough for anything," I said. "But I want to solve some of these mysteries, so I'll follow Mr Lunan tomorrow evening."

"Don't get caught," Agnes advised.

~

I seemed to spend a lot of time sneaking around the steading at night, which is strange considering my fear of the dark. "Are you coming, Agnes?"

"Not me." Agnes lay on the bed. "I'm not up to adventuring the night."

That suited me, for I would be quieter alone. As Agnes was heavily pregnant, I did not think she should creep about in the near-winter dark anyway.

The wind carried a bite as it slid from the hills, cutting through my coat and skirt, and scouring my exposed face and hands. Wrapping my scarf around my face, I stepped into the night, searching for the lantern-light that would show where Mr Lunan walked. It took only a few moments to find him, with the yellow glow bouncing against the steading's rough stones and the steady tramp of Mr Lunan's feet echoing in the dark. As always, he had his three black mastiffs with him, bulky shadows that padded at his back.

Keeping downwind of the dogs, I followed Mr Lunan as he made his circuit of the steading. He shone his lantern into every nook and cranny, while the dogs followed, vague shapes against the black.

"I know you're here somewhere," Mr Lunan muttered from time to time. "And when I find you, I will kill you."

When he had completed his tour of the steading, Mr Lunan headed onto the path, walking with a steady gait that covered the distance at speed. I kept further back here, for, with no sheltering buildings, the fields were open, bare, and bleak, with the lantern briefly illuminating patches of ploughed earth. The dogs walked at Mr Lunan's heels, occasionally stopping to sniff at the wind or inspect an appealing tuft of grass.

"Where are you going, Mr Lunan?" I asked. I had always been inquisitive, but somehow, I knew that Kingsinch would help solve the mysteries of my life.

Who was I? What caused the whistling that tormented me?

After only ten minutes, Mr Lunan left the track to follow the line of a fail dyke, the turf-boundary between two fields. I knew he was headed for the ruined chapel I had seen the day I arrived at the steading, although I could not imagine for what purpose.

I waited half-way down the dyke, crouching low to avoid being seen and thankful I was downwind of the dogs. Mr Lunan placed his lantern on a convenient stone, possibly one that had fallen from the ruin, then fiddled with a padlock. I heard a creak as he drew back a bolt, then he vanished inside the building, with the dogs eager to follow.

I waited, unsure whether to creep closer or return to the farmhouse. I inched towards the ruin, keeping as low as I could. An owl hooted, once, twice, and again, the sound reassuring rather than eerie. Owls had never bothered me. Even as I hesitated, Mr Lunan reappeared, with the dogs around him. Somehow, I could tell that the dogs were pleased with themselves; I could sense their happiness. However, now I had to move quickly, for the alteration in our relative positions meant the wind would carry my scent to them. Keeping low and holding the hem of my skirt out of the mud as best I could, I scurried deeper into the field, trusting to the dark to hide me.

The wind was fickle, gusting this way and that, howling through the gaps in the dyke and around the ruin's ancient stones. I crouched in the night, a black hump amongst the clouded darkness as Mr Lunan and his dogs stalked past, and only then did I approach the ruin.

The padlock was in place, clamped around the lock, with a heavy bolt securing the door to the jamb. I rattled both more in hope than expectation. What was Mr Lunan hiding in here?

I paused, shaking my head. My curiosity had got me into trouble on more than one occasion in the past, and then I heard the whistling.

"Oh, dear God, no!"

I froze as the whistle undulated out of the dark. I could not see from where it came, or to whom it was directed. I only knew it scared me. I belatedly remembered that same sound when I first walked to Kingsinch, and near this place. I looked around, with goosebumps forming that had nothing to do with the cold. "Who's there?" I asked querulously. "Is there anybody there?"

As always, there was no answer, only that same low, undulating whistle that seemed to come from nowhere and everywhere. I hugged the chill stone of the ruin, wishing I had never left the security of the farmhouse. I felt very vulnerable, unable to see the Whistlers, ignorant of their purpose, or what they were.

The whistling grew louder, as if it was all around me, and even within the ruin. "You won't frighten me," I lied, raising my voice above the pitch of the wind. For the first time, I thought the whistling was pulling at me, dragging me somewhere. I resisted, pushing against the sound. "You won't take me," I shouted, feeling for the gutting knife I carried up my sleeve.

Yet, even as I shouted, I felt a strange compulsion to give up. Part of me wished to follow the music and allow it to ease me away. It would have been easier to lose myself in the soft music and surrender to whatever force created the sounds.

"Dear God, no!" I shook my head as my instinct for self-preservation fought the whistler's subtle invitation.

I stepped away from the ruin, with the noise urging me back, trying to make me open the padlock and enter. "No," I said, and forced myself away, with each step an effort on the muddy, newly ploughed field. "I can't open the lock!" I cried. The whistling continued, a siren-call in the chill dark, an enticement to somewhere I did not wish to go, yet something I had known and feared all my life.

"Go away!" I covered my ears with my hands, desperately wishing that I had not come, yet knowing that I had to solve the mystery. My sanity depended on finding the truth, or I would condemn myself to a lifetime of uncertainty and doubt. People had already believed me insane; perhaps they were correct.

The lights of the farm-toun glowed in the dark and I pictured all the homely, familiar scenes. The bothy boys would be crouched around the fire, boasting of their conquests, maybe playing cards as Jim twanged a tuneless song on his Jew's harp. Mrs Lunan would be in her room with Mr Lunan, maybe reading a book or going over the farm accounts. Agnes would be in our room, lying on the bed and dreaming of her baby and the delights of married life with Andrew. And here I was, exposed to the wild blast of the wind, being assailed by I-knew-not-what, terrified by the honey-sweet invitation to a mystery I was too scared to solve.

My nerve broke then. Lifting my skirt high above my ankles, I ran towards the farmtoun with my boots sinking in the soft earth, stumbling over the pristine plough-furrows. I could hear my breath rasping in my throat, feel my lungs burning and my legs aching, and then I reached the path and ran into something tangible, something that should not be there, something of flesh, bone, and blood.

I screamed. I emitted a full-blooded scream that would have carried right across Strathmore if the wind had not dissipated the sound.

The thing I ran into roared as well, and we stared at each other in mutual terror. I recovered first.

"Peter!" I could hardly contain my relief. "Peter! What are you doing here?"

"Lighting the lantern, Ellen," Peter was immediately defensive. "I'm meant to be here. Mr Lunan says that I'm to light the lantern every night."

"Of course, you do," I said, putting a hand on his shoulder. "What a fright you gave me!"

"I wasnae scared," Peter denied his earlier reaction. "I just got a bit of a surprise, that's all."

Even although Peter was still a boy in his mid-teens, I was glad of his company. "I'll come with you," I said.

Peter nodded, with his eyes gleaming in the dark. "Aye. I'd like that."

We walked side by side on the path, with the wind now flitting the clouds away, so a fitful half-moon shone down on us.

"Did you hear that whistling a few minutes ago?" I asked as Peter seemed reluctant to speak.

"No. I never heard anything."

"I thought I heard a whistling," I said.

"It was probably the wind," Peter told me. "Or an owl. It's all right, Ellen; I'll look after you."

I looked at him with new eyes. He was a sturdy lad, stocky, with an ugly pug face and a determined jaw. I knew he would be a staunch man when he grew up.

"You aren't scared at all, are you?" I asked.

"No," Peter said with his feet thumping down on the path. I listened to his footfall for a few moments, a steady, measured stride. Peter was a country boy through and through, unimaginative, hard-working, and eager to be a man.

When we reached the lantern that swung madly from its hook, Peter scratched a match alight on his third attempt and applied the flame to the wick. The little gleam grew, and he pushed shut the glass, so the lantern spread its circle of yellow light onto the path.

"Are you going to light your lantern, too?" I asked.

"No," Peter said. "I know the way. He looked at me. "Unless you're feared. If you're feared, I can light it."

"Would you light it, please? I don't like passing that old, ruined chapel in the dark."

"I'll protect you," Peter said, obligingly lighting his lantern.

I smiled at Peter then. Although he was much younger than I was, he was also a couple of inches taller and began to walk with a swagger, very much acting the protective man.

"Thank you, Peter," I said softly.

"If you want to go out at night again." Peter exaggerated his swagger, "you just let me know. I'll look after you if you're feart."

I smiled, looked around and, with nobody else looking, reached over and kissed his cheek. "Thank you, Peter," I said, knowing I had made his day and, very probably, his year. Halflins did not have much chance of meeting girls, let alone being kissed by one.

As Peter touched his cheek, I whispered to him. "Please don't tell anybody you met me."

Peter nodded, still with a hand on his face. "It's our secret," he said. "Here's the farmhouse, now, Ellen." Like a true gentleman with tangled hair and rough clothing, he waited until I was inside before he marched away. I heard the thud of his boots disappearing to the bothy and knew he felt six inches taller for having helped a lassie.

The back door of the farmhouse opened directly into the kitchen, so nobody saw me enter. I had to wash the mud off the bottom of my clothes and clean my boots before returning to our room, but I need not have worried about Agnes. She lay diagonally across the bed, taking up all the space, and was fast asleep. Rather than wake her in her delicate condition, I spent that night on the chair, half-dozing as I listened for the whistling that never came.

~

Peter never said a word about our meeting in the dark, but from that night, he became very protective of me. Whenever I had something heavy to lift or carry, Peter would arrive, with a shy smile and a show of muscles to prove he was a man.

"You'd better be careful, Ellen," Dougie shouted. "The halflin thinks you're his sweetheart."

"Well, Douglas Mitchell," I said, smiling archly, "he's already a better man than you'll ever be."

I saw Dougie's face darken, wondered if I should add, "In every way" and decided not to, in case Dougie took some cruel revenge on Peter. A halflin's life was hard enough, as he was at the beck and call of everybody in the farmtoun, from Mr Lunan down to Agnes. Only I was lower down the pecking order. Yet in some ways, I was better regarded, for, while Mrs Lunan had the exclusive right to raise a hand to me, every day seemed to be open season for poor Peter.

Perhaps I viewed him as the little brother I never had, for I took a liking to the young lad, and favoured him with the smiles and quiet conversation that I denied to Dougie. I had always craved a brother or sister, somebody close to which I could confide my fears and secrets.

"You are nobodies," Miss Deas told us daily. "Unwanted rubbish, fit for nothing." She would fix us with that cold, blue-eyed stare. "If it weren't for the orphanage you would live in the gutter, where you belong."

Occasionally, one or other of us would retaliate with a word or gesture, which Miss Deas would instantly repress with cutting words reinforced by the swing of her tawse, the two-tailed strap she carried at all times. I do not know which was worse, her strap with its burning pain across hands, legs or buttocks, or the cruel lash of her tongue, which could reduce a boy or girl to tears. Miss Deas had the knack of finding what hurt us most and exploiting it to the full.

"You are things," she would say. "You are not fit to mix with decent people. Your parents were not married, and your disgraceful mother did not even want you."

There was not a single day when Miss Deas did not reduce some child to sobbing wreckage with her words or her belt, and often she would have two or three of us in such a state.

I learned early not to make friends, for there was nothing Miss Deas liked better than to turn friends against each other.

I have met many terrible people in my life. Yet Miss Deas sticks in my mind as the most wicked, for she preyed on the most vulnerable in society, helpless orphan children and destroyed any confidence they may have had.

"Leave him," said as Dougie cracked the back of his hand on Peter's head for some imagined fault. "He's done you no harm."

Dougie looked up in surprise, for bullying the halflin was one of his prime sports. "He's got to learn!"

"You don't teach somebody by hurting them," I said.

It was a measure of Dougie's astonishment that he argued with me, rather than hitting Peter again.

"It's the quickest way," Dougie said. "We've all been through it."

Andrew had been brushing the mud from his boots. "That doesn't make it good," he said. "The lassie's right. You're too hard on Peter."

"I'm the first horseman," Dougie said as Peter took the

opportunity to escape. He hovered at the bothy door, near to me.

"Aye." Jim had been strumming his Jew's harp and ignoring the ruckus in the bothy. "And I've got the best girl in Scotland."

Andrew laughed as Dougie began to boast of all the women he had known. I left the bothy then, with Peter at my heels.

"Thank you," Peter said, and I saw something in his eyes I had never seen before. I sensed the depths of his feelings for me.

"Try to avoid giving Dougie any excuse to hurt you," I said.

"Yes," Peter said. He hesitated a moment. "Thank you, but you didn't have to do that. I'm tough stuff, Ellen. I can take it."

"I know you are tough," I said. "But you don't have to take it."

"It makes me a man," Peter said.

Something inside me twisted at Peter's words. "You're already a man," I said. "In everything except years."

Peter looked around, as if fearful of being overheard. "I'm not a man yet," he said. "I've never," he paused, "never, you know, with a woman."

I tried not to smile. "There's plenty of time for that," I said. Why did boys put such store in an action that would occur when they were ready?

"You'll be my first," Peter said.

I sighed, for I had guessed at Peter's feelings. "I look on you as a brother," I said, and probably hurt him more than anything Dougie did.

Peter was quiet for a moment. "I don't look on you as a sister," he said and ran away, his legs clumsy.

CHAPTER 7

AGNES HAD GIVEN me specific direction to the Pictish House, augmented with a warning never to visit.

"It's an unchancy place," Agnes said.

"So I've been told," I agreed. "That's why I want to visit."

"You'll be alone then," Agnes said. "Nobody will accompany you."

I did not want anybody with me. After a lifetime of being shunned and running away from people, I told myself that I preferred my own company. I had long adopted a defensive shield that some considered aloofness, never dreaming of the lonely woman inside, screaming for human companionship. Other people were unreliable; they always let me down or walked away when they discovered who I was, or rather, who I was not. Circumstances had forced me to depart from the few exceptions, those few for whom I cared.

There was no path from Kingsinch to the foot of the hills, so I followed the rough tracks to the upper fields. Once there, I walked carefully along the base of the fail dykes that separated one park from another.

Our cattle grazed the lower slopes of the hills, with Charlie Fleming's sheep higher up, their fleece white against the grey-green of late autumn grass. A few scattered trees added variety, with some boulders and the occasional ribbon of a rain-fed burn. I saw the skeletal tops of a group of trees half-hidden in a dip of the hills, bleak and naked under the lead-dull sky. Two hundred yards away, a rounded hillock swelled from the slope, wind-and-sheep cropped to be as smooth as a bald man's pate.

The Pictish House stood in solitary splendour, the only building between Charlie Fleming's cottage and Kingsinch steading. Despite its name, the Pictish House was only a strange, humped structure that dug into the ground. Rather than approach, I sat on a nearby lichen-furred boulder and studied the place.

I could see at a glance that it was old, but I guessed, rather than knew, that the Picts had not built it. I did not know much about these elusive Picts, except they had fought the Romans and disputed the country with encroaching Angles, Scots, and Norse. They must have been an enduring people to last as long, and survive so many waves of invasion, so I doubted they lived in secretive, semi-underground buildings.

"Who built you?" I asked. I wondered, not for the first time, why it was mostly men who attended university, for I would love to gain more knowledge about the Picts and the even more elusive Sidh. I knew I could join the public library if I had the time, but I wanted more than that. I wanted access to a whole world of information to satisfy my curiosity, for my schooling had been both brutal and patchy.

Schooling?

The image came clearly to me as if it had been yesterday, rather than more than a decade ago. I *was standing in the school classroom with the tall, multi-paned window to my left and a seagull screaming outside. Miss Deas had entered the room and caught me staring at the shelf of tattered but enticing books. The titles were so evocative, Robinson Crusoe, A Geography of the World, The Waverley Novels, Tytler's History of Scotland. I wanted to devour them all and learn everything that was between the pages.*

"What are you doing here?" Miss Deas's voice was like breaking glass. I still shivered at the memory.

"I was just looking at the books, Miss Deas." I knew I was quaking with fear. "I didn't touch any of them.

"You've no right to be here," Miss Deas said, closing the door behind her. She stepped towards me with one hand outstretched to grab my shoulder.

"I was just looking!" My voice rose in panic as Miss Deas advanced towards me with slow, deliberate steps. Behind her glasses, her eyes were huge and very blue.

"Come here!"

I panicked. Miss Deas terrified me. I tried to slip past her, but she grabbed my hair, twisting it in her hand, so I screamed. That brought a backhanded slap across my face.

"I'll teach you," Miss Deas said and grabbed the long tawse that lived on top of her desk when it was not ready in her fist. "I'll give you something to cry about!"

The whistling brought me back to the present. I saw a small man standing beside the Pictish House. He was watching me through almond-shaped eyes.

"Hello," I said, still shaking from my memory of Miss Deas.

The small man said nothing, yet for a strange moment I thought I knew him, or perhaps he knew me. I certainly did not feel threatened, as I usually would if I met a strange man on a lonely hillside.

Only when the man smiled did I notice the birthmark on his face and the slightly pointed ears. I started, and he vanished. It was as quick as that. One moment he was there and the next he was gone.

"Wait!" I stood up. There was no trace of the small man. "Where are you? Don't be scared! I won't hurt you."

Lifting my skirt, I ran across the rough grass to the Pictish House, wondering if he had maybe fallen through a gap in the stonework. He had not. The masonry was as secure as if the builders had left last week rather than a thousand or ten thousand years ago.

"Hello!" I shouted with my voice drifting in the wind. "Where are you?"

I could not see the small man. "Hello!" I shouted again.

"Hallo!" The reply came a few moments later, and a long, lean man strode towards me, holding a shepherd's crook in his hand. "Who are you to be making so much noise?"

"I'm Ellen Luath," I said, "I'm working at Kingsinch."

"You're the new kitchen maid," the man said, "I'm Charlie Fleming. What are you doing here?"

I liked this man with his direct approach and the slow, lazy smile as he stood two yards away, leaning his hands on his crook.

"I came to see the Pictish House," I said. "And I thought I saw a wee man here."

"Ah." Charlie Fleming nodded. "The wee man. I've seen him. He won't harm you."

"Who is he?"

"I'm blessed if I know," Charlie Fleming said. "He doesn't do me any harm, and I don't bother him."

I liked Charlie Fleming even more. "Is he a tramp? A gypsy perhaps? I've seen gypsies near here."

"Neither one nor the other," Charlie Fleming said. "He's a ghost, I think. Either that or one of the Sidh."

"A ghost?" I repeated foolishly, "or one of the what?" I

pretended ignorance to elicit more information from Mr Fleming. I knew that men of his age liked to speak to young women; it appealed to their fatherly instincts if nothing else.

"The Sidh," Mr Fleming said. "The old folk, the People of Peace who lived in these parts before even the Picts."

"I thought they died out centuries ago." I did not hide my confusion.

"Maybe they did," Mr Fleming said, "or maybe they went underground and learned how to live among us without being seen." He grinned, showing uneven, tobacco-stained teeth. "As I said, they don't bother me, and I don't bother them." He tapped his crook on the ground. "I'd better be getting on. I wouldn't stay too long here, Miss Luath. It's getting dark."

"Are the Sidh dangerous after dark?"

"I was more thinking of you falling over and breaking an ankle," Mr Fleming said, "I've never heard of them bothering anybody." He winked and loped away, long-striding over the mingled heather and rough grass.

I finished my inspection of the Pictish House without finding anything except stone walls that fitted without mortar and extended thirty yards under the hill. Not far away, I climbed to the top of the bald-smooth hillock, more to look at the view than for any other reason, sat on a rounded boulder and allowed the wind to caress my face.

From up here, I could see the whole valley, with the flat fields the bothy boys were gradually ploughing, and Kingsinch looking more like an island than it did from ground level. The name inch gave a clue, for it was the old Scots word for an island. The ancient ruin was also on a small hump, I realised. I heard somebody singing, presumably Mr Fleming, admired his musical voice and saw two more people watching me.

This time, I knew without asking that they were Sidh. I lifted a hand to wave to them, and they disappeared. I did not see them move. What I did see was Mr Lunan, striding over the hill with his shotgun under his arm and his three dogs at his heel. He was so intent on his walk that he did not see me, which was strange as I was little more than a hundred yards distant.

Mr Lunan walked around the Pictish House, with his dogs sniffing at the ground, occasionally giving tongue.

"We're not after rabbits," Mr Lunan growled. "Come on."

The dogs stopped at one area of the hillock, pawing at the turf, and barking. Mr Lunan joined them, poking at the ground with his toe.

"Come on, dogs." Mr Lunan pushed them away. "There's nothing here."

I remained perched on my boulder until Mr Lunan was gone, and shaking my head, I stood up and began the steep walk home. After my childhood experiences when I told people I heard whistling, I knew better than to mention the Sidh.

I spent that night with my mind in turmoil. I had been familiar with the whistling since I was very young, but only today had I seen the Sidh who presumably caused it. I tried to analyse the little that Charlie Fleming had told me about them. They lived in our world but were different; they might have been here before we were, and they seemed to have the ability to appear and disappear without effort.

Why? I asked myself.

Why were the Sidh whistling to me? Were they hunting me? Or were they only whistling and nobody else could hear them except me?

The questions filled my head, driving me further towards insanity with every moment. I knew that the Pictish House had given me a partial answer to my questions, and I wondered if there were more answers I could tease out in Kingsinch. I resolved to dig deeper and lever up whatever I could.

~

"Has that old chapel got a name?"

"We just called the ruined chapel," Agnes replied at once. "And the skelp of land it's on is called Chapelinch."

"What does Mr Lunan use it for?"

Agnes shrugged. "He doesn't use it for anything," she said. "It's dangerous, so Mr Lunan warned us all to keep clear of it."

"I see," I said. "There must be a story behind it."

"There's a story behind everything here." Agnes tried to settle herself comfortably on the bed. "It was about a thousand years ago when King Malcolm the Destroyer was fighting the Vikings. He passed through here and got lost in the Moss."

"Is that why it was known as the Kings Moss?"

Agnes shrugged. "Probably," she said. "You know that we're on an island here in the steading, don't you? All the flat land, all the fields around us were once moss land – bogland. The farmers have been working to drain it for generations, with Mr Lunan doing most of all, I think."

"I know that," I said. "Tell me about the old chapel."

Agnes had found a comfortable position, with a pillow supporting her belly. She smiled, quite happy to educate me, and I wondered if I had found a true friend at last. "Well, King Malcolm was trying to raise an army to fight the Vikings, or the Danes or the English or somebody, and he got lost in the hills. He was a great warrior, but no good at hill navigation, and he wandered into the bogland. It was raining, so he was in danger of drowning as he floundered in the deepening mud. He prayed to God to save him, and God led him to these inches, these raised areas of dry land amidst the moss."

"That was very kind of God," I said.

"It was," Agnes agreed. "King Malcolm was so relieved to

be saved that he promised the Lord he would build a church on the smaller of the two islands."

"I see the king kept his word," I said.

Agnes nodded. "He marked out the boundaries of the building with his sword, and after he defeated the enemy at the Battle of Barry, the king kept his promise and built the church."

"It would be a lonely place for a church back then," I said.

"Aye, and it was an unlucky site, too," Agnes said. "The priests, or whatever they were all disappeared, and so did the next lot. The holy folk gave up and abandoned the chapel."

"What happened to the priests?"

Agnes shrugged. "I don't know," she said. "Nobody knows. They just vanished." She lowered her voice. "The legend says the Sidh took them."

I fastened onto the word to see if Agnes could tell me more. "The Sidh?" I sighed. "I've heard that term used since I came to Kingsinch," I said, "who are the Sidh?"

"We don't talk about it, here," Agnes said.

"Why not?" I asked.

"We just don't," Agnes said.

I nodded. The Sidh, whoever they were, seemed to throw a malign influence over Kingsinch steading. While part of me wished to find out who these mysterious Sidh were, another part warned me to keep clear. Yet I knew I had to find out to clear my mind.

"That's why folk don't like to take this farm, except the desperate," Agnes said. "They're afraid of the Sidh."

"I see." Mr Fleming had mentioned the Sidh up by the Pictish House, and I had seen the small, friendly man who had appeared out of nowhere and vanished just as quickly. Why were people afraid of the Sidh that did not worry Charlie Fleming, who lived close by them?

"Are the Sidh so dangerous?" I asked.

Agnes nodded. "Yes. They steal babies and sometimes women." She clammed up, looking down at her belly with sudden concern.

I could not imagine the small, friendly man I had seen stealing babies or women. "I see," I said, again. I felt I was piecing together a mystery, brick by brick, without any idea of the structure I was creating. I had lived my entire life in the shadows, despite my best attempts to discover who I was. Those attempts had often got me into trouble.

"What are you doing here?" Mr Snodgrass's voice made me jump "You've no right in here?"

I looked around from the cupboard, aware of my wrongdoing. "No, Mr Snodgrass," I said. "I was just looking for something."

Mr Snodgrass stepped into the office, with the candle in his hand throwing dark shadows over his face. "You're Ellen Luath, aren't you?"

I nodded, wondering if I could dive out of the window and escape. Mr Snodgrass's hand crushing my shoulder ended that hope.

"I've heard about you. Miss Deas told me you were a troublemaker."

"I'm not causing trouble, Mr Snodgrass," I tried to defend myself. "I was just looking."

Mr Snodgrass placed the candle on his desk so yellow light pooled around the room, revealing the open drawers and the files I had piled on his desk.

"What are you looking for?" Mr Snodgrass asked, with his eyes bright inside deep pits.

"I was looking to see who I was," I explained truthfully.

Mr Snodgrass sat on his chair and sighed, looking more patient than I had expected. I began to hope I might escape from his study without him beating me. "You are an orphan, Ellen," he said. "We did not know your name, or from where you came. Somebody, perhaps your mother, left you at our doorstep and that's all we know."

Mr Snodgrass sounded so kindly that I nearly believed him. The candlelight softened the hard lines of his face as he held my shoulders with both hands. "You are an orphan of the storm, little Ellen nobody, an unwanted waif, a piece of litter blowing in the wind."

"Yes, Mr Snodgrass." I was growing uncomfortable in his hands and wriggled to escape. He was too strong for me.

"Nobody wants you," Mr Snodgrass's voice was growing harder as his grip tightened. "You are fortunate that Miss Deas and I look after you, feed and educate you and teach you right from wrong."

"Yes, Mr Snodgrass," I said, now desperate to escape. I did not know what Mr Snodgrass planned, but I knew it would not be pleasant.

"Right from wrong." Mr Snodgrass's right hand slipped down my arm to my leg, while his left hand held me tight. "What happens to unwanted little girls who nose into places they are not allowed?" His right hand was on my leg now, his fingers cruel as they thrust into me.

"I don't know!" I said, hearing my voice shrill.

"Well, if you don't keep quiet, I'll teach you." Mr Snodgrass's voice was harsh, his breathing hard as his fingers probed my immature body. "If you utter one more word, I'll belt you naked before the whole orphanage!"

Despite Mr Snodgrass's threats, I tried to scream, but his hand covered my mouth. He lifted me and threw me on the floor, lifted my dress and spread my legs. I struggled, kicking, and scratching as hard as possible, but a nine-year-old girl cannot fight off a grown man in his forties. His fingers were cruel inside me, preparing me for the worse ordeal to come.

When Mr Snodgrass finished, he buttoned himself back up and glared down at me as I lay sobbing and bloody on the ground. "Wash yourself," he said, "and remember what will happen if you mention this to anybody."

Later, as I lay in my hard bed in the dormitory, I opened the crushed piece of paper I had held throughout my ordeal. I read the words:

"Unknown child," they said. "Left on the doorstep on the 31ˢᵗ ᵒᶠ October 1882. Ellen's name was tied to her wrist and the letters LU embroidered on the shawl in which we found her."

Nobody even knew my last name.

Ellen Luath; that was me. I was unwanted and unknown. I was Ellen Luath, and I would survive whatever this orphanage threw at me.

I cried myself to sleep that night, as I had so often in my life. I did not remember the newspaper; I remembered a green shawl, although I knew I should not have a memory from such an early age. I always knew I was strange. I was different: perhaps that was why my parents abandoned me so young?

The first I knew that Heather Jock arrived was the sound of a startled hen in the small hours of the morning. My first thought was of a fox, and I turned over to go back to sleep, for the henhouse was Mrs Lunan's responsibility, and if she had not locked the door properly, the fault lay with her.

I could not sleep, for fear of the whistling was upon me, yet there was no whistling that night. Nature blessed me with acute hearing, and the sound of the footfall was distinct. By that time, I could recognise Mr Lunan and any of the bothy-boys by their footfalls. I knew the feet I heard did not belong to anybody in Kingsinch.

"Go to sleep," Agnes complained when I sat up in bed.

"Somebody's walking about outside," I said.

"I can't hear anything. Go to sleep," Agnes said, but I was already up and at the window.

"You're too restless," Agnes complained. She was sleeping within a minute, lying on her side, and breathing steadily.

I opened the curtains slowly, determined not to disturb anybody outside, and peered into the dim. Starlight and a new moon fought the dark, and I saw the bedraggled figure of a man passing furtively past the henhouse. I knew at once that it was Heather Jock. He was about middle-height, lean and wiry, with ragged dark clothing and unkempt hair. Yet, although he was evidently stealing from the henhouse, I could not feel any badness in the man. He was a rogue, of that I was confident, but that was all. I had felt sufficient badness in my life to recognise it. Even as I watched Heather Jock, I knew he had not been responsible for digging up Mr Anderson's grave.

"Come back to bed," Agnes stirred and looked at me. "I need to sleep."

I obeyed, for there was no more for me to see.

"Bloody Heather Jock!" Mr Lunan roared the next morning. "It must have been him! The henhouse was locked and secured, and a fox would have massacred everything inside. Only Jock would have taken two hens and secured the door after him."

"It's time the police locked away that man for good," Mrs Lunan said.

I hid my smile, although I rather liked the idea of a thief who closed the door behind him. I continued to black-lead the kitchen range, wondering if I would ever see Heather Jock again. I hoped so.

CHAPTER 8

THE MOON WAS FULL, with silver beams seeping through the panes in the window I had cleaned to perfection. It may have been the moonbeams playing on my face that awakened me, or something else. I only knew that one moment I was in my usual disturbed sleep, reliving the bad old days of childhood, and the next I was awake.

Agnes slept beside me, with every breath moving a stray strand of hair that crossed in front of her lips. I glanced at her fondly and slid from the bed carefully so as not to disturb her.

The moonlight made the steading nearly as bright as day, casting short shadows from the stark stone buildings, high-lighting the shape of the cobbles on the ground, and disturbing the beasts. The cattle were lowing softly, while I saw a couple of bats flitting past. They called to each other, or something else, with their high-pitched squeaks pleasant in the night.

I know that some people are afraid of bats, but I do not fear them. No bat has ever attacked me, nor have they ridiculed or belittled me, as many people have. On the contrary, they mind their own business and hunt the insects of the night, which can bite when one is least ready for them.

An owl called, the wavering hoot friendly. I like owls as well, for they live lonely lives, hunting for food. They are the terrors of the mouse population and eat rats, which spread diseases.

Yet it was neither an owl nor a bat that I saw as I peered out of the window. I did not know what it was at first. I saw it, and then it was gone as if it had never been.

I blinked and looked a second time. I was sure I had seen something out there, something that moved on two legs, like a man, yet no man could disappear so suddenly and so completely.

I stared outside, wondering if I had been dreaming. I started when I saw the man if it was a man again. He moved on two legs, like a man, but so softly and swiftly that there was no sound as he passed across a moonbeam and vanished.

"Who are you?" I asked. "What are you?"

I already knew the answer. He was one of the Sidh, the strange people I had seen at the Pictish House, the entities that scared everybody except Charlie Fleming.

Should I also be afraid of them?

I was not sure. My life had sent me so many mixed messages I was unsure what to believe or who to trust. At one time, I had welcomed the night as giving me relief from the daytime tyranny of Miss Deas. Then I had feared the long, lonely hours of the night, with only my dark thoughts for companionship in my bleak cell. When I returned to the dormitory, I had feared both, for the tortures of my fellow orphans replaced the torments of Miss Deas. I had longed for the day the Orphanage released me, and I was free to pursue my life. Yet freedom brought other trials.

"Who are you?" The woman smiled to me from her side of the open door.

"If you please, miss," I said, "I am Ellen Luath from the Orphanage."

"Oh," the woman opened the door, "you're the new girl."

"Yes, miss." I bobbed in a curtsey, as Miss Deas had taught us.

"Come in and welcome." The woman's smile broadened. "I am always happy to see a polite, well-mannered girl."

I stepped into the house, where a dozen more young girls were busily sewing. None looked up when I entered; they all kept their heads down at their work while a coarse-featured man walked around, glowering.

"I am Mrs Lindsay," the smiling woman said. "You'll be happy here. There is plenty to keep you busy and busy hands are happy hands."

Within ten minutes of my stepping through the doorway, I was sitting at the table, with a thin-featured girl explaining what I had to do.

"We stitch shirts together," she said. "You will attach the sleeves. No stopping, no breaks and no talking."

I glanced at the brutal-looking man and shivered. I could guess what would happen if I stopped work. I had run willingly from the frying pan to fall into the fire.

Mrs Lindsay remained for the remainder of that day, smiling over our table as she supervised our work, occasionally stopping to do a little sewing herself. We slept at night wherever we could, crowded together on the floor, huddled in a human clump to contain each other's warmth.

"What is Mrs Lindsay like?" I asked.

The thin-featured girl, who called herself Mary, answered in a small whisper. "Don't talk unless somebody asks you a question. Sleep when you can and eat if you can."

I saw behind Mrs Lindsay's smile the next morning when one of the girls, a huge-eyed little creature called Sarah, dropped a stitch. Mrs Lindsay continued to smile as she lifted Sarah by her hair and thrust a needle deep into her hand before dropping her back on her chair, with the needle still in place.

After that, I made sure I did not drop any stitches.

I remained with Mrs Lindsay for a few months, for it was winter, the rain hammered off the windows, and the wind roared in the chimney. If the days were unremittingly ugly, my nights were better. None of the other girls tried to bully me; either because they were all too exhausted, or perhaps because I did not mention the whistling in my head. The brutal-faced man proved the friendliest person in the house as he produced the occasional potato or piece of dry bread when Mrs Lindsay left to take the shirts to wherever she sold them.

The months passed until the spring when news of my ancestry reached the house.

"You're from the lunatic hospital in the orphanage," Mrs Lindsay said and told the girls not to speak to me. "Her disease might be catching," Mrs Lindsay said.

"It's not a disease, and it's not catching," I was foolish enough to reply.

Mrs Lindsay's smile broadened as she wrapped my hair around her hand and lifted me high in the air.

"Little girls don't answer back," Mrs Lindsay said as she lifted her longest needle, held it to the candle until the point was hot, and slowly thrust it in into the fleshiest part of my thigh. "Little lunatic girls do as I say."

I screamed, once, and kicked out as hard as I could. The point of my boot caught Mrs Lindsay in her belly, and she yelled. I kicked again, until she dropped me, so I fell on the floor with my scalp in agony and the needle still protruding from my thigh. I had no desire for any more of Mrs Lindsay's smiling company *so scrabbled for the door handle and fell into the street outside, limping and with blood oozing slowly down my leg.*

I do not know how long I ran or where I went. I only know that my sewing career ended that day, and my leg burned like nothing on earth. My attempt to be normal had failed, and to make things worse, the whistling met me as I limped to nowhere.

The advent of November brought the day of the wedding. As was the custom, we called it a Penny Wedding, with all the guests contributing a penny to the festivities and most bringing food and drink to help the couple begin their journey through life.

Some of the local farmers attended the wedding on horseback. Others arrived on dogcarts crowded with farm-servants in their Sunday best, all shaved and groomed and in high good humour. Nearly everybody knew each other from the feeing-fairs or through a long acquaintance, with me being the only stranger.

The wedding was at the Free Kirk at Newtyle, a planned village a few miles to the east. Few of the bothy lads had much time for the established Church of Scotland, which they viewed as a tool of the establishment that had supported the forced evictions in the Highlands. Instead, they favoured the Free Kirk, which had broken away from the established church, or Kirk. The congregation appointed the Free Kirk ministers, while the austerity of the buildings and sincerity of the services reflected the hard life of the land. The minister had railed at Agnes's pregnant condition before marriage, but he also approved of Andrew marrying the women he had got into trouble, as he called her pregnancy.

"It's a natural state," Mr Lunan said as he met the minister, the Reverend Ogilvy, face-to-face, "and no reason for shame between lad and lass."

"Restraint is a Christian virtue," the minister said.

"So is forgiveness," Mr Lunan said, "and I've seen damned little of that among the unco good of the Kirk, even the Free Kirk."

The Reverend Ogilvy nodded. "I'm glad you're back in the fold, Mr Lunan, and I forgive you your lapse of attendance this past nine Sabbaths." He walked away before Mr Lunan could retaliate.

In the Free Kirk, the wedding ceremony is simple, with no music except the psalms of the congregation, and no fuss except the long sermon intended to keep bride and groom on the straight and narrow path to redemption. Expecting heaven is a bit much to hope for in the Free Kirk, where the Sabbath was a time to think of eternal damnation, and playing cards were known as the Devil's Bible.

When the minister announced that Agnes and Andrew were man and wife, one of the coarser elements in the congregation – I think it was Dougie – shouted out "you can now legally do what you've been doing for months." There was a subdued murmur of laughter and a disapproving glare from Mr Ogilvie. I managed to keep my face straight, despite Agnes's sudden embarrassment.

After the ceremony, we thanked the Rev Ogilvie and headed back to Kingsinch for an evening of music, dancing and singing. It was only when we left the kirk that I realised I had heard no whistling all day. The absence of noise in my head was a blessing that I enjoyed, and when I wiped a tear from my eye, Agnes misconstrued my reason.

"Weddings always make me cry too," she said. "It will be your turn soon, Ellen. I know it."

I felt Peter's eyes on me and did not need to force my smile.

"Come back in five years, Peter, my lad," I thought, "and you'll still be too young for me."

The jovial atmosphere altered when we turned off the public road onto the track to Kingsinch. Two of the dogcarts pulled up.

"This is as far as we go," the farmers said.

"It's only a couple of miles," Andrew protested.

"We're not going to Kingsinch," the farmers refused to even turn into the road-end. "We wish you the best of British luck."

"Don't believe all the rumours," Mr Lunan pleaded.

"If only half were true, we'd still not come," the farmers said.

The remaining dogcarts followed us along the track, jolting in the ruts. I noticed that while the farmer's wives and daughters studied the people, the men examined the state of the fields, remarking on the quality of the ploughing and farming. Mr Lunan and Dougie listened anxiously for the comments of their professional peers.

"No' bad," was the primary comment, which was high praise from a Scottish farmer.

Once we arrived at the farm, I was hard at work in the kitchen, with Agnes excused work for the evening as she was the bride.

"You enjoy yourself, Agnes," Mr Lunan said. "Ellen will cope. Ellen's our new kitchen lass," Mr Lunan explained as people enquired who I was. "She's from up north."

"What brings you down here, lass?" a middle-aged farmer asked me, not unkindly.

I could not tell him the truth, for fear of appearing a fool. "It's hard to find a position in Moray." I mustered a crooked smile. "There seems to be a glut of kitchen maids up there."

"Aye." He nodded his grizzled head, with his shrewd eyes

appraising me as if I was a stunted cow at the market. "And you might find a husband down here, too."

"I might, at that," I agreed, for it was better to appear pleasant than to argue.

The farmer nodded and moved away. I knew that my name and history would spread around the company within half an hour so everybody would know all about me. That suited me, for I disliked repeating the same story, and nobody in the south knew about the asylum.

As I toiled in the kitchen with plates, glasses, and Mrs Lunan's precious best china, the food and whisky flowed freely. I could judge the progress of the drinking by the volume of wild laughter, raised voices, thumping of dancing feet on the ground and coarseness of the humour and language.

I listened to one of the more repeatable songs, humming to the tune.

"Come, ye jolly lads and lasses,
Ranting round in pleasure's ring
Join wi' me, tak up the chorus,
And wi' mirth and glee, we'll sing."

Scottish farmers can be a reticent bunch, but give them an excuse and a few drams, and the barriers fall, the hair comes down and the repressed joviality of months of achingly hard work explodes into life. When a couple of fiddlers arrived to add music to the evening, I knew we were in for a noisy time.

Every so often a guest or one of the bothy-boys would erupt into the kitchen for more food or another bottle of something sensible, and I was busy carrying bannocks, scones, oatcakes, and other delicacies through the house. Twice in the first hour, I had to fend off the roving hands of drunken horsemen, and once I interrupted a courting couple as they slipped into a quiet corner for some purpose of their own.

I was scouring the house for discarded plates and glasses and saw candlelight reflecting on a glass outside the press – the walk-in cupboard – in the back passageway. Tutting at our guests' inconsideration, I stepped forward to retrieve the glass. I realised the cupboard door was open and moved to close it when I heard the rustle of clothing and subdued laughter. Naturally, I glanced inside the press.

Neither of the two people inside saw me. They were too busy exploring each other's bodies, with more animal lust than any pretence at affection. I lingered for a fraction longer than I should, more out of astonishment than any other reason. I was not surprised that the man was Dougie, showing his muscular buttocks to great purpose. However, I had not expected his partner-in-sin to be Mrs Lunan. Yet, why not? She would have the same desires as any other healthy animal, and Mr Lunan was at least twenty years older than she was. With her eyes closed and her mouth open, she looked just like any other mature woman in such a situation.

"Sorry," I said politely and withdrew. I doubt that Dougie or Mrs Lunan even noticed I was there, and certainly neither ever mentioned the incident. I felt some sympathy for Mr Lunan as I refilled his glass five minutes later.

"Thank you, Ellen," he said, deep in a discussion about lung-disease in cattle. I doubt he knew his wife was missing, given such a fascinating conversation.

Perhaps it was the excitement, but Agnes's voice grew shriller as the evening wore on. I watched her, but I did not need to worry, for Andrew proved the most attentive of new husbands, ensuring he was at hand and ushering her to a chair whenever the burden of pregnancy grew irksome.

As the clock ticked away the evening, Mrs Lunan

appeared, glanced around the company, patted her husband's arm, and pulled me aside.

"Ellen," Mrs Lunan said sharply. "You'd best attend to the cows. I'll look after the kitchen until you're back."

"Yes, Mrs Lunan," I said, for, in truth, I was glad to escape the noise and confusion for a few moments. Bothy-boys and drink is not the best combination, and as the whisky flowed, the men's behaviour deteriorated. I was tired of stray hands patting and pinching my rather plump bottom. It would have been bad enough if the hand's owners were handsome young men, but most came from the older, married men, and in the presence of their wives, as well.

I welcomed the cool air of the steading and walked briskly to the byre, where the cows bellowed in expectation of being milked.

"Here I am, girls," I said as I entered the byre.

They greeted me with a welcome chorus, and I began work, talking to them, as was my way. In common with most animals, cows respond best to a friendly word, and by that time, I knew each animal by her nature and personality.

"You're agitated today," I said as one of my favourites butted me with her head. "Has the excitement of the wedding affected you?" I laughed and patted her face. "You'd like to join in, wouldn't you?"

It was then that I became aware that I had company in the byre. The cattle lowed in warning, and I turned around with the memories of the whistling returning to my mind. I had neglected to carry my knife in my sleeve and looked around the byre for a suitable weapon.

"It's only me," Peter stood in the doorway, smiling. "I wanted to make sure you were all right."

"Thank you, Peter," I said as he stepped closer. "Wouldn't you prefer to be at the celebrations than in a gloomy byre?"

"I'd rather be with you," Peter said. "I like you."

I stopped milking the cow and smiled across to him. "That's very flattering," I said, "Thank you, Peter. I like you, too." That was true; I did like Peter, but not in the manner he hoped. "If I ever had a wee brother, I hope he'd be like you."

Peter stepped further into the byre. "I don't think of you as a sister," he said.

I swivelled around on my stool to face him. "What do you think of me as, Peter?"

"My girl," Peter said, placing his thumbs in his braces to imitate the stance that Dougie often adopted.

"Oh, Peter." I shook my head. "Peter, Peter. What a lovely thing to say."

As Peter stepped even closer, I held out my hand. "How old are you, Peter?"

"Fifteen," Peter said, "nearly sixteen, and I am big for my age."

"I am far older than you, Peter," I said, as kindly as I could.

"Yes, but you kissed me," Peter said.

"I did," I agreed. "I kissed you to thank you, as I would kiss my brother."

"Kiss me again," Peter said.

"Do you want to be my friend?" I asked.

Peter nodded.

"Then make yourself useful." I made my voice as businesslike as I could. "Mrs Lunan asked me to place a rowan branch above the byre door to protect the beasts from witches, but I don't like heights."

"I'll do it for you!" Peter brightened at once as the genuinely decent boy emerging from the masculine image.

"Thank you, Peter," I said, favouring him with a smile.

"It's not to keep witches away, though," Peter said. "It's to keep away the Sidh."

I sighed and asked my usual question. "Who are these Sidh?"

"The Sidh are the People of Peace," Peter was pleased to educate me. "That's what we have to call them, anyway. We pronounce it as Shee but spell it as SIDH – and they lived all over this area."

"Lived?" I fastened on the word, determined to glean every scrap of information I could from every source.

"They are the old folk." Peter sat down on the ground, ruining his best clothes. The hills – the Sidlaw Hills – were named after them." He produced a pipe to look more manly. "There are hundreds of stories about the Sidh all over the Sidlaw Hills and in Strathmore."

The People of Peace, the Sidh. I shivered as the name seemed to hang in the dusty air of the byre. "Have you ever seen one?"

"Me?" Peter laughed at the idea. "Not me!"

"Have you heard them talking?" *Could nobody hear them except me?*

Peter looked surprised. "No, of course not. You do ask the strangest of questions."

"That's because I'm the strangest of women," I said. "Are the Sidh dangerous?"

Peter screwed up his face. "They used to be, but they're all deid now," he said pragmatically. "Deid folk cannae hurt anybody, but the old folk like to keep the stories alive."

"You're not scared of them," I said.

"No," Peter said and repeated. "Deid folk cannae hurt anybody." He laughed. "Did you not hear about auld Lunan?"

"No," I said. "I didn't hear about Mr Lunan."

"Well," Peter said, warming to his subject as I returned to the milking, "auld Lunan likes to say that the Sidh stole his first wife. He says that he was farming over Carlungie way, past the old Pictish fort of the Laws, and he was out one night."

I did not know the old Pictish fort of the Laws but allowed Peter to continue with his story.

"So auld man Lunan was coming home from the inn at Monikie, when he heard a noise, like singing, except with no words. He said it was like folk humming or whistling."

"Whistling?" I repeated.

"Aye, so auld Lunan said," Peter spoke with all the wisdom of a teenager. "Mind you; he was drunk when he told the story."

I nodded. "Carry on, Peter, please." I felt my heart hammering. Mr Lunan had heard the whistling; I was not alone, and here was proof that the Sidh were the Whistlers. I placed another small brick in my wall of knowledge.

"Aye, so anyway, auld Lunan was going home when he heard this low, penetrating whistling, and then a whole host of the Sidh passed him, running with a litter in their midst. Now, the Sidh liked to grab new-born bairns, so auld Lunan thought the litter held somebody's baby, maybe his. He carried a stout rowan staff and shouted for the Sidh to stop. They whistled all the more and ran faster, with auld Lunan chasing after them. He wasnae so old then and caught the hindmost."

I shook my head. "I thought you said the Sidh were all dead."

"Aye, I did," Peter confirmed and continued, "When Mr Lunan caught the Sidh, he shouted "Got you, by God, and all the others ran away, leaving him with a woman of the Sidh. He held her fast and hurried home, to find that his wife and bairn had gone, and a long wooden figure was in Mrs Lunan's place in their bed."

"The Sidh stole Mr Lunan's first wife and his baby?" I asked.

"Aye, that's what he claims," Peter said. "They took babies before they're safely Christened, and sometimes the mothers, to care for the bairns, ken?"

"I see." I felt my heartbeat increase even further. "What did Mr Lunan do?"

Peter smiled, evidently enjoying having my undivided attention. "Mr Lunan kept the female he captured as a prisoner to try and get his wife and baby back, and he holds her still, in the ruined chapel; the one you're feared of."

I remembered the whistling around Chapelinch. "Dear God," I said.

I could see the Sidh woman in there, chained to the wall, shivering with cold and fear, listening to the howl of the wind and the batter of rain. I remembered what it was like in my cell in the lunatic asylum and imagined suffering in that manner for endless years. "That poor woman," I said.

Fortunately, Peter misinterpreted my words. "Aye, poor Mrs Lunan," he agreed. "It must be awful for her."

I nodded. "Maybe the Sidh will release her sometime."

"Aye, maybe." Peter stood up, brushing some of the straw from his trousers. "That's why auld Lunan patrols with his dog, hoping the Sidh come back to get his captive, and he can swap her for his old wife, except then he'd have two."

"The present Mrs Lunan won't like that," I said. "Nor would Mr Ogilvie. The Kirk disapproves of bigamy."

Peter smiled. "Do you want to know what I think, Ellen?"

"Yes," I said. "Tell me what you think."

"I think old Lunan found his first wife with another man, and he killed the man and keeps his wife in the old chapel. I think all the rest is a lie to hide his murder."

"You are a very pragmatic young man," I said, smiling as I tried to digest all the information. "Turn around."

I brushed the loose straw and dirt from Peter's trousers and gave him a little slap for luck because I believed that's what elder sisters did to younger brothers. "Now off you go and replace the rowan twig for me. We can't have the dead Sidh bothering the cattle, can we? Wait!" I called him back. "One more thing!"

"What's that, Ellen?" Peter asked, eager to please me.

"This," I said, and planted a kiss on the end of his nose. "Thank you, Peter."

"Oh." Peter touched his nose with the colour rushing to his cheeks. It was so easy to please him that I wanted to kiss him again.

"That's your lot," I said. "Off you go, now."

I watched Peter swagger away and returned to my work with a hundred thoughts cramming my head, and my hands busy at the udders.

If Mr Lunan had confessed to hearing the whistling, I was not alone. More importantly, I was not insane. The shadow of insanity had hovered over my head for so long that its removal made me dizzy with relief. I felt myself gasping for air as I nearly fainted. I was normal. I was normal; the words ran through my head as I finished milking the cattle.

Dear God in heaven; I was normal! The Whistlers were real; others had heard them, and I had no reason to hide away.

"Ellen!" That was Mrs Lunan's carping voice. "What a time you're taking! Hurry! Agnes is having her baby!"

CHAPTER 9

Leaving the byre at a rush, I ran to the farmhouse, nearly knocking Peter down in my haste. We were fortunate that so many women were present, and most had experience in helping births, human or animal.

"All you, men, leave us!" Mrs Lunan took charge as we supported Agnes to the room we shared.

"I'll come," Andrew said with whisky slurring his words.

"You'll do no such thing," Mrs Lunan said. "Childbirth is no place for a man! Davie, take Andrew away!"

Mr Lunan obliged with a heavy arm around Andrew's shoulders.

"She should be in her husband's house," one hard-faced farmer's wife said. She's a married woman now."

"No," Mrs Lunan said. "She's better in a familiar place."

So, to our room, we went, half a dozen women, all full of wisdom and practical advice, and poor Agnes, moaning with the agony of her first child.

Mr Lunan sent Dougie for the doctor at Meigle. "Take my horse," Mr Lunan said, "and ride like the wind."

Dougie nodded, and followed the instructions to the letter, racing along the dark track as if the devil was on his tail. I only watched for a moment, and my opinion of Dougie rose. Not only did he keep Mrs Lunan happy, but he also galloped for Agnes.

I was too busy to watch the birth as I fetched and carried, acting as general dogsbody to half a dozen farmwives. Agnes was a fit, strong woman, and although the delivery was as painful as first births usually are, she delivered her child like a champion, with the minimum of fuss and no complications.

"That's the quickest labour I've ever known," a plump woman said. "Only three hours for a first baby."

"It's a boy!" Mrs Lunan said, holding up the child as Agnes lay back, exhausted but happy.

The farmer's wives and daughters clustered around, clucking like hens as they congratulated the mother and tried to hold the baby for longer than their neighbours. I helped clean Agnes as the older women gave her free advice, and then we gave the child to its mother.

"You'll have to sleep in the kitchen tonight," Mrs Lunan told me. "Agnes will need her rest with the baby. Not that there's much of tonight left!"

We became aware of the men outside the door, with Andrew first to enter. Like a good husband, he ran straight to Agnes with anxious enquiries even before he glanced at his son.

"I'm fine," Agnes said, smiling. "What a day, a new husband and a new baby."

Mr Lunan glanced at the fancy silver watch that he wore in his waistcoat pocket on significant occasions. "Two days, Agnes," he said. "It's one in the morning now. You son was born at midnight."

"Midnight!" Agnes smiled, holding the baby to her breast.

"How romantic! Which day will be his birthday? Yesterday or today?"

"Whichever day you choose," Mr Lunan said. "We'll get him Christened as quickly as we can. It's best to be safe. I'll speak to Mr Ogilvy tomorrow," he permitted himself a small smile, "or later today, rather."

"What's his name?" Mrs Lunan asked.

"Robert; Andrew's middle name," Agnes said at once, as the baby released his mother's nipple and roared lustily. I have never heard a newborn baby cry as loud in my life.

"My!" Mrs Lunan said, "you've got a healthy pair of lungs, haven't you, Robert?"

We all laughed as Agnes tried to hush the child.

"Best keep him quiet." Mr Lunan glanced out of the window. "You don't want to attract attention before he's christened."

Nobody laughed. I remembered Peter's story about the Sidh abducting babies, and hurriedly closed the curtains, which gained me an approving nod from Mr Lunan.

Within two hours, Dougie arrived with the doctor.

"You made good time," Mrs Lunan approved, touching Dougie on the leg.

"Out, out!" Dr Fenton said, flapping his hands at us. "Everybody get out and give me peace to examine mother!"

Ten minutes later, the doctor opened the bedroom door to pronounce Agnes fit but tired.

"Keep her in bed for a few days." Dr Fenton was elderly, grey-bearded, overweight, and kindly. "She is strong, young and healthy, and the child is as fit as a fiddle. I don't foresee any complications, but if anything happens, just fetch me." He accepted a warming glass of whisky, added another for the road and left on his gig, facing the lonely track with a phlegm that many younger men would have envied.

I heard the whistling again that night, and a scrabbling outside the farmhouse, and then came the deep baying of the dogs, and silence.

I remembered Peter's story about the Sidh stealing babies, and I felt a chill run down my spine. Ellen's was the first human birth I had seen and left me with a feeling of wonder. I did not wish any harm to come to young Robert, that helpless little creature, who was so dependent on his mother.

"Set the dogs loose, Mr Lunan," I said, softly, and gripped my gutting knife. I resolved to stay awake that night, to help protect Robert and Agnes. The dogs barked again, an hour later, and I smiled at the reassuring sound.

I never minded dogs. When I left Mrs Lindsay's sewing factory, I limped away, biting my lip at the pain in my thigh. Mrs Lindsay had shoved the needle in deep, so I was scared to extract it in case it bled faster than I could control. It was a dog who discovered me whimpering under a hedge, beside a farm road, with my thin dress little protection against the spring wind.

The dog's nose was cold on my leg as it sniffed at me. I looked into its deep brown eyes and knew I was in no danger. I was never afraid of animals. They were honest creatures, except foxes, which killed for fun, and cats that played with their prey. Dogs either liked you, or didn't, and did not pretend otherwise. Kept dogs followed the character of their humans, so a decent human had a decent dog.

This dog was a cross between a Border collie and something else. It possessed all the intelligence of a collie without the brittle temperament, so when it discovered me lying under the hedge, it licked the blood on my leg and barked to summon its master.

"What have we here?" The man was as ragged as any I had

ever seen, with a rough pepper-and-salt beard and dirt engrained in his face and hands.

I cowered away, for so far, life had taught me not to trust anybody.

"Don't be scared," the bearded man said. "Old Glen won't hurt you."

I was unsure whether old Glen was the dog or the man. Either way, I pulled back as far as I could, preparing to roll to the far side of the hedge and run, or rather limp, for my right leg was stiff and throbbing fit to scare Lucifer.

"You're bleeding," the ragged man pushed his dog away. "What happened?" His voice was as rough-edged as his appearance, which a scar from eye to jaw did nothing to enhance.

"It doesn't matter," I said.

"It does matter." the tramp examined my leg with hard, gentle hands. "If you leave that needle in your leg, it will fester and poison your blood."

"I'll take it out later." I pulled away.

The tramp nodded. "I'm Donald," he said. "The dog's called Glen. Do you have a name?"

"Ellen," I said. "I'm Ellen Luath."

"Come with me then, Ellen, and don't be scared." Donald slipped off his ragged coat and draped it across my shoulders.

For some reason, that simple act of kindness brought hot tears to my eyes. Although the coat was torn and filthy and smelled of smoke and dirt, it was the most comforting thing I had ever felt.

"You're all right, Ellen," Donald said. "Come along with Donald and Glen."

Beneath the coat, Donald wore a faded scarlet jacket, much patched and worn, with a row of medal ribbons on the breast and double stripes on the arms.

"Were you a soldier?" I asked, losing some of my fear as Glen sniffed at my hand.

"I was," Donald said, standing more erect as old memories returned. "79th Foot, Cameron Highlanders." He threw a smart salute, then took hold of my hand. "Come on little Ellen and don't be scared."

Donald led me to small lean-to shelter in the lee of a dry-stane dyke, with a couple of old blankets inside and a fire outside against the nip of April's wind. "Here's home," he said. "It's not Balmoral Palace but better than a scrape under a hedge."

I hesitated, unwilling to enter such a place with a strange man.

"It's all right," Donald said. "You've no reason to fear Donald and Glen."

I remembered Mr Snodgrass at the orphanage and pulled back. Donald stepped away with understanding in his haunted eyes. I saw deep shadows there, and I sensed tragedy and sorrow. When I reached over and touched Donald's shoulder, I heard the thunder of artillery and the long crackle of sustained gunfire, the hoarse shouts of soldiers and the hopeless screams of mutilated, dying men.

"Thank you, Donald." I squeezed his shoulder, knowing that life had tormented this soldier too deeply for him to hurt me. Although he moved in the present, his mind remained confused by some terrible battle in his past.

"Let's see that leg of yours," Donald said. "Lie down lassie and relax."

I lay down in Donald's hut, with the wind rustling the branches above and Glen by my side with his cold nose pressed against my hand and his tail slowly wagging.

"Lift your skirt," Donald said.

I recalled Miss Deas giving the same command, and Mr Snodgrass, two people whose veneer of respectability hid inner depravity. Old Donald was not of that ilk. I did as he requested, still trembling, and pressing my legs together.

"How on earth did you manage to stick a needle into your leg?" Donald asked. He was on his hands and knees, examining my wound. "Never mind; I'll soon have it out. This will hurt, so brace yourself."

I took a deep breath as Donald grasped the end of the needle, gave me a short nod, and smoothly pulled the slender steel out of my leg. I stifled my yell as Glen licked me, and then Donald held the needle up in triumph.

"I'll have to clean the wound," Donald said. "This will sting." He offered me a swallow of his whisky before pouring a drop or two onto my leg. It stung like the devil's tail, but a kindly meant hurt is no bad thing.

"Brave lass!" Donald said, and for a second, I saw him as he had been, a handsome young soldier, proud in his scarlet jacket as he marched to meet the Queen's enemies in some foreign land. I wondered if Victoria would speak to him now, a man broken in body and mind, yet generous in spirit.

"Sleep now," Donald said, and I did, knowing I was safe. When I woke, Donald was gone, taking Glen with him, and leaving me with a crust of stale bread, which was probably all he had to give. The widow's mite is worth infinitely more than a hundred pounds from a wealthy man, and I never forgot Donald and Glen. Genuine kindness resides in the hearts of the poor.

As I said, I never minded dogs, and have never been feared of them, and perhaps because of that, dogs have never bothered me. Mr Lunan's hounds were no exception, so while others shunned their broad, slavering jaws, I sought them out, clapped their rough fur and fed them with whatever I could find. In that farmstead of mixed emotions, Mr Lunan's dogs were my faithful friends.

I met the mastiffs next morning, washed the dried blood from their muzzles and thanked them for performing their duties like faithful soldiers. They accepted my thanks, sniffed me all over and returned to their patrolling.

I had come south to escape the whistling, yet in Kingsinch, my attitude had altered. I no longer wanted to evade the sound, and no longer believed myself insane. Now, I wished to find out more. I knew I was not alone, and I knew the mysterious Sidh were the Whistlers. I wanted to discover what they wanted with me.

The Sidh were all around. Their whistling followed a pattern; three nights of whistling followed by three nights of peace. I had heard them at Chapelinch and sometimes in the dark of the fields; I knew I could not escape here. If anything, it was worse, surrounding me, creeping up on me as I was trapped in that isolated farm with only one road in or out.

I did not know who the Sidh were or why they should plague me so terribly. I only knew what Peter and Charlie Fleming had told me; I knew that the Sidh had stolen Mr Lunan's wife and might also steal newborn and unchristened babies.

Peter's words haunted my mind. If Mr Lunan did indeed hold one of the Sidh inside the old chapel, perhaps I could talk to her. She might help me find an answer to a mystery that had tormented me since I was a child. Why were the Sidh bothering me?

I would have to find the key to the chapel and sneak out after dark once more. In normal circumstances, that would be difficult, but after the excitement of the wedding and birth, the steading was more unsettled than usual. With Agnes and Andrew occupying my room until Agnes was deemed fit enough to move, I slept on the kitchen floor. I was there when Mr Lunan returned from his nightly patrol, hung up his keys on the hook beside the range, wished me a terse goodnight and stomped upstairs to his bed.

I allowed him a few moments to settle with Mrs Lunan, then slid my gutting knife up my sleeve and quietly lifted the keys. They rattled slightly, which increased my heartbeat, but when no sound came from upstairs, I raised a lantern, slipped open the door and stepped out into the night.

The night was cool rather than cold, with clouds concealing the moon and that pair of owls calling each other in the dark. I made good time out of the steading, hurrying past the buildings, and hearing the restless tramp of the cattle in the byre. I saw the glitter of light from the hanging lantern, knew that young Peter had already done his duty, and left the track for the fail dyke that led to the chapel.

Although the ground was soft underfoot, it was less muddy than on my previous visit, allowing me to hurry beside the wall to Chapelinch. I was trembling long before I reached the building, wondering if, after all this time, I would answer one of the questions that blighted my life.

Beside me, the rowan's branches raised in supplication to the uncaring sky, like the fingers of a soul in eternal torment.

I tried three keys before finding the correct one for the lock and then struggled to prise open the padlock. I took a deep breath and dragged back the bolt, with the sound seeming to echo around the silent fields.

The door was heavy, of a wood I could not identify, reinforced with iron bands, and I opened it with difficulty before peering inside the ruin.

"Hello?" I said, and then louder. "Hello? Is anybody there?"

There was no reply. I stepped inside the building, shivering as the temperature suddenly plummeted. "Hello?"

Remembering the lantern I carried, I scratched a light and applied it to the wick. The increasing glow revealed a stark interior of dressed stone, with stone slabs on the floor and a single carved cross against one wall, with a small wooden cross beneath, crudely fastened with red cord.

"Helloa?"

Again, there was no reply. I had wasted my time, and hours of precious sleep, coming to an ancient building in the middle of the night. Peter was mistaken, and the stories were all lies or, at best, exaggerations. The ruin was empty, if surprisingly watertight, with a roof of closely fitted stone and barely a trace of damp on the walls. Mr Lunan did not hold a Sidh captive here, nor had he imprisoned his first wife. The chapel was bare and as bleak as a Free Kirk sermon on a November evening.

I heard the noise then, a curious rustling, like mice behind a wall, yet louder, and more concentrated in one area. I stopped to listen, feeling my heart pound in my chest. That sound came again, from beneath my feet.

Lowering the lantern, I examined the slabs. They were even and tightly fitted, except for the building's furthest corner, underneath the carved cross, where one slab protruded. I stepped towards it, hearing my feet echo and with the sound of my breathing harsh in my ears. The thick walls prevented any sounds penetrating from outside. Chapelinch was not only an island rising from the surrounding fields; it was also an island of silence in a noisy world.

The end flagstone was undoubtedly raised, with a slight gap between it and its neighbour. I placed my lantern on the ground and examined the stone, wondering if I could lift it to see what lay beneath. I was not sure what I might find, but I suspected something was there. Perhaps Peter was correct, and

Mr Lunan had indeed imprisoned his first wife. I scrabbled around the edges of the stone until I found a slight declivity, a fingerhold in which I could get purchase.

I heaved at the slab using all the strength I had, feeling it rise slightly, a quarter of an inch, half an inch, and then an inch. I rested then, aware of a draught of stale air from beneath the slab. Finally, I placed both hands underneath the cold stone and pulled, gasping with effort.

My lantern revealed a flight of stone steps, dark with age, worn with the passage of feet over many centuries. "Helloa?" I called, with my voice little more than a whisper.

When no reply came, I lifted the lantern and, guided by its wavering light, descended step by nervous step. I would have expected to see spider-webs down here, and scuttling insects of all sorts of shapes, yet there was nothing: no silver-grey webs, no many-legged creatures hiding from the light. Instead, there was sweet air and a mixture of scents. One was of dog, and the other was familiar, although from where I did not know.

There were thirteen steps, leading to a short passage of closely linked stones, beautifully fitted together although I could not discern a trace of mortar. I could nearly stand upright here as I walked along, holding the lantern in front of me. At each step, I fought my inclination to turn and run. I had come this far and would see this investigation to the end, for as well as insatiable curiosity, my faults include a grim stubbornness.

The passage had a dogleg turn at the end, where the roof sloped downwards, which would make it awkward for a tall man. Again, I barely had to stoop and found a wooden door set in the wall, studded with iron, bolted, and locked. Above the door was a cross of fresh rowan, complete with faded berries and tied with red thread.

"What sort of beast has to be held in such a terrible place?" I asked myself as I tested Mr Lunan's keys in the lock. The first key did not fit, and neither did the second, but the third snicked into place.

Unsure if I was doing the right thing, but determined to see my quest to the end, I took a deep breath, turned the key, and drew back the twin iron bolts.

"Helloa," I whispered, yet again. "I mean you no harm."

I pulled open the door.

CHAPTER 10

THE AIR WAS SWEET, without any of the foul, stale stenches I would expect so far underground. I smelled dog again, and something else.

"Helloa?" I lifted the lantern and allowed the yellow glow to pool inside the chamber. The walls were of dressed stone, perfectly fitted so not a trace of moisture entered from outside. A wooden cross embellished one of the walls, with a twisted red cord holding the crosspiece in place, and on the furthest wall, crouching before the intrusion of my light, was a small, entirely naked woman with huge eyes and pendulous, misshapen breasts.

"Dear God in Heaven," I breathed. "What have they done to you?"

Peter's story was accurate. Either Mr Lunan had imprisoned his wife here, or this unfortunate woman was one of the Sidh. However terrible her crime might have been, I felt immediate sympathy for anybody kept in such barbaric conditions.

Kneeling at the woman's side, I could see she was tied wrist and ankle with the same red cord that looped around the crosses, while a cruel iron chain held her to the wall.

"You poor soul," I said. "Who are you?"

The woman looked up at me through a tangle of dark brown hair, with her eyes slightly almond-shaped and evidently terrified.

"It's all right," I said. "I won't hurt you." I looked behind me in case Mr Lunan had followed. "Who are you? Are you Mrs Lunan? Or are you one of the Sidh?"

The woman said nothing, cringing away from me and blinking in the light. I could not tell when she had washed, although, by her ripe scent, I would have said many weeks, if not months, had passed since she last experienced soap and water.

"Can you talk?" I knelt at the woman's side. "Are you Mrs Lunan?"

The woman shivered at the name as if I had invoked a half-forgotten memory. "My name is Ellen," I said.

I was unsure of what to do. I knew I should free the prisoner, but what then? I could hardly take her back to the steading, where her jailer lived. Yet I could not leave her here, in such terrible captivity. I hovered for a moment in indecision, looking at the poor woman. I could not determine her age. She may have been twenty or forty, and her eyes were pleading for help.

"I'll set you free," I decided. "But you cannot go to the farm. That's where your captor lives, you understand?"

The woman seemed incapable of speech, or perhaps she had forgotten how to talk after months or years of captivity.

I wrestled with her bonds, remembered my knife, and sawed at the bindings. The knots were tight, folded in on themselves, and the cord was thick with tar, slowing the progress of my blade. "Who are you?"

The woman still did not speak - my candle cast deep dark shadows which hid the woman's eyes.

"I wish I had brought some food," I said. "I have nothing for you."

I sliced through the last of the woman's bonds, and then I examined the chain. It was rusted, yet still strong, and without any evident lock. I lifted it, link by link, tracing the chain to its junction with the wall, where there was a simple catch, out of reach of the prisoner.

"Got it!" I said and pushed the link apart.

The chain fell to the ground with such a loud clatter that I thought it might awaken the steading, a full quarter of a mile away. I stood back, appalled at the noise, and waited until the final echo died away.

"You're free!" I told the woman who continued to crouch against the wall with her arms wrapped around her knees. "Let me help you up."

I stretched out my hands, holding her by her upper arms, and eased her to her feet. "Take it slowly," I said. "You'll be stiff after so long sitting down."

The woman was even smaller than I was, with no weight to her at all, although she was undoubtedly not a child. She looked at me through her curious, almond-shaped eyes and, without a sound or any expression of gratitude, stepped away.

"You can't go like that," I said. "You're not wearing anything! Take my coat!" I may as well have spoken to the moon as the woman gave me one last glance, then ran along the corridor, with me in pointless pursuit.

"Wait!" I shouted as the woman scrambled up the stairs. For a woman who had spent an unknown time chained up, she was fast on her feet, so I struggled to keep pace with her.

"Wait!" I shouted. "I want to help you!"

The woman reached the outer door of the chapel and halted, cringing on the ground.

"What's the matter?" I asked as I reached her. She pointed upwards, towards the rowan twig.

"You are a Sidh, aren't you?" I had to stretch to reach the end of the twig, and even then, I required three attempts before I could flick it to the ground. When the woman edged even further away, I kicked the rowan into the nearest field.

"There you are," I said, and took hold of her arm to help her up. "Take my coat now!"

The woman's face altered; the mouth tightened, the eyes narrowed, and she snarled at me, showing a row of pointed teeth. I started back, suddenly alarmed. "I'm trying to help!"

I had seen such a face before, glaring through the windows of my cell in the lunatic asylum. And I had seen it again in the carved figure in the Muckle Barn during Jim's initiation.

"Oh, dear God!" I said as the realisation flooded me.

Peter's story had been accurate. The Sidh had stolen Mr Lunan's wife and child and had left that hideously carved figure as a replacement. Mr Lunan had captured one of the Sidh and hoped to recover his first wife, and now I had set the Sidh free.

"Stop!" I tried, belatedly, to reverse the harm I had done. I plunged out of the chapel into the darkness of the night.

The Sidh woman was gone before I reached the outside world, and the last I saw of her was a flash of pale flesh as she vanished into the fields.

"What have I done?"

Then I heard the whistling, long, low, undulating, and sinister.

"No," I said. "This is not the night for it!" I looked around again, with fear replacing my concern for the released captive. I saw somebody, or something, lurking in the fields and began to head back to Kingsinch, increasing my speed as the dark shape headed quickly towards me.

"Go away!" I pleaded as I began to run. "Who are you? Go away!" I felt for the knife in my sleeve, wishing I had remained safely within the farmhouse.

The thing moved faster than me, and even before I reached the path, it lunged forward, wrapped sinewy arms around my legs and brought me heavily to the ground.

"Leave me alone!" I begged as a rough hand clamped across my mouth.

"Keep quiet, if you value your soul!" a harsh voice breathed in my ear, and strong arms turned me around, so I was face-up on the ground.

The lean, brown face of Heather Jock glared at me.

"Jock!" I tried to speak and glanced around for a way of escape, but Jock's wiry strength was too much for me. I tried thrusting with my knee, but he blocked that attempt with ease, and when I flicked my knife from my sleeve into my hand, he held my wrist.

"Lie still!" he hissed. "I'm not going to hurt you! Lie still!"

With no alternative, I could only glower into his brown eyes.

"Stop moving and keep quiet!" Jock whispered.

With no alternative, I did as Jock said, lying on the damp ground with his weight pressing down on me. After a few moments, I saw something flitting past us. It was only a shape, a shadow of darkness in the lesser dark of the night, and then it was gone.

Jock removed his hand from my mouth. "What have you done? Oh, God, what have you done?"

"What do you mean?" I asked.

"Have you released," he paused for a moment. "Did you release *it*?"

119

"I freed the woman that was chained up if that's what you mean!" I retorted, more tartly than I had intended.

"You fool! Oh, you fool!" Jock was shaking his head. "You have no idea what you've done."

"Mr Lunan held that woman captive, and I helped her." I refused to mention the Sidh.

"That was no woman," Jock said. "That was one of them, one of the People of Peace, the Sidh!"

"No," I said, denying the truth while I grappled with the fact that Heather Jock knew about the Sidh.

"Do you know what you've done?" Jock said. "Do you realise what evil you have unleashed?"

"She was a prisoner," I said.

"Can you hear them?" Jock whispered savagely in my ear. "You can can't you? I can feel it in you!"

"The whistling?" I asked. "Can you hear it?"

"That's them, the things, the Sidh! They're all around us."

I shivered, appalled at the implication. "I've been hearing that whistling all my life, wherever I go," I said. "I didn't think other people could hear it."

Jock looked at me. "All your life? The Sidh want you, then," he said.

"They want me?" I repeated, hoping Jock knew more than I did. "Why would they want me?"

"Get back to the steading," Jock told me. "Get onto the path and run for your very soul. Don't look behind you and don't stop for anything."

Jock's words scared me more than anything that had happened at Kingsinch. The instant he released me, I stood up and ran for the steading. I did not understand what I had done, or the trouble Jock had mentioned; I only knew it was serious. As I ran, I heard the undulating whistling, as if there were a hundred Sidh, as well there might have been.

In my mind, I saw that terrible face again with the glowing eyes and rows of sharp white teeth, and I knew I was right to run. I heard the harsh gasping of my breath and the soft thump of my feet on the path, and ran on, nearly panicking in my hurry to get to safety.

By the time I reached the farmhouse, I was damp with sweat and panting like an old horse fit for the knacker's yard. I fumbled for the keys, opened the door, and sat beside the embers of the fire for a good five minutes before I gathered my wits together.

The thoughts and images tumbled through my head like dry leaves dancing in an October gale. I saw the Sidh woman chained to the wall, cowering in fear, and I saw her snarling at me with her sharp teeth bared. I saw Heather Jock's angry face as he glowered at me and heard his voice in my ear. And I realised again that others also heard the sounds that plagued me, and the Sidh were real, dangerous and lived among us.

"Ellen?" That was Mrs Lunan's sharp voice from upstairs. "Is that you?"

"Yes, Mrs Lunan," I replied. "I thought I heard a noise outside. I was going to investigate."

"It's only the wind," Mrs Lunan told me. "Go back to sleep."

"Yes, Mrs Lunan," I said.

I was not sure what to do. Should I admit that I had let the captive free and take the consequences? Or should I say nothing and allow events to take their course. When I was young, I naively mentioned the whistling to Miss Deas in the orphanage in Elgin. She looked at me in disgust and told Mr Snodgrass, who in turn referred me to the nearby lunatic asylum.

I was too young to lie, so when a couple of kindly-looking doctors questioned me, I told them the truth.

"How often do you hear this whistling?" the younger of the two doctors asked, hiding behind his wing collar.

"It comes every three days," I said, counting the days on my fingers, *"and lasts for three days."*

The two doctors looked at each other. *"Do you think it is God talking to you?"* the older man asked.

"No," I said.

"Who then?" the younger man asked.

"Somebody whistling," I said.

"Can you see them?" The older man leaned closer to me. *"Or is it a voice inside your head?"*

"It's like a voice inside my head. Whistling."

The doctors locked me up and subjected me to a harsh regime of sparse food, cold baths, and beatings to cleanse me of my supposed insanity. Only when, much later, I told them that I no longer heard the whistling, did the doctors allow me back into the orphanage, but I knew I was different from other people.

I resolved, there and then, never to mention the whistling again. When the orphanage released me, sending me to work with the smiling Mrs Lindsay, I told nobody about the whistling. From there, I moved from place to place, always leaving when people learned my history, or when the Whistlers caught up with me. Now, some foolishness had forced me to tell Heather Jock, and I hoped he would keep the information to himself. I did not wish the bothy boys to think I was insane and mock me as others had. However, as Jock also heard the Whistlers, I told myself that he might be loath to reveal by secret.

I was preparing breakfast the next morning when Mr Lunan returned from his regular inspection of the fields.

"Good morning, Mr Lunan," I said as he slumped onto his chair with his head in his hands. Unusually, he allowed his dogs into the kitchen, and one came to me, tail slowly wagging and nose sniffing.

Ignoring me, Mr Lunan spoke directly to his wife. "It's escaped," he said.

"What?" Mrs Lunan thumped herself down on a chair. "What do you mean, it's escaped."

"The doors were open, and it's gone." Mr Lunan fumbled for his pipe and stuffed tobacco into the bowl. "The bonds were cut clean, the chain was unfastened, and somebody has shifted the rowan."

I listened intently, unsure whether to confess or hold my tongue. Given my history of creating trouble for myself, I thought it best to keep silent and allow developments to take their course.

"The Sidh will be after the baby," Mrs Lunan said at once. "As soon as Agnes is fit enough to travel, we'll take her and the baby to be Christened. If I had some trailing pearl wort, I'd feed a cow with that and make Agnes drink its milk."

"Aye; pearl wort would do the trick, but we've none. I'll see Mr Ogilvy today," Mr Lunan said. "We can't delay things any longer, and maybe he'll come to us."

Mrs Lunan took his hand. "We'll be all right," she said. "We'll guard her and the baby. We haven't done all this work here for the Sidh to force us out." She looked over to me. "Ellen said she heard noises last night."

I nodded, feeling miserable that I had caused so much trouble.

"Noises? What sort of noises?" Mr Lunan asked, quickly looking up.

I felt so guilty that opened my mouth to confess my stupidity when there was a rap on the door, and Heather Jock calmly stepped inside the kitchen.

I expected the dogs to launch themselves at him, but

instead only one snarled, and the others looked up from my feet, where they lay in comfort, and looked away again.

"What the hell are you doing here?" Mr Lunan asked. "I've told you not to come back!"

"The creature's escaped." Jock sat down without a by-your-leave and leaned across the table. "You'll have to take precautions."

"Did you let it out?" Mr Lunan asked.

"Don't be bloody stupid, Davie, man," Jock said. "When I passed Chapelinch last night, the door was swinging open."

"What the devil were you doing on my land?" Mr Lunan asked.

"Poaching," Jock said calmly. "You must have left your keys unattended, or the things found out how to open locks."

"Poaching!" Mr Lunan rose with his fists clenched.

"Never mind that now." Mrs Lunan put a hand on her husband's arm and nodded to me. "The lassie heard something last night, remember?"

"What did you hear, lass?" Mr Lunan asked me.

Grateful that Jock had not given me away, I told the truth. "It was like a whistling," I said. "I've heard it before, but last night it was louder."

"A whistling?" Mr Lunan nodded. "Aye, that's them. That's how they talk to each other, they give a low, musical whistle or sing, damn them to hell and buggery. What time was that, girl?"

I screwed up my face to think, for, in all honesty, I did not know what time. "I'd guess about midnight," I said.

"Aye, near enough," Jock said. He smelled of fresh earth and living things, a man dressed in drab browns and greys, with a long, weather-battered face and darting, intelligent eyes. I favoured him with a nod, for he could have landed me in grave trouble, but chose to hold his peace.

"You'd best warn the lads," Jock said. "They'll need to know. Warn Andy to look after his woman and the newborn."

"The baby's called Robert," Mrs Lunan reprimanded Jock.

"I'll warn everybody," Mr Lunan said. "With that creature free, there's nothing to hold them away."

"I don't understand," I said.

"When Mr Lunan held the Sidh hostage," Jock explained, "the other Sidh could only whistle and pester. They might steal the occasional hen or shoot at a cow now and then, but they knew if they tried more, Davie here would destroy one of theirs. Now," he pulled a face, "they are free to do what they will."

"But who are the Sidh?" I asked, pushing for as much information as I could gather, and from as many people as I could. "And what do they want with us?"

"They're the old ones," Jock said, "the Sidh, the things that were here before humans. When we took over the land, they retreated underground and waged an intermittent war against us, stealing babies, killing livestock, and even stealing people."

"Why?" I asked, still confused. "Why would these Sidh steal babies and kidnap people?"

Mr Lunan looked directly at me. "We are not sure," he said. "We think that each generation of Sidh is less fertile than the last, so they steal our babies to keep their race alive."

I nodded, not sure how else to respond.

"And, as for people," Jock said. "Every seven years, the Sidh have a ceremony when they sacrifice a human being to their god." He looked at me, as though assessing my ability to comprehend his words. "They want a virgin, somebody pure."

Mr Lunan jumped in, speaking to the fireplace as if remembering, rather than explaining. "Fourteen years ago, they took my wife. I swore then to fight them with every bone and muscle I have, and until last night I did that. I captured a female Sidh, which held the others back from my farm. They've crept closer; I found one of their arrowheads in the fields recently. Now, the Sidh will seek their revenge on us."

"Can't we leave the farm?" I asked.

"I'm damned if I'll run," Mr Lunan said. "I've drained this land by the sweat of my brow, dug ditches, built dykes and walls and held back the Sidh. They won't take my land from me."

I saw the determination on Mr Lunan's face and knew he spoke only the truth. "Is that what the dogs are for?"

"Yes," Mr Lunan said, caressing the nearest behind its ear. "They are trained to sniff out the Sidh."

I remembered the blood on the dog's muzzles and nodded. Although the mastiffs were friendly with me, I could imagine the terror they could install in the lightly built Sidh.

"What do you want me to do?" I asked.

"Keep out of the way," Mrs Lunan snapped at me. "There's nothing you can do against the Sidh."

"Yes, there is," Mr Lunan said. "The people are afraid of rowan wood and iron. I had both protecting the creature I captured, so I don't understand how it escaped."

"Somebody must have helped it." Mrs Lunan looked pointedly at Jock.

"Not me," Jock said. "I know how dangerous they are."

"And it wasn't the girl," Mrs Lunan said. "I saw her in the kitchen last night."

I said nothing, although I felt the blood rush to my face.

"Maybe the halflin," Mrs Lunan said.

I wondered again if I should confess until Jock met my eyes and gave a warning shake of his head.

"As soon as the men are at work, I'll have Ellen and the halflin hammering rowan wood and horseshoes above every door and window."

I could hardly believe what I heard. We lived at the end of the nineteenth century, not the middle of the seventeenth, and we were putting up pieces of wood and iron to protect us from some mysterious creatures from the long past. If I had not lived my life on the fringe of unreality, I would have laughed. As it was, I remembered the Sidh woman's snarl, the creature at my cell window and that horrible figure at Jim's initiation.

"Yes, Mr Lunan," I said.

Mrs Lunan nodded. "That's what we'll do, then. Jock, you're a thief and a vagabond, but you know about these Whistlers from the dark. What do you say?"

"Warn everybody," Jock said. "The Sidh will target the beasts first, and then the baby, at least until we get him Christened."

I looked up, even more ashamed of what I had done, yet too scared to admit my faults. When one has spent much of one's life being victimised and abused, one tends to hide one's mistakes for fear of further hurt. Life had made me secretive, avoiding confrontation and denying guilt. "I want to help guard the baby," I said.

Mrs Lunan gave me an approving nod. "We'll all do that, Ellen. Now, get on with the breakfasts; it's past time the boys were up."

"I'll get on patrol," Mr Lunan said. He fetched his shotgun from its position in the lobby cupboard, broke it, loaded it, and snapped the weapon shut. "Come on, dogs!" With the briefest of nods to us, he withdrew outside, dogs at his heels.

CHAPTER 11

THE BOTHY-BOYS TOOK the news better than I had expected. As first horseman, Dougie took the lead. "I knew about the stories before I accepted the position at Kingsinch," he said. "There's no secret about the Sidh having been here. I'm not going to run."

"Nor am I," Jim said. "I'll have to warn Brenda, though."

Andrew toyed with his spoon before he looked up. "I'm not sure," he said slowly. "I don't want Agnes and the baby to be in danger."

"We'll look after her," Peter said, planting his fist on the table. "Give me a few moments with any of these things, and they won't come back a second time."

I favoured Peter with a smile, for despite his supposedly manly posturing, he had a good heart.

Andrew shook his head. "I know you will, Peter, but this is something beyond our ken. I'm responsible for Agnes and the baby. I don't want to leave them in a danger I don't even understand."

"You've got a position here, Andrew," Dougie said. "Maybe

best wait until term-time and seek a new place at the feeing fair."

"That's months away," Andrew said. "I don't want my family in danger that length of time."

"Where will you go?" Jim asked.

Andrew considered for a few moments. "I don't know," he said. "I'll speak to Agnes about it."

"That would be best," I said. "Agnes is a sensible woman. She won't make any rash decisions."

All the time we spoke, I hated myself for the trouble I had caused. In trying to do good, I had done immeasurable harm. I had acted like a foolish, irresponsible child rather than a thinking adult, and at my age, I should have known better. At my age? I laughed at myself. I did not even know how old I was, or even what my name was, except the name the orphanage had given me.

"I must warn Brenda," Jim said. "I'll see her tonight and tell her to stay away for a while. Either that or I'll bring her down to Kingsinch. She can stay with us."

Dougie grinned. "You'll bring a girl into the bothy?" he asked. "At least we'll get to see her."

"No, not in the bothy," Jim said. "She can share with Ellen."

"She'll be welcome," I said, desperate to undo some of the harm I had caused.

"Mrs Lunan will be glad of another mouth to feed," Andrew said sarcastically. "Would she not be better at her own home?"

"I want here safe with me," Jim said as the bothy-boys gave him bawdy advice that brought a blush to his face.

"Enough," Andrew said. "Lady's present!"

"Where?" Dougie asked. "I can only see Ellen."

I left then, not because of the ribald comments, but because the boys would talk more freely without a woman present. Despite the danger from an unknown adversary, the lads were in good humour, or perhaps, I told myself, they used humour to combat their fear.

If they knew what I knew, they would need more than humour.

Mr Lunan made what preparations he could. While I took over all the kitchen duties, Mrs Lunan supervised Peter in cutting branches from the rowan tree and attaching them above the farmhouse's doors and windows.

"This feels silly," Peter said as he stood on the ladders with a hammer and nails.

"You'll feel the back of my hand unless you do it properly," Mrs Lunan said. "These creatures are dangerous."

"I've never seen one in my life," Peter said with all the scepticism of youth.

"Just get on with it!" Mrs Lunan slapped his leg, grunted, and slapped again, evidently drawing some satisfaction from the procedure. "Ellen! I want you here!"

I left the kitchen and joined them, drying my wet hands on the back of my skirt.

Mrs Lunan ordered me to hold the basket as Peter cut the lengths of rowan.

"Enough for every door and window in Kingsinch," Mrs Lunan snapped. She fashioned the twigs into miniature crosses and tied them together with a thin red cord. "If we had the berries, the crosses would be even more effective," she said.

Peter gave me an elaborate wink. "If you say so, Mrs Lunan."

"I do say so." Mrs Lunan gave him another slap to emphasise her point, this time across his rump. "Now I want you to place one of these crosses above every window and door in the steading; every single one. If you don't, by jingo, you'll know all about it!"

As soon as Mrs Lunan walked away, Peter grinned to me. "Every one," he repeated. "If I don't, by jingo, I'll know all about it!"

"We'd best get on with the work," I said.

"Aye," Peter said. "By jingo!"

I could not help laughing, for Peter caught Mrs Lunan's intonation perfectly. Peter grinned at me, mature in attitude and young in years. I smiled back, knowing that if I ever had a son, I wanted him to be as handy, brave, and cheeky as Peter.

We completed the task, with me holding the basket and Peter doing the work until we decorated every building in the steading with the rowan crosses and I was giddy with looking upwards.

"There we are," Peter said as he descended the ladder. "Now, you'd better get back to the kitchen, by jingo."

"So I had, by jingo," I said. "Or I'll know all about it."

We laughed together, Peter and I, sharing our simple joke as the darkness descended and the surrounding heights glowered at us from behind their damp grey curtain.

That night, Charlie Fleming's light went out. I used to watch the single bright speck halfway up the hillside like a beacon of hope, a shred of sanity in an insane world. I often wondered at Charlie's lonely existence, up there with the wind and only the bleating of the sheep to keep him company. Naturally, the bothy-boys made obscene jokes about his habits, but their coarse humour concealed a genuine liking for the man and respect for anybody who tried to farm on such unfavourable ground.

Charlie never extinguished his light. Even on the darkest nights when the wind screamed across the slopes, Charlie's lantern hung outside his house, dancing to the whim of the blast. That night, as I peered out through the window, the light vanished.

I knew without thought that something was wrong. I did not need the low, undulating whistling to confirm my fears.

Charlie's cottage was close to the Pictish House, where I had seen the small man with the birthmark on his face. I remembered Charlie's pragmatic response to the Sidh and wondered if they had finally decided to turn against him. I also remembered Mhairi's sudden disappearance and shivered.

I did not like to think of Charlie like that, and wondered, as I had so often if I was the catalyst of disaster. Mhairi had vanished when I heard the whistling, and now Charlie Fleming's light had gone out not long after I spoke to him. I had not thought about Mhairi since I arrived at Kingsinch; now, her memory returned.

The gang master looked me up and down. "You're rather small," he said. "Do you think you can keep up with the other women?"

"Yes," I said.

"It's hard work, ye ken."

"Aye," I said. "Hard work never killed anybody."

"Aye, maybe not." The gang master was about fifty, with a neat grey beard and eyes like gimlets. "All right then, Ellen. We'll give you a try. If you fall behind or drag my ladies back, I'll get rid of you like a shot."

"Archie's all right," the oldest of the gang told me. "His bark is worse than his bite. Have you done this sort of work before?"

I shook my head, still unsure of myself in company.

"Follow what we do, and you'll be all right. I'm Cathy."

I had never heard of an agricultural gang until I saw them forming. As Archie said, it was hard work. We moved from farm to farm, twelve women under Archie's watchful eye, harvesting the turnips or potatoes with the cold rain pattering down on us, and sleeping at night in bothies, all together in one room. My initial shyness soon vanished, for the women had bawdy humour that transcended any difference of age or appearance. Archie left us alone, ensured we had reasonable accommodation, and paid us regularly.

We travelled the north for a season, working the fields, forming a strange camaraderie, and seeing the countryside. I found Caithness bleak and beautiful, Sutherland desolate and sad.

"What's happened here?" I could feel the hurt pressing down on me.

"The Clearances," Mhairi said. She was a MacLeod from Skye, with her race's fey eyes and the high cheekbones of Norse ancestry. "The landowner evicted all the people to make way for sheep, then evicted the shepherds to create a personal playground for killing deer."

I looked around the sparse fields where we worked. "There used to be people here." I could sense the old laughter beneath the tragedy of emptiness.

"Aye." Mhairi stretched her back. "There were, and there will be again. The Gaels will return after the great desolation has passed."

I did not ask for details. Mhairi lived her life on the misted border between this world and another. She intrigued me, yet she was as wary of companionship as I was.

In the spring and early summer, we planted potatoes under the vast skies of Caithness and along Ross's fertile east coast. We were working before dawn set the sea silver and worked until the sun slid behind the blue-grey granite hills of the west. Yet I was not unhappy. I had food and shelter, and the company did not seek to intrude on my mind.

After a few months, I even found myself joining in the conversations. I told some of the truth about my past and found most of the women in the gang had similar tales and similar gaps in their life stories. I learned that few people were fully candid about themselves, and fewer have no shadows in their past.

After a year, I was settled into the life, and making friends with the women who were becoming more than work colleagues.

It was then that the whistling began again. At first, I thought it was my imagination, and I ignored it. Then, I knew it was real, and I could have cried. In my past, tears had not helped any, and I was too cynical to use them. I just moved on with life and hoped for better days. However, as one of Archie's gang, I felt I belonged, but now the Whistlers were tearing away my happiness.

Mhairi sensed something was wrong. We were working a field in the shadow of Mount Keen when the easterly wind brought the whistle. I heard it and looked up, to find Mhairi looking directly at me.

"Did you feel that?" Mhairi asked in her Skye accent.

I nodded.

"Somebody is calling," Mhairi said and continued working.

The other women had not noticed anything unusual. I returned to gathering potatoes, but my soul was not in the work. My fingers were cold and muddy, and my heart hammered inside my chest as I listened for the Whistler again. Every few moments, I glanced across to Mhairi, who seemed as distracted as I was. She would look up and glance around her as if searching for somebody, or something.

At night we lived in a stone-built bothy with an open fire at one end.

"You are very quiet, Mhairi," Cathy said cheerfully.

Mhairi gave a small smile. "I'll be better tomorrow," she said.

But she was not. I heard the whistling during the night, and in the morning, Mhairi was gone. Nobody had noticed her leave the bothy, most of her clothes were beside her bed, and there was no note.

"She must have had enough of gang work," one of the women said. "She was a queer fish anyway."

"Maybe she found a man." Cathy was more worried than she pretended.

I said nothing. Although I did not know what had happened, I guessed that the Whistlers had something to do with Mhairi's disappearance. We were all quiet the next day, and in the evening, I told the gang I was going for a walk.

"A walk?" Cathy stepped back. "Don't you get enough exercise in the fields?"

"I just want to be alone for a bit," I said.

I did not want the Whistlers to take Cathy next or any of the other women. I knew my presence there put them in danger. On an impulse, I gave Cathy a quick hug, which brought forth a laugh of surprise, and then I walked away and kept walking. As the north was so dangerous, I would try my luck elsewhere. I would find a position in one of the Lowland towns, or a farm-toun as a kitchen maid. I would go anywhere that I could escape the Whistlers and restart my life.

I thought of Mhairi when Charlie Fleming's light vanished and wondered where she was.

"It might be something simple," Mr Lunan said when I told him about the light. "I'll have a look next time I'm over that way. Charlie's a good man; he knows how to take care of himself."

I did not mention the whistling or the Sidh. I merely

nodded and returned to my work, and Mrs Lunan ensured there was always plenty of work. I cannot say that I was unhappy at Kingsinch, for the bothy boys were friendly, and I could cope with Dougie's advances without much trouble. I was only apprehensive about the Sidh. That was not entirely true. I was frightened of the Sidh, yet I knew I had to face them to settle my mind, and when one's mind is unsettled, one can never have peace in any form.

As I had initiated this new period of trouble, I resolved to bring it to a conclusion. I was responsible for increasing the danger to Kingsinch; I must end it. I would wait until the three nights of whistling stopped, and then leave under the blanket of night. I would cross the fields to the Pictish House and confront the Sidh. Either that or I would run again, and perhaps the Sidh would follow me and leave Agnes and the others alone. I could hurry down the long track to freedom and head for Dundee. It was a long road, perhaps fourteen or fifteen miles, but there was work in Dundee. I could work as a mill-girl and rent a single-end, a one-roomed flat in a tenement and surely there, amidst the bustle and crowds, I would be safe.

Yes, I thought, I would be safe, but at the expense of everybody at Kingsinch.

I knew that running solved nothing. I had run all my life, and trouble followed me like a grasping shadow.

No. I would not run. Not this time. I would face the Sidh, and if they wanted me as a sacrifice, well, my life had not been entirely successful, and nobody would miss a half-crazed orphan. I sighed, shrugged, and prepared myself to meet the Sidh. The culmination of all life was death, so I may as well die with a purpose.

And then, as if the fates had read my thoughts, the rain began.

CHAPTER 12

"Aye," Andrew said, with a glance at the glowering sky, "we're in for a devil of a downpour."

"We are at that," Dougie agreed as they led their horses from the stable to the fields. "It'll be a wet few days."

"Or weeks," Andrew said.

I was as able to judge the weather as any Moray quinie, but local men who worked outdoors knew the weather-signs as well as they knew their faces. They could tell when the rain would come, and from what direction, and how long it would last. I listened to their conversation and wondered at the content, for rain is not uncommon in Scotland, whatever the season, and hardly worth mentioning.

The clouds gathered above the hills, grey at first, then gradually becoming heavier, and darker, bruising themselves on the summit-ridges of the braes before the rain came. The first drops were slow and heavy, as though the Lord was reluctant to release his wrath on the fields below. The early rain landed with a distinct splash, a miniature explosion on the furrowed land below.

Mrs Lunan looked skyward, shook her head, said, "Aye," and returned to her work of ensuring I was toiling with black-lead at the range. "Sidh or no Sidh, Ellen, I want the work done right." Mrs Lunan emphasised her words with a sharp dig in my ribs.

From meagre beginnings, the rain increased by the hour. Single drops multiplied to dozens, to scores, to hundreds and thousands until the whole sky seemed to be falling upon us in a constant deluge of water.

I thought of the damp miles between Kingsinch and the Pictish House and wondered how wet I would be before I arrived. Then I thought of my ultimate aim and told myself that it did not matter. The cycle of whistling continued that night, although the hammering rain muted the sounds. I heard the drops hissing in the embers of the fire, decided that one more day in Kingsinch would do no harm and closed my eyes.

Within five minutes, I thought I heard something scraping at the window. I lay under the covers, facing away from the window, praying, and not daring to turn around. The scraping sounded again, like fingernails against the windowpanes.

"Go away," I said. "Leave me in peace; please leave me in peace. I'll come when I am ready."

I may as well have bayed to the moon or tried to call down the stars. The scraping continued for perhaps five minutes, and only when it ended did I summon the courage to pull my head free of the coarse blankets and set a light to the candle. A draught set the flame a-flicker as I held the brass candlestick in my trembling hand and slid out of bed. The stone-slabbed floor was cold under my feet as I moved to the window to peer outside.

The rain continued, as it had all the previous day and all that night, battering at the glass and snaking down the window in rivulets of cold water. Fighting my fear, I wiped away a small circle of condensation and peered outside, with the reflection of my candle-flame distorting my image. I could see my eyes as larger than normal, nearly tear-drop shaped, with my face small, triangular beneath a broad brow. Outside, there was nothing except darkness and the teeming rain.

And then I saw movement. Only a hint, only a suggestion, a flicker of deeper dark against the lesser dark of the night, but undoubtedly somebody or something was out there. It was not Heather Jock, and it was no animal, so must be the Sidh.

I stifled my scream as I stepped back, still miraculously holding my candlestick although the wax was dripping onto my fingers.

My heartbeat had increased, and I could hear my breathing as harsh and uncontrolled. I sat on the bed, shaking, and analysed what I had seen.

Was it only a deer, pushed down from the hills in search of food? Or a fox perhaps, lurking around the henhouse? No; I shook my head. It had not been an animal, or rather it had not been an animal that I had ever seen before. I tried to recall what I had seen from the glimpse I had.

It had been standing upright, on two legs, not four. Of that, I was confident or nearly confident. I shook my head. I did not know, I could not tell, and now the wind had strengthened, blattering the rain against the windowpanes, threatening to lift the slates from the roof and howling around the farmtoun as if all the demons of hell were gibbering at our gates, clamouring to enter.

I shook away such fantasies and returned to the window, with the reflection of my candle-flame wavering on the glass. Whatever I had seen was gone now or was hiding in the dark. Two legs. It had been a Sidh, prowling around the farmhouse, perhaps searching for an entrance unguarded by a rowan cross or an iron horseshoe.

"What are you doing in there?" It was nearly a relief to hear Mrs Lunan's voice outside my room. "It's three in the morning! Either get back to sleep or get up and work. This rain will upset the kye: best check them soon."

"Yes, Mrs Lunan." I opened the door a crack. "I thought I saw somebody outside the house."

"Nonsense!" Mrs Lunan said. "Nobody in their right mind would be abroad on a night like this. Not even the Sidh." She stood with a candle in her hand and bare feet peeping from under the hem of her nightgown. "It's just the rain that awakened you, Ellen. Go back to bed now and try to sleep."

"Yes, Mrs Lunan," I said meekly and closed the door. I did not sleep; I lay on the floor with the candle slowly melting beside me, and my mind racing with images and thoughts. As I lay still, I heard Mr Lunan leave the house by the front door, whistling for his dogs. For all Mrs Lunan's words to me, I knew she had sent her man outside to see who, or what was there.

I already knew and wished that I did not. The image of that creature I had released remained with me as I fought my fear and indecision.

"We're flooding now," Mr Lunan said as he sat at his breakfast. Milk-based porridge for him, not the simple brose of the boys. "The rain is creeping over the fields."

"We've had rain before," Mrs Lunan said.

"Aye, but not like this; not in my time."

For centuries, farmers had tried to make a living from the Kings Moss, draining the land by muscle power, spade and sweat. They had gradually reduced the moss, the bogland, to create a fertile oasis amidst the hill's green swells, but now nature had decided to intervene. The steady deluge began to undo the slow toil of centuries. At first, there were only puddles in the fields, long stretches of water in the plough-furrows. By mid-morning, the puddles had merged, and after that, the fields resembled small lochs.

"Kingsinch indeed," Mrs Lunan said as I returned from the byre with my milk churns. "There'll be nobody leaving here until the rain subsides."

"It might stop soon," I said.

Mrs Lunan looked at the sky. "It won't," she said. "This rain is set for days yet, and even then, it will have to drain away. We're here for weeks, I'd say."

"The road is higher than the fields," I pointed out.

"Not high enough," Mrs Lunan said.

I failed to hide the dismay that crossed my face.

"You'll live," Mrs Lunan said. "I presume you have a sweetheart somewhere, that you're so anxious to leave us?" She took the milk churns from me. "Well, you'll have to do without his embraces, Ellen. Does Agnes's situation not teach you anything? An early pregnancy and marriage and that's her tied down for life; no more freedom for that young woman."

I was not thinking of Agnes. I was thinking of the whistling and whatever it had been outside my window. I looked at the downpour and the water that rippled across the path and knew I was trapped.

"Is there no other road out of here?" I asked.

Mrs Lunan stopped her work to look at me. "You are surely desperate to get away," she said. "It must be love." She nearly smiled. "If he's keen on you, Ellen, he'll wait. If he doesn't, then he's not worth thinking about." She considered for a moment. "I have heard there is an ancient causeway to the old chapel, but nobody knows where it is now. It is said to float on the surface of the bog. The old whisky smugglers used it, and I am sure that Heather Jock knows it."

"Heather Jock knows a lot of things, Mrs Lunan," I said.

Mrs Lunan was talkative that morning. "Aye, he does," she paused to step closer to me. "They say that his granny was one of them."

"One of whom?" I asked.

"Them," Mrs Lunan repeated, glancing around in case the pots and pans might hear her, for God knows there was nobody else in the kitchen. "Them," she lowered her voice even further. "You know, the Sidh."

I must have been stupid not to make the connection before that conversation. "Is that why Jock's treated as an outcast?"

"Aye, that and his behaviour," Mrs Lunan said. "He was ayeways a wild loon."

"Where is he from? Is he a local man?"

Mrs Lunan gave me a sideways look. "Local? I suppose so. Why the questions? Go and feed the hens, and check the lads are busy. They should be in the stables, attending the horses."

I realised I had asked enough questions and stepped out into the driving rain. *Was Jock one of the Sidh? That would explain how he knew about them. Did they throw him out? I must find out.*

CHAPTER 13

I HEARD the whistling that night, low and prolonged, and then the soft shuffle of feet. Perhaps my hearing was becoming more acute, or maybe I was tuned to the noises the creatures made, for I was the only one awake in the farmhouse. Andrew and Agnes still slept in our old room, with Baby Robert snug between them and a cross of rowan tied to the foot of the bed.

"Andrew." I shook him awake. "Andrew!"

He woke slowly, staring at me through the yellow glow of candlelight. "Ellen? What is it, lass?"

"I heard the whistling," I said. "The creatures are out tonight."

Andrew slid out of bed. "Did you see them?" He pulled on his trousers.

"No; I heard them."

Andrew checked Agnes and the baby. "I'll keep watch." He reached for a staff, with a heavy knob at one end.

"Andy?" Our talking had wakened Agnes, who sat up, blinking, with her hair tousled and her mouth slack.

"It's all right; get back to sleep," Andrew said.

"The baby?" Agnes stretched her arm over her child.

"Robert's fine," Andrew said.

The whistling started again, close to the walls of the house, three distinct sounds. "Can you hear that?" I whispered.

Andrew shook his head. "No," he said. "Douse the candle; it might attract them."

I blew out the flame, so we stood in the shivering dark, with Agnes's quiet breathing the only sound inside the room.

Without the candle-flame, the world outside the window became more visible. Andrew stood with his stick ready while I slipped into the kitchen and returned with my gutting knife. I could still hear the undulating whistling outside, and then I gasped as a hand appeared at the window.

"Andrew!" I whispered.

"I see it," Andrew said, tight-voiced. He raised his staff as the hand, small but with long fingers, scrabbled at the glass. "It's scraping at the putty, trying to take away a windowpane."

"Andrew!" Agnes woke again, saw the thing at the window, and screamed. "Andy!"

A second hand joined the first, both scraping busily, and then a face appeared, staring inside the house. It was nearly human, but not human, triangular-shaped, with almond eyes, a small nose, and a mouth like a slit that grinned at us from the opposite side of the window. I had seen a similar face, at my cell window, and on the carved object in the Muckle Barn. It was the face of a hundred nightmares, but real and here.

"Get back!" Andrew brandished his staff, just as Mrs Lunan burst open the door, joined Agnes in screaming, and yelled for her husband to do something.

Mr Lunan was in his night-shirt, with great clumsy boots on his feet and his shotgun in his hand. He swore mightily and roared at Andrew: "stay there and look after the women!"

Shouting for his dogs, Mr Lunan opened the kitchen door

and ran outside the house, foully swearing as he dashed to where Agnes's bedroom window overlooked the yard outside.

I heard the barking of the dogs, then a high-pitched squeal.

"Go on, boy!" Mr Lunan roared. "Tear its bloody head off!"

Unable to resist my curiosity, I gripped my knife and followed Mr Lunan outside the house, in time to see him aim his shotgun at a shape in the far corner of the yard. The sound of the gun echoed around the stone buildings, rapidly followed by the bright flash from the muzzle. Mr Lunan fired again, with a second crash and flare, and white smoke drifted over the battered granite setts on the ground.

The muzzle-flare temporarily destroyed my night vision, and when it slowly returned, two of the dogs were worrying something that wriggled and squealed like a rabbit caught by a stoat. Something else lay in a shapeless bundle in the far corner, a pile of rags and meat lying in a spreading pool of blood. Mr Lunan stalked forward, looked at the thing he had shot, and grunted in satisfaction.

"Got you, you bugger from hell," he said, turning the body over with his feet. I only caught a glimpse of the small, near triangular face I had seen a few moments before, and then Mr Lunan saw me watching him.

"Get back indoors, Ellen," he snapped. "This is no place for a girl."

I obeyed, with Mrs Lunan berating me for my foolishness in leaving the house, shaking, and slapping at me as if I had been a child. Agnes was sobbing, holding Baby Robert in her arms, with Andrew sitting at her side, still holding his stick.

"The rowan should have kept them away," Mrs Lunan said after she finished shouting at me. "How did the Sidh get past the rowan? They're meant to be frightened of that."

"We'll have to get to the kirk," Agnes said between sobs.

"We'll have to get this wee man Christened, so he's safe. I'm no' letting thae things get him."

I nodded with my guilt mounting by the minute. I had caused this assault by releasing the Sidh woman. I pondered how to make amends.

The Sidh hunted babies before the Kirk christened them. I was unsure if the Kirk had ever christened me. Somehow, I doubted it. As far as I was aware, my parents, or somebody else, had dumped me on the front of Grant's Orphanage in Elgin. If that was what they thought of me, I don't think they would have spared the time and trouble to have me Christened. Maybe I was a damned soul in the next world as well as this one. Perhaps the best thing for everybody was for me to hand myself to the Sidh.

The whistling had stopped. Only then did I realise that I had not been afraid. From the moment I heard the initial whistling until I saw the dead creature on the ground, I had not been afraid. Somehow, I knew I would not come to any harm.

I shook myself; the whistling had scared me all my life. Why should I lose that fear now when I knew what caused it?

"You women stay inside the house." Mr Lunan reloaded his shotgun as he stood within the kitchen, dripping rainwater onto the stone slabs. He snapped the weapon shut. "We have work to do." He looked up as the bothy-boys arrived, enquiring loudly what the shooting was all about and with their lanterns casting elliptical shadows around the steading. A couple of bats fluttered overhead, providing a suitable eeriness to the scene. At Halloween, youngsters enjoy the spookiness of ghost stories and turnip lanterns; out here, with the sinister Sidh hovering around our home, the atmosphere was merely ominous.

"What's the to-do, Mr Lunan?" Peter asked, wielding a long hoe as if it were a spear.

"Come with me, and I'll show you," Mr Lunan said, taking

the bothy-boys to the yard. I watched out the window as the men dragged away the two bodies, with the dogs following. As farmworkers, the men were used to blood and slaughter, although they all paused to examine the creature's corpses. The Sidh looked like men, but smaller, with slanting eyes and slightly pointed ears. As far as I could make out, neither had a tail or cloven feet, so they were not the classical demons of mythology. I presumed that the men buried the bodies, or otherwise disposed of them, but I never found out where. They were out of my sight, and that is all that mattered.

"I wonder why the rowan did not work," Jim said as we all gathered in the farmhouse kitchen soon after dawn. I was busy with the kettle, making strong sweet tea for the crew, listening to the conversation, and trying to keep silent.

"I heard somewhere that it was less effective if there was one of the Sidh already in the house," Dougie said. "If one of the creatures was allowed inside, the others could breach the barrier."

"Has one of the Sidh been inside?" I asked fearfully.

"Heather Jock was here," Mrs Lunan reminded.

Everybody at the table fell silent at those words. By now, we all knew the rumours that Heather Jock was part Sidh, which explained his ability to navigate the countryside by dark.

"I don't think he was to blame," Dougie supported Jock once more. "He knows how dangerous the Sidh are."

"He might not have done anything deliberately," Mrs Lunan said, "but if he's got Sidh blood in him, he would have breached the barrier and left us vulnerable."

"We don't know if he has Sidh blood," I said.

"We don't know that he hasn't, either," Agnes said, nursing her baby. "I've always thought there was something not quite canny about that man. I wouldn't trust him as far as I could throw him."

I said nothing, although I knew that fear for her baby drove Agnes to speak as she did. I had heard that motherhood changed women.

"I agree," Mrs Lunan said. "A man should have a steady job, not wander the countryside, poaching and living off what he can find. I don't want him back in the house."

I spoke out. "Jock helped us," I said, only for Mrs Lunan to tut me into silence.

Dougie gave me a slight, wondering nod. "I agree with Ellen," he said. "Jock might be the best friend we could have in this situation."

"Don't let him back in the house, Davie," Mrs Lunan said. "If he comes, drive him away from the steading."

"He's hardly likely to come back when we're under flood," Mr Lunan said mildly.

"Heather Jock knows the secret paths and causeways," Mrs Lunan said, "and that's another indication he's part Sidh."

"If he comes back," Mr Lunan said, "I'll give him a flea in his ear."

"No!" Mrs Lunan said. "I want more than that. Give him a boot up the doup, or even better a dose of lead shot. Prove to him that he's not wanted."

"He's not a bad lad," Dougie said. "Shooting Jock won't help drive away the Sidh."

"He's a threat to my baby," Agnes held Baby Robert closer to her.

Andrew nodded. "Agnes is right." He placed his hand on his wife's shoulder, already acting like an old married man.

I was surprised how quickly fatherhood, or perhaps matrimony, had altered Andrew. A few weeks ago, he would have spoken up for Jock. Now he was stoutly supporting Agnes; Mr and Mrs Andrew Ferguson were separate from the rest of us, a family unit within the comradeship of Kingsinch.

We spent the next day improving the security of the steading. As it seemed that rowan was no longer effective against the Sidh, Mr Lunan sent Jim and Peter to collect as many horseshoes as they could.

"Why are the creatures scared of iron?" I asked.

Dougie shrugged. "Blessed if I know," he said.

"It's because they didn't have it," Mrs Lunan said. "The Sidh had not discovered iron yet. They only used bronze or flints."

I nodded. "I suppose the strong new metal would be like magic to them."

With that question answered, we again attempted to improve the defences of Kingsinch. Augmenting the rowan wood crosses, we hammered iron horseshoes above the doors, hoping that, if the rowan failed, the iron would keep us secure.

"Of course," Mrs Lunan said, "the horseshoes won't work for any building that Heather Jock has entered."

"If Jock is to blame," Dougie said stoutly.

"That man is a menace," Agnes said. "I hope we can get rid of him soon." She glowered at Dougie. "When the water recedes, we should hand him to the police."

"For what reason?" Dougie asked.

"Poaching, trespass, helping the Sidh and theft," Agnes said, as her pretty little mouth twisted upwards.

Dougie shook his head. "Jock's no' that bad," he said and walked away with his boots splashing in the spreading puddles.

With the horseshoes nailed in place, Mr Lunan organised more traditional defences. There are many discarded materials, wood, corrugated iron, planking, and the like on any farm. The bothy boys and Mr Lunan boarded up windows and added makeshift bolts to the doors. Peter scoured the outbuildings for old lanterns, which Mr Lunan placed around the steading, ready to pool their light, showing us where the Sidh came.

"Weapons," Dougie said. "We need something to fight them with."

"We'll make them," Mr Lunan decided. "You may as well do something, now that you can't plough the fields."

Peter was the most innovative, suggesting weapons such as pikes and axes, which the practical horsemen created with a minimum of fuss and a maximum of skill. I watched as Dougie cut down the hafts of broken hoes and spades, while Mr Lunan formed the blades into points.

"Not as good as a blacksmith could make." Mr Lunan examined his work with a critical eye, "but suitably lethal for our purpose."

As we worked, I looked around the small island on which Kingsinch stood. The rain had reduced to a drizzle, yet still increased the surrounding loch. Nature had negated generations of farmers' work in a single wet week.

"Ellen!" Mrs Lunan shouted. "The cows still need to be milked! Stop standing talking to the boys and do your job!"

Jock came to the door an hour or so before the sun set. Mrs Lunan had expected him, and locked the door, with the bolt drawn and turned.

I heard Jock's hammering, but Mrs Lunan pushed me aside.

"Go away, Jock," she said sharply. "You're not welcome here."

"It's me, Mrs Lunan. It's Jock." The rough voice sounded through the solid wood.

"I know very well who it is," Mrs Lunan said. "Get away with you! Go on! We don't want your sort here, bringing in the Sidh and causing all sorts of trouble."

"I didn't bring the Sidh," Jock said. "They were here long before I came."

It took that long for Mr Lunan to arrive. "Get away, Jock. Go back to where you came from, or I'll set the dogs on you!"

Jock's reply was muffled, but I thought I heard some obscenities.

"Aye, you too, Jock. Now get and don't come back!" Mrs Lunan responded with a few foul words of her own.

"You can't leave him out there with the Sidh around," I said, trying to get to the door. "It's not safe."

Mrs Lunan's response was a back-handed swipe that caught me across the face and threw me against the wall. "You mind your own business, Ellen, or I'll send you out with him!"

I held a hand to my face, startled at Mrs Lunan's reaction.

"Mrs Lunan's right, Ellen," Mr Lunan said not unkindly. "It's best if Jock stays outside the house. Best for the baby, and the rest of us." He patted my shoulder. "Jock can look after himself. Now you put the kettle on and make us some tea."

The noise had attracted Andrew and Agnes, who held Baby Robert tight to her breast and looked, wide-eyed, at my reddening cheek. "Has he gone?" Agnes asked, in a small voice.

"Aye, Agnes, he's gone," Mrs Lunan said. "No thanks to your friend Ellen here. That's one less fear for the little one."

"Thank you, Mrs Lunan," Agnes said. "I'm sorry to cause you trouble."

Mrs Lunan nodded. "It had to come sometime, Agnes. We knew taking on Kingsinch was a risk. Now we have to cope with it. Davie!" she snapped. "Take the gun and see if Jock's gone. I don't trust that man."

With a last glance at me, Mr Lunan fetched his shotgun, loaded it with two cartridges and stepped outside. The moment he was gone, Mrs Lunan slammed shut the door and drew the bolts.

"As for you." She looked at me with bitter, hard eyes, "you had better keep out of my way, girl."

I kept out of Mrs Lunan's way until she had calmed down. In her mood that night, she was quite capable of throwing me outside in the rain.

Mr Lunan returned a few moments after dark, still carrying his shotgun. "No sign of him," he said tersely.

"Good," Mrs Lunan said.

That night we waited for the Sidh to return. I lay in my makeshift bed on the floor of the kitchen, listening to the wind in the lum and hoping, praying, not to hear that terrible whistling.

I had a fear that the Sidh might try coming down the chimney into the kitchen, so ensured the fire continued all night, sending sufficient heat up the lum to deter the hardiest of the Sidh. I did not find much sleep, only dozing and waking with a sudden start, to stare around me.

The Sidh did not come that night, nor the next, as we continued with what work the farm demanded, and strengthened our defences for the next assault.

"Maybe they won't come back," Andrew said hopefully.

"And maybe I can jump to the moon," Dougie said. "They've got their eyes on the bairn now, and the flood's trapped us here."

I nodded, still sick with guilt at having released the captive. We were indeed trapped, for the rain had not relented. Sometimes it was a heavy downpour that bounced off the dull slates, more often it was a steady, insidious drizzle that painted the landscape grey, but always it added to our dilemma. Until the waters receded, we were as trapped in Kingsinch as if we had been on the moon.

On the third night, the whistling returned. Peter heard it first and passed on the news.

"They're coming," he said, gripping the steel-tipped pike that was his pride and joy. "Now we can fight them!"

I thought that Peter enjoyed the situation, for, in his eyes, he could prove himself equal to the horsemen. I also thought it strange that others could hear the very sound that had condemned me to a lunatic asylum when I was a child. Perhaps we were all mad in Kingsinch, and none of this was real.

"Let's hope we don't have to fight," Mr Lunan said. "I want everybody in the farmhouse tonight."

We obeyed, for it made sense for the men to be close to the baby. The bothy- boys crammed into the farmhouse, with Jim trying to look nonchalant, Dougie fierce-eyed, a Scottish warrior if I ever saw one, while Peter was proclaiming his eagerness to fight. Mr Lunan positioned them around the building.

"If you hear anything, or see anything," Mr Lunan said. "Shout out right away."

I was in the kitchen, making tea and brose, scones and oatcakes, and listening for sounds at the backdoor. Occasionally Mrs Lunan would look in on me, make a critical remark or merely run her cold eye over me before withdrawing.

The whistling came again, louder, and closer than before. It came from all around us, penetrating even the persistent hammer of the rain.

"Here they come," Mrs Lunan said.

"Dougie! Take charge inside the house!" Mr Lunan shouted. "Andrew: stay with your wife. Jim; you're with me!" Lifting his shotgun, Mr Lunan called up the dogs, opened the door into the yard and strode outside into the night.

"Take a lantern!" Mrs Lunan said, but it was too late. She spoke to the closed door.

We waited inside, heard the whistling, and then the frantic barking of the dogs. I raced upstairs to peer out the nearest window and saw only the dim shapes of the buildings.

"What's happening?" Mrs Lunan shouted.

"I can't see anything," I replied, looking through a crack in the new wooden barrier. "All the lanterns are out."

Then I heard Mr Lunan shouting and the resounding thud of the shotgun. In the sudden light of the muzzle flare, I saw the images of Mr Lunan with the gun at his shoulder, and Jim lunging at something with his pike. I did not see the dogs, although their barking altered to a high snarl and I heard one or more of them worrying something. The darkness returned, more intense in contrast to the preceding brightness. One by one, the lanterns flared into life, casting sharp shadows as they forced back a fraction of the night.

The dogs sounded again, snarling, and barking, and then I heard Jim's voice: "There's another one," and Mr Lunan shouting something incoherent. Then silence save for the barking of a single dog.

"What's happening?" Agnes asked, her voice plaintive.

"I don't know," I called down. "I can't see."

We waited, listening, and then Baby Robert decided to cry. So far, he had been a very well-behaved little boy, but now he made up for his previous reticence with bawls that filled the house and no-doubt carried far beyond the confines of Kingsinch.

"What a pair of lungs that boy has," Mrs Lunan approved. "He won't be backward in coming forward."

"The Sidh will know he is here," Agnes said.

"They already know that," I said.

Baby Robert was still crying when Mr Lunan and Jim returned to the farmhouse. Jim was gasping, with blood dripping from his pike, while Mr Lunan looked white and strained.

"I don't know how many of these things are out there," Mr Lunan said as the dogs flopped on the floor beside the fire, tongues out. I fondled the closest, ruffling the rain-sodden hair around his neck.

"Did you get any?" Mrs Lunan asked.

"Jim spitted one," Mr Lunan said. "Shoved his pike right through it as if it was cheese. I shot at a group. I don't know if I killed any, but I wounded a few." He jerked a thumb at the dogs. "These are the best weapon we have. The Sidh are terrified of them."

Only then did I notice the blood on the dogs' muzzles. I fetched a cloth and basin and washed the blood away, with the dog making little playful growling noises that fooled nobody.

"It's time Ellen fed the dogs," Mr Lunan said.

"No." Mrs Lunan shook her head. "Don't feed them. Let them find their food outside. There's nothing better to defend us than a hungry dog. Let them loose outside, and they can hunt down the Sidh all night long."

"That's a good thought," Mr Lunan said, opening the door. "Go on, dogs. Seek and kill."

The dogs did not require any further encouragement. All three bounded out of the door and into the pounding rain.

Mrs Lunan grunted. "God help the Sidh when the dogs get hold of them." She gave a twisted grin. "There will be blood and bones to clean the morn, Davie."

We heard no more whistling that night, and with all the men waiting in the farmhouse, we had little fear that the creatures could break in and seize Baby Robert. I slept beside the fire, curled up like a child with the red embers hissing a few feet away. Bad dreams interrupted my night, with the sharp-toothed Sidh roaming through my head, following me as I recounted Peter's story.

As I prepared the breakfasts in the dark of the morning, Mr Lunan opened the door and shouted into the rain.

"Come on dogs!" he roared. "It's time you were in!"

I stood back, expecting a deluge of wet dog. Nothing happened.

"Come on, damn you!" Mr Lunan shouted again. "Dogs!" he swore when the dogs did not appear and stepped outside, still calling. After a few moments, he cursed again, loudly, and then there was silence.

"What's that man doing now?" Mrs Lunan said. "Ellen, go and find out what's happening."

I lifted a lantern and ran out into the semi-darkness. I knew Mr Lunan had gone towards the byre, so followed, and saw him on his knees, holding something in his arms.

"They're dead," Mr Lunan whispered when I arrived at his side. "The Sidh have killed my dogs."

CHAPTER 14

MR LUNAN WAS CORRECT. All three dogs lay together outside the byre, each perforated by a dozen arrows. The dog's blood had pooled around them and lay in a sticky mess outside the byre.

"Oh, good God in heaven."

I stared for some time, feeling the pain of each dog. Although Mr Lunan had never named them, each had a distinct character; I knew them as individuals in a way that Mr Lunan could not. I touched each body, feeling the residual warmth. The life force had left them now, so they were merely meat, bone, and rough fur.

"Rest easy, my friends," I said, but quietly. Nobody would understand my words save the dogs. They would be in whatever afterlife God created for animals that are not as dumb as the humans who maltreat them.

"Dear God; the Sidh will pay for this," Mr Lunan said. He raised his voice to a roar that the good neighbours of Meigle must have heard. "Do you hear me, you creatures from hell? You'll pay for this!"

His words echoed in the growing light as the rain continued to weep from an uncaring heaven.

"Come on, Mr Lunan," I said. "I'll take you back to the house. We can bury the dogs later when you've recovered."

I heard the music then, for the first time. It was more harmonious than anything I had heard before and originated beneath the ground. I stood entranced. I could hear men and women singing, and the sound of musical instruments, lutes and fiddles, and soft bagpipes without the Highland drone.

"Can you hear that?" I asked.

"Yes, damn them." Mr Lunan was nearly in tears at the death of his dogs. "The creatures are celebrating. I'll not have that. I'll give them something to celebrate; you see if I don't! They won't kill Davie Lunan's dogs and get away with it."

I had never seen Mr Lunan in such a taking. He was shaking with anger, stamping his feet and the veins in his neck protruded as he swore vengeance on the Sidh.

"Come on, Mr Lunan," I said. "Come with me." I led him back to the house, feeling him tremble, either with anger or grief, or perhaps both.

"My dogs," Mr Lunan said as he sat at the kitchen table. "My poor wee dogs."

"I'll go and bury them," Dougie said until Mrs Lunan shook her head.

"No, Jim. Wait for full dawn." She put a hand on his arm. "The Sidh might still be out there, waiting."

"I'm not scared of the Sidh." Peter gripped his pike. "I'll go."

"The dogs weren't scared of the Sidh, either," Mrs Lunan said dryly. "You'll stay here until it's daylight, Peter, or you'll know all about it, by jingo."

Dawn came slowly that morning. We were all edgy, looking out the gaps in the window and jumping at every sound. The hoot of an owl had us reaching for our weapons, with Mr Lunan cursing fit to scare a marine.

"Get the fire banked up, Ellen," Mrs Lunan said. "Make yourself useful."

I added coal, with a covering of dross to eke out the fuel and poked a couple of air holes to ensure the heat continued. The men grumbled and spoke in low tones. As I made the brose, Baby Robert woke up, calling for food, so we all ate together, thinking of the horrors outside the house and wondering what full daylight would bring.

"That's the lighter hours beginning now," Mrs Lunan said. "Best get to the dogs, lads."

The men looked at each other, with time having diminished their initial enthusiasm. Dougie gripped his pike. "Come on, lads," he said. "There's work to do."

Peter was next, making a chest as he stepped boldly outside, with Jim third. Andrew hesitated, looking over his shoulder at Agnes, who shook her head.

"I'll be all right," she said, waving her hand to the door. "Off you go and do your work."

There was always work at Kingsinch, whatever happened. A farm cannot stop working just because of a death, or an attack by creatures beyond our ken.

I got myself ready until Mr Lunan put a heavy hand on my shoulder. "Where do you think you're going, lass?"

"To see to the cows," I said. "It's past their time for milking."

"You'll not be going alone, Ellen," Mr Lunan said. "Not this morning. Wait until the men come back."

"You could go with her, Davie," Mrs Lunan said.

"And leave you and the baby without a man in the house?" Mr Lunan shook his head. "No. Anyway, I can't hear them bellowing. They'll soon let us know when they want Ellen to milk them."

Mr Lunan was correct. My cows were strangely silent that morning as if they knew there was trouble abroad and decided to wait for the easing of the dark. I wriggled with impatience, for I knew how much my girls needed me. They would be missing my company, as I missed theirs.

"Have patience, Ellen," Mrs Lunan said, strangely motherly.

The bothy boys removed the arrows and buried the dogs in a single deep pit. I heard the boys' voices through the patter of the rain and closed my ears to the language. Men had to swear when they worked; I did not know why. They returned to the farmhouse with a heavy tread and threw a handful of bloodied arrows onto my scrubbed table.

"Thirteen," Jim said with a catch in his voice. "There were thirteen arrows in each dog." He slumped onto a chair. "We threw most away and brought some back."

I examined the arrows. They were straightforward, with a light shaft of a single reed or length of wood, and a small tip of sharpened flint.

"That's what I found last week." Mr Lunan opened a drawer and produced an identical arrowhead. "My father called them elf-shot and thought they had mystical properties. Some folk thought they were poisoned."

I held one of the arrows close to the lantern. "I can't see any trace of poison," I said. "It's only sharpened flint."

"Are you an expert in poisons?" Mrs Lunan asked.

I shook my head.

"Don't be so presumptuous, then," Mrs Lunan said. "With the loss of the dogs, that's one of our most effective weapons gone. We'll have to be extra vigilant now." She nodded at me.

"Off you go and see to the cows. One of the men will go with you."

"I'll go." Peter grasped his pike. "Come on, Ellen; I'll look after you."

"Thank you, Peter," I said.

A chill wind blasted the spaces between the buildings, ruffling my skirt and threatening to lift the bonnet from my head. Peter looked around, holding his pike in two hands.

"I'll go first," Peter said. "Just in case the Sidh are waiting for you."

I nodded, for, despite my show of nonchalance, my heart was hammering like an Irish drum. I shivered at the thought of one of those sharp flint arrows penetrating my cringing flesh.

Peter opened the byre door a crack and stepped inside, to emerge a moment later with his face white and shock in his eyes. "Don't go in, Ellen."

"What? Of course, I'm going in!" I pushed past him to tend to my patient cows, and immediately wished I had not.

Every single one of my cows, my charges, the animals I had tended for weeks, lay dead, pierced by a multitude of arrows. I knew these cattle as friends; I knew their habits and personalities. I knew them, and they trusted me. Now they lay dead, murdered by the Sidh.

I stood inside the byre, staring at the scene of slaughter, with Peter at my side. I felt his hand slide into mine and was grateful for the physical contact. He patted my arm, more mature than men twice his age.

"Come away, Ellen," Peter said. "You can't help them."

"No." I stared into the gloomy byre, now tainted with innocent blood. "No, I can't help them."

At that moment, I began to hate the Sidh. Until then, I had felt slightly detached from events at Kingsinch, as though this entire sequence of events did not concern me. Now I knew that

I was central to the whole thing. By killing my cattle, the Sidh had struck directly at me.

I had often been better able to relate to animals than humans.

"You know about dogs?" The man eyed me up and down as if I were one of his pets.

"A little," I said.

"Can you feed them and take them for walks?"

I looked at the man's collection of dogs. They looked back at me through wary eyes. I was wrong; these animals were not pets; the man kept them for quite another reason. The dogs told me that through their attitude.

"Yes, I can do that." The dogs had found me as I slept in a barn and gave tongue until their owner stomped across to see what they had found.

"Don't feed them too much." The man was in early middle age, with broad forearms and a scarred face. "Just enough to keep them alive."

I resolved to feed them more than the man wanted.

"My name is Ellen," I said.

"You call me Mr Edwards."

"Yes, Mr Edwards," I said.

"Most people are scared of my dogs," Mr Edwards said.

I said nothing to that. People scared me; animals did not.

I lived in an outhouse, with the dogs in a cellar next door, underneath the cottage that Mr Edwards shared with his slatternly wife. I knew at once that she did not like me, perhaps because her husband did. Sharp-tongued and hard of hand, she spoke to me as if I were one of her animals, but the outhouse provided shelter from the unseasonable weather, and the dogs appreciated my company.

They were lean and scarred, these dogs, unhappy with their lives. They devoured their meagre rations with much snarling and bared teeth, but that was through hunger rather than malice.

I took them for walks through the fields that surrounded Mr Edwards' lonely cottage, and if we wandered into the odd farmstead, the dogs did not mind. Their numbers and hunger gave them an advantage over the farm dogs we met, and from time to time, we stole the meat from the farm dogs' plates. My dogs appreciated the extra and followed me as if I was the leader of the pack.

It was on a Saturday that I walked further and, greatly daring, visited the market town of Keith. I could feel the stares of the good neighbours of Keith as they saw me, a thin-faced, diminutive girl as rough and uncouth as my dogs, infesting their douce little town.

The smell of the butcher's shop enticed my dogs, and five minutes later, the enraged proprietor was chasing us away, joined by a vociferous crowd of his townsfolk. My dogs rather enjoyed the run, but not as much as they enjoyed the free food the butcher had unwillingly supplied.

The next day, Mr Edwards told me to select two of the most aggressive of his dogs.

"They're not aggressive," I said. "Only hungry." That was true, for the animals had never been anything but friendly with me.

Mr Edwards selected two himself, a rough-haired Alsatian I knew as Alie and a mixed-breed, snarling wee thing I had called Toothy.

Leaving the rest of the pack in the cellar, Mr Edwards took Alie, Toothy and me to an isolated steading somewhere in the hill-country south of Keith, where other men, and a few women, had also brought their dogs.

"What is this place?" I asked.

"It's a dog fight," Mr Edwards told me. "What did you think

it was? I'll throw the cross-breed in the ring first, and then the Alsatian will fight the animal that kills it."

I could sense the fear of the dogs; they knew that something terrible was about to happen. Toothy looked at me with a question in his eyes. He licked my hand in the hope that I could help.

"I thought it was something like that," I said. "Is there much money involved?"

Mr Edwards laughed. "You catch on quick," he said. "Yes, we gamble on the dogs. I'll be paid for using the cross-breed as bait, and then win when the Alsatian kills his opponent."

I nodded, feeling sick.

Both my dogs were looking at me as I came to fetch them. Toothy opened his mouth, with his tongue hanging out, pleading for help. I opened the boxes that contained them, tied the rope-leads around their necks, and ran.

"Come on, boys," I said, with my dogs at my heels. "Run!"

And that was the end of my job looking after dogs.

CHAPTER 15

"Come on." Peter pulled me away from the byre.

"You weren't long." Mrs Lunan looked at me through suspicious eyes.

"They're all dead," I said.

"Who's all dead?" Mr Lunan asked.

"The cows," I said, speaking as though in a daze, for in truth the sight had shocked me more than anything else I had seen in Kingsinch.

"What do you mean, dead? I'll see about that!" Mrs Lunan stormed out of the house as if her hot temper had some magic quality of restoring life. She was back in minutes, looking as stunned as I felt.

"The girl's right," Mrs Lunan said. "They're all dead. All of them."

Mr Lunan looked up from the table. He had barely stirred since discovering the death of his dogs. "The Sidh," he said.

"The Sidh," I repeated.

"Get the boys to check the stables," Mr Lunan spoke

offhandedly as if he did not care. "Cows are livestock, but the horses are valuable property."

After witnessing Mr Lunan's reaction to his dog's deaths, I knew his apparent callousness was an act. I watched as Dougie and Jim left for the stables, with Peter at their heels, pike in hand.

They returned in ten minutes, white-faced with shock. I did not have to ask what was wrong.

"They're all dead," Jim whispered. "All of them."

I knew how attached the men were to their horses, so said nothing when Dougie, big, hard-as-nails Dougie the first horseman of Kingsinch and would-be soldier, surreptitiously brushed a tear from his eyes.

"More money lost," Mr Lunan said. "We'll be hard-pressed to meet our creditors."

"Aye." Mrs Lunan was the most stoic person in that house. "We'll have to get a loan from the bank next term, Davie, if we're to keep this farm running."

Mr Lunan nodded. "Aye, Lizzie, that's what we'll have to do."

I sat at Mr Lunan's side, listening to the quiet ticking of the kitchen clock and the slow crackle of the fire. That was when the whistling started again.

"It's daylight," Mrs Lunan said. "The Sidh don't come in daylight."

"They don't kill cattle and horses either," Mr Lunan said. "Or dogs. Something is different."

The clock ticked on, slowly, remorselessly, each tick removing a second from our lives. Time is such a precious commodity; we waste so much of it, although we only have a limited supply, and nobody knows how much he or she has left. We are such foolish creatures, not to make full use of the most marvellous gift of all.

"Something is different," Mrs Lunan repeated her husband's words.

"I know what's different." Dougie stood inside the door with a mug of steaming tea in his fist. "The Sidh have a leader. When Mr Lunan had the Sidh woman locked up, the Sidh were restless but harmless. Now they have somehow freed her, and the Sidh are more aggressive."

I nodded assent. I had thought the same. The image returned to me, with my cows lying dead in their stalls and the little arrows protruding from them like the spines of a hedgehog.

"They're not only attacking us," I said. "Mr Fleming's light hasn't been on these past few nights."

Andrew leaned against the wall with his eyes never straying far from Agnes and the baby. "Charlie Fleming was always vulnerable out there," he said. "Farming marginal land is chancy at the best of times but farming near the Sidh?" He shook his head. "He wouldn't stand a chance."

"How about Brenda?" Jim was sitting on the floor, holding his pike as if his life depended on it, which it might do, I realised. "How about Brenda? I am meant to meet her tonight, up at the Pictish House."

"She won't be foolish enough to go," Andrew said. "Not with the rain and the Sidh."

"Rain won't stop her," Jim said. "She loves me, and she won't know about the Sidh. How could she know unless she's met them? I never told her in case she thought I was crazy."

"How will she know indeed," Dougie said, "and she'll be right in the heart of Sidh territory." He dragged the toe of his boot along the floor, a habit he had while thinking. "Hopefully, the rain will keep her at home."

"She might know about the Sidh," I said. "And they might leave her alone."

"They've not bothered anybody for years," Jim said. "Dougie's right. The woman that escaped must be their queen."

"They've always been up there." Mr Lunan altered the course of the conversation. "The hills were named after them, and the area is filled with folklore and stories about the Sidh." He glanced at his wife before continuing. "There were two reasons I took on Kingsinch. One was because it was inexpensive, and the other was because of the Sidh."

Mrs Lunan stretched across the table to hold her husband's hand.

"I wanted to hunt them down," Mr Lunan said quietly. "I wanted to destroy them like the vermin they are. That's why I came here. I used my prisoner as bait." He looked up. "I trained my dogs with the milk of the Sidh so that they could sniff them out, and I would kill them."

"The milk of the Sidh?" I asked the question that the others must have been thinking.

"My dogs suckled at the breasts of my captive," Mr Lunan said.

"Ah." I said no more as I felt sympathy for the woman I had set free. She may have been responsible for the slaughter of my cows, but Mr Lunan's treatment of her was reprehensible. I remembered her distended breasts, thought of the dogs sucking at her and shuddered. That poor woman must have suffered in her dungeon; no wonder she was taking revenge on Kingsinch.

"Now," Mr Lunan said, "the Sidh are hunting us." He looked around. "I have brought you all here, without telling you of the danger."

Dougie finished his tea. "I grew up in Meigle," he said. "I knew about the Sidh long before I came here."

"I'm a Strathmore man, too," Andrew said. "I'm no stranger to tales of the Sidh."

"Nor am I," Agnes said. "I'm a farm lassie, born and bred."

Peter brandished his pike. "I knew about them, and I'm not scared."

"How about you, Ellen?" Mrs Lunan said.

I considered for a few moments before I replied. "I had never heard of them," I said, "But I've always been aware of something." I explained that I had heard the whistling all my life, with it rising every few years until it invaded every part of my life. I stepped back, waiting for the ridicule and verbal assaults.

"Every few years?" Dougie said. "Every how many years? Five, six, seven?"

I tried to work out the times, screwing up my face with the effort as I cudgelled my memory. "Seven," I said, at last. "Every seven years, I think."

The room became deadly quiet as everybody stared at me. Even Baby Robert left his mother's breast to focus bright eyes in my direction.

"Oh, dear God," Dougie said quietly. "Every seven years."

I sat in uncomfortable silence.

"The Sidh are said to make sacrifices every seven years," Mrs Lunan repeated what Jock had told me. "They seek out a human virgin." The room was hushed as she continued. "Are you a virgin, Ellen? Have you ever enjoyed a man?"

It was not the sort of question I would have expected in mixed company, especially with Dougie listening expectantly for my answer. The ticking of the clock seemed very loud.

"I have never enjoyed a man," I said, honesty. I did not trust people sufficiently to speak of Mr Snodgrass's invasion of my body, which was not a thing I enjoyed.

The silence continued for a few seconds, with Dougie running a speculative gaze over me, as if sizing me up for future use, and Agnes trying to hide her slightly superior smile as she held the sleeping Robert.

"Then that's the reason," Mrs Lunan said with an air of finality. "The Sidh have marked you down for sacrifice."

Although I was not pleased to hear Mrs Lunan's words, nor was I surprised. I stared into the fire as the others discussed my situation.

"Is it only because she's a virgin?" Agnes asked.

"I believe so," Mrs Lunan said. "The Sidh have two reasons to attack us now; they want the un-christened baby, and they want a virgin sacrifice."

"Can't we christen the baby ourselves?" Andrew asked. "There must be a Bible somewhere in the house. Can't we use the book and say the holy words?"

"Do you know the holy words?" Mrs Lunan asked him pointedly.

"No," Andrew said.

"No," Mrs Lunan repeated. "And do you happen to have a bottle of holy water handy?"

Andrew shook his head. "No."

"Nor do I," Mrs Lunan said.

"I have an idea," Dougie said, smiling to me.

"I can imagine what it is," I said, just as we heard the scrabbling upstairs.

"Jesus!" Jim blasphemed before Dougie could explain. "They're inside the house!"

The men grabbed their weapons and dashed for the door.

"Stay with your wife, Andrew!" Mr Lunan said, snatching at his shotgun. He rammed in a couple of cartridges as he followed the men into the body of the house.

"Where are you going?" Mrs Lunan demanded as I lifted the poker and left the kitchen. If the Sidh intended to sacrifice me to their god, I wanted to retaliate.

"I want to fight," I said.

Mrs Lunan laid her hard hand on my shoulder. "You'll stay put!" she said.

We sat around the kitchen table with the door locked, listening to the rain outside as the hands of the clock continued their passage around the face. Agnes made small sounds to Baby Robert while Mrs Lunan and I sat in tense silence.

The men returned, swearing softly. "Not a sign of them." Mr Lunan leant his shotgun in the corner of the room beside the pantry. "Just a bird in the chimney."

That was a quiet day, with the men patrolling the steading every half hour as the daylight gradually faded into night.

"You don't have to sleep in the kitchen tonight," Mrs Lunan said as darkness crept over us.

"I'm fine here." I preferred having a room to myself, rather than sharing.

"Are you not scared in case the Sidh come in the door?" Agnes asked.

"It's locked and bolted," I said.

As the boys made a guard-rota, I lay down next to the range, where the embers of the fire continued to glow. I had barely settled down when the noise began.

Agnes screamed, high pitched and frantic, then Andrew yelled for help. "They're in the room!"

"We're coming!" Dougie shouted, followed by a string of obscenities and another shrill scream. I could hear the incoherent roars of fighting men, with gasps and thuds that I could not identify.

I reached my old bedroom last, poker in hand, to see the bothy-boys engaged in a desperate encounter with several of the Sidh. Although the Sidh were smaller in stature than any of our lads, they were wiry, fighting back with long-taloned hands and small, leaf-shaped knives. I stood at the doorway, gripping my poker as the bothy-boys gradually overcame the Sidh's resistance. There was blood on the floor and spattered on the walls, with Jim gasping in pain, holding his thigh, and two of the Sidh writhing on the floor. The others, whistling to each other, slid into the fireplace, and scrambled up the lum, with Dougie having a final swipe at the last creature to leave.

"The devils!" Mr Lunan said, gasping for breath. "Well done, lads! You chased them away."

Jim sunk onto the bed, holding his thigh, from which blood was seeping, while Dougie and Peter looked at the Sidh that lay on the ground. One lay still, and the other writhed and moaned, with an ugly stab wound in its midriff.

"One's still alive," Peter stared, white-faced. The boy had discovered that there was more to being a man than strutting and postulating.

"What will we do with it?" Dougie asked.

"This," Mr Lunan said and battered the thing's skull with the butt of his shotgun. "Now it's dead."

"They came down the lum," Peter said with a nervous giggle. "I never thought they could do that." He lifted a bronze, triangular-bladed knife from the floor. "I'll have this."

"Dougie," Mr Lunan pointed to the dead Sidh, "get rid of those things. Jim, get to the kitchen, and we'll look at your leg. Ellen, you and Peter make up every fire in the house."

"We'll soon run out of coal if we do that, Mr Lunan," I said.

"Then we'll burn wood, and if that runs out, I'll tear the barns to pieces and burn them," Mr Lunan said. "The Sidh found a weak spot in our defences, so we must bolster them."

"Yes, Mr Lunan," I said.

"Come on, Jim." Mr Lunan put an arm around Jim's shoulder and supported him to the kitchen as I hurried downstairs for kindling and coal.

"Let's see that leg," Mrs Lunan said. "Take your trousers off."

"What?" Jim looked askance.

"Don't be silly, Jim," Mrs Lunan said. "Ellen! Give a hand here!"

I helped remove Jim's trousers while Mrs Lunan examined his wound. It was deep, with a steady flow of blood.

"We'll have to clean it," Mrs Lunan decided. "Lie on the table, Jim."

There was no ceremony and damned little sympathy as Mrs Lunan poured some of her husband's precious whisky directly onto Jim's wound. He bore it like a man, grimacing in silence, but he made little noises as Mrs Lunan stitched his wound together with needle and thread.

"That's not great." Mrs Lunan reviewed her work. "It'll hold until we get you to the doctor." I helped Mrs Lunan wrap lengths of torn sheets around Jim's leg, and immediately we finished, she turned on me.

"Have you got these fires made up, yet?"

"No," I said.

"Then get it done!" Mrs Lunan screamed in my ear.

With Peter carrying coal for me, I made up every fire in the house, although Mrs Lunan said not to light them yet.

"There are surely enough of us in the house to watch for the Sidh," she said. "I'm not wasting coal for no purpose."

I never understood that woman.

CHAPTER 16

"How DEEP IS the water in the fields?" Andrew asked as we gathered around the kitchen table the next day.

Mr Lunan frowned. "I'm not sure," he said. "It covers the fail dykes."

"The fail dykes are five feet high," Dougie said, "so the floodwater is more than that. What are you thinking, Andy?"

"I'm thinking that the path is higher than the fields," Andrew said.

"You mean to follow the path out," I said.

"That's right." Andrew nodded. "Why stay here, waiting for the Sidh to come to us. Why don't we get away?" He glanced at Mr Lunan. "I don't mean to desert you, Mr Lunan; I want to make sure our baby, and Agnes, are safe."

"Ellen had better go too," Mrs Lunan said, "if the Sidh want her, she's safer away from here."

"We should have taken the dogcart when we had horses," Jim said, wincing as he rubbed his leg.

"If wishes were horses," Mrs Lunan said, "we'd all be the Queen of Sheba. Is that leg bothering you?"

"No, it's fine," Jim said.

"Then leave it alone."

"Can you find the path when it's underwater?" Dougie asked.

"I reckon I can," Andrew said. "It's straight most of the way. There's only that one dog-leg bend and the post marks that."

"It's a sensible suggestion," Mrs Lunan agreed. "The boys will escort you, and then they can leave or stay, as they wish."

"I'm staying," Peter said at once. "The Sidh aren't going to chase me away."

"I'm staying as well," Dougie said.

"And me." Jim was still in pain from his wound. "I want to make sure Brenda is all right."

We lit the fires half-an-hour before dusk, with the men stationed in the various rooms of the house to watch for the Sidh. Rather than have lanterns scattered around the farmtoun, Mr Lunan had concentrated them around the farmhouse, lighting them himself as the darkness gathered.

The men stood watch-and-watch, two hours on, two hours sleeping, watching through the cracks in the boarded-up windows and listening for the Sidh outside. I slept fitfully, dozing beside the kitchen fire with the table propped against the door for extra security.

"They're not coming tonight." Agnes arrived in the kitchen, bleary-eyed. "I need to change the baby."

"I hope they don't come," I said. "Try and get some sleep, Agnes. You might need all your strength tomorrow."

The Sidh did not come that night. Only the owls called, lonely in the dark.

~

"Perhaps we scared the Sidh away," Andrew said hopefully as we rose well before dawn.

"Maybe we did," Dougie agreed. "Maybe that attack down the chimney was their last, and now they'll leave us in peace."

I felt the tension as we prepared for the journey, with Mr and Mrs Lunan watching through haunted eyes. Jim's leg was troubling him, so he remained in the house, with the Lunans. We left the house half-an-hour before dawn, with the steady drizzle weeping on us and the floodwater extending to the hills on either side.

Dougie took the lead, probing under the water with his pike, feeling for the raised track, with the rest of us following, step by slow step. Agnes and I were in the centre, with Peter acting as rear-guard and Andrew never straying far from his family.

"It looks so different underwater," Agnes said. "I must have walked this track twenty times, yet I hardly recognise a thing."

"Use the shape of the hills as landmarks," Dougie advised, "and look for the marker post. Once we're past the dogleg, it's only a long stride to the public road and then the Black Yett."

The Black Yett. When I had first heard that name, I thought it sinister. Now it seemed a beacon of hope in a world I did not understand. I pictured the Yett, metalled and tarma-cked, that would take us from this place of fear to civilisation, where people worked in factories and women spent time gossiping and shopping. I resolved never to leave a town again. I would live in a city, surrounded by laughing, struggling, ordi-nary humanity, rather than out here with the spirits of crea-tures from the distant past. My idea of sacrificing myself to save others had died when the Sidh murdered my cows.

"Keep close," Dougie called, still probing with his pike.

When we left the steading, the water was up to our thighs, with the occasional deeper dip as we stumbled into a hole. Now the path rose slightly, so we were only knee-deep, and Dougie was moving slightly faster. He still tested each step, but our route seemed easier to follow, with the increasing daylight showing us the line of the hills on either side.

"This is easier than I thought," Dougie said. "We're making good progress."

"We should have done this days ago." Agnes held Baby Robert close, ensuring no part of its clothing touched the peat-cloudy water.

"Maybe we should have," Andrew said, with his eyes never still. A sudden splash to our left startled me, and all three men faced in that direction, pikes ready to fight.

"It's only a bird," I said, as the white blur of a seagull lifted off from the water, followed by half a dozen others.

"I thought so," Peter said, keeping his pike raised.

"Come on, let's hurry," Agnes said. "I want to get away from here."

"We're doing fine," Dougie said.

We moved on, with Agnes urging speed and Dougie advising caution. As daylight strengthened, we could see our position with more clarity, identifying the run of hills.

"We'll be close to Chapelinch now," Andrew said. "That's our first landmark."

"I'll be happier when we're past it," Agnes said. "I'll be happier when we're out of this valley completely."

"So will we all," I said.

An owl called from the left, with her mate answering with a similar hoot on our right. Peter readied his pike.

"It's only an owl," Andrew said. "Nothing to worry about."

I shivered, for I had never heard an owl in this section of the path before. They were further back. "No," I told myself. "It's all right. The weather will have forced the owl to new hunting grounds, that's all." I knew that was not true; I knew my wildlife.

I peered ahead, hoping to see a friendly light somewhere in Strathmore, although I knew the valley's twist obscured our view of the outside world. We would see nothing until we passed the dog-leg bend.

"There's Chapelinch now," Agnes said. "See? That darker hump to our left."

We all looked at the shape, pleased that we had made progress.

"We'll be at the post next," Peter said. "Once we're past that, it's only a mile or so to the road."

That news cheered me up immensely, and Dougie began to sing one of his ballads, with Andrew and Peter joining in the chorus.

> *"There's burstin buds on the larick now,*
> *A' the birds are paired an' biggin'*
> *Saft soughin' win's dry the dubby howe,*
> *An' the eildit puir are thiggin'"*

"Shush!" Agnes said. "The Sidh might hear us, and I can't listen for them if you lads are making a noise."

The men stopped singing at once. Baby Robert began to cry.

"I can't change you now," Agnes said crossly. "You'll have to wait!"

Robert continued to protest about his discomfort, increasing the volume to let the world know.

"Can't you keep it quiet?" Dougie asked. "It's making more noise than we ever did!"

"Robert's not an it!" Agnes said. "He's a he! And I'm trying."

I saw the light first. It was only a faint glow, little more than a flicker in the half-dark as if somebody held a candle behind a thin cotton sheet. I stared across the dark waters in the direction of Chapelinch.

"There's a light in the old chapel," I said, quietly.

The others looked in that direction. "I see it," Peter said.

"It might be Heather Jock," Dougie sounded hopeful. "We haven't seen him for a few days."

"Not since Mr Lunan kicked him out of the house," Peter said. "Should I give him a hail?"

"No." Andrew shook his head. "Jock can look after himself if anybody can. We should keep moving."

I agreed although I would have liked to see Jock's sober, capable face once more. Something about that wild man gave me confidence.

We entered a stretch of deeper water now, as the path dipped between two fail dykes. The men were all right, but as the water reached above my waist, I began to worry a little.

"This flood will wash the dykes away," Dougie spoke like a farmer. "We'll have to build them up once it recedes. Old man Lunan will have us working twenty hours a day."

"Agnes and I won't be here," Andrew reminded. "We'll not set foot in Kingsinch again."

I gasped as I stepped into a dip and plunged deeper into the water. I was a full half-a-head shorter even than Agnes, so when the water reached her knees, I was mid-thigh, and when it lapped her thighs, I was waist-deep. Now I was up to my breasts and not enjoying the experience.

"Are you all right, Ellen?" Peter placed a supporting hand on my arm.

"Thank you." I struggled up, searching with my foot for firm ground. "I found a hole."

I could see Peter's face distinctly now. He was smiling to me, his teeth gleaming and his broad, smooth face friendly.

The vision came to me, a shocking image of Peter lying on a stone slab in some subterranean chamber. He was on his back, spread-eagled naked within a shimmering barrier, with his eyes staring, pleading for clemency that nobody was willing to grant. I was there, watching, beyond the barrier, while in the background, people chanted and sang one of the most beautiful songs I had ever heard.

"Peter!" I reached for him.

"It's all right, Ellen," he smiled to me with his supporting hand strong on my arm, "I won't let you drown."

The vision had only lasted a moment. I was back on that flooded road, with the grey-light revealing the hill slopes around and the rain still falling in a slow, relentless drizzle that soaked us all to the skin.

The only thing that remained was the music, soft and insidious. "Can you hear that?" I asked.

"Hear what?" Agnes asked. "With the noise that the baby's making in my ear, I can't hear a thing!"

"Listen." I held up my hand. "I can hear singing."

We all stopped for a moment, so the constant swirl and splash of water ended. We stood there, thigh-and-waist-deep in cold water, with the rain pattering around us, trying to hear beyond the raucous calls of Baby Robert.

"I hear it," Peter said. "It's like a choir, a church choir." He raised his head. "It's beautiful."

It was beautiful. I had never heard tunes like them before. "Peter's wrong, though," I said. "Church choirs are normally men grating and women shouting out the words, with at least one person coughing and hacking in the middle. That is far nicer."

"It's like angels singing," Peter said. "A heavenly choir."

"It may be a choir," Dougie said, "but it's not from heaven. More likely, the other place."

"It's far too sweet for that," Peter said. "I want to go and listen."

"It's a siren call," Dougie said. "And it's coming from Chapelinch where the light is."

"What's a siren call?" Peter asked, taking a step closer to the church.

"It's an old Greek legend." Dougie proved himself better educated than I had previously imagined. "The Sirens were a group of women who lured old-time sailors onto rocks by singing."

"There are no sailors here," Peter said.

"Peter!" Dougie grabbed him roughly. "That's not angels in there, and it's not Jock; that's them; that's the Sidh."

Dougie's words broke the spell, and we moved on, faster now as we strove to put the ancient chapel behind us.

The singing continued for a few moments before it faded away, leaving us only with the splash and surge of the flood-water and our gasps as we strove on. Even Baby Robert had decided that his complaints were pointless and resumed his sleep in his mother's arms.

All around us, the soft rain pattered onto the flood as the daylight improved visibility. The hills were clear now, if mist-shrouded, the grey-green slopes easing into the grey sky above.

"There's the post." Peter gestured ahead. "I'm glad it's there, as I thought the path veered more to the left."

"So did I," Dougie said. He prodded under the water with his pike. "Be careful, people. The path narrows here."

We walked in single file, with the cold water biting at us and the memory of the sweet singing bitter in our ears. I glanced over my shoulder for the fifth or sixth time since we passed Chapelinch, knowing that the Sidh were watching us.

181

The post thrust up from the water, looking vaguely skeletal in the dull light. I peered ahead, where a spur of the hills concealed our valley from broad Strathmore. If only we could round that spur, we could see the outside world. Only another three hundred yards and our escape was clear.

"Stop!" Dougie lifted a hand. "Something's wrong." He thrust his pike into the water. "I can't find the path here."

Peter felt his way forward to stand on Dougie's right and poke into the water. "Nor here," he said. "You try, Andy."

Andrew was already prodding into the water, swearing softly as he failed to touch anything substantial. "Nothing here," he said. "No bottom."

The men prodded all around, with no success. The post taunted us, unreachable despite its relative proximity.

"There's no track," Dougie said as Agnes fought her tears. "Either the Sidh have cut it, or the flood has washed it away. It was only built on bales of straw, remember."

"What now?" Agnes asked. "Can we swim to the post?"

"What if there's no track there, either," Andrew said. "I'll go ahead and see." He began to strip off, then glanced at me.

"I'll turn my back," I said, although in our present situation I was hardly likely to be concerned by the sight of a naked man.

I heard the splashing and a gasp or two as Andrew slipped into the cold water. "He's going well," Dougie approved.

"Very well," Agnes said and added in a sudden sharp tone, "What's that over there? On top of the flood? It's a man, walking on water!"

I turned around, no longer caring if I embarrassed Andrew or not. Agnes was correct; a man was walking on the water, or rather gliding over the water, towards Andrew, who was swimming with slow, steady strokes towards the marker pole.

"I don't believe what I'm seeing," Peter said.

"That's not a man," Dougie shouted. "It's one of them, one of the Sidh."

"Andrew!" Agnes screamed. "Andrew! Come back!"

Andrew grabbed the post and clung there, gasping at the chill. He looked very white as he lifted a hand in acknowledgement. The Sidh continued to glide across the water, slowly decreasing the distance to Andrew.

"Andrew!" Agnes screamed again. "Look out!"

"What is it?" Andrew shouted back.

"Behind you! Look behind you!"

Andrew turned around, to see the Sidh produce a short bow that had been slung across his back. Standing on the water, the Sidh pulled back the bow, took deliberate aim and fired at Andrew.

"Andy!" Agnes screamed with Baby Robert joining in.

The arrow missed, landing in the post with a soft thud. As the Sidh fitted a second arrow to his bow, Andrew lunged forward, while we all yelled encouragement.

"I'm coming, Andy!" Dougie yelled, and threw himself, fully clothed, into the water.

I stopped Peter from following. "Stay here, Peter," I said. "We need you to protect us."

Peter looked at me, and then at the drama unfolding before us.

"Please, Peter," Agnes said. "Don't leave us alone."

The Sidh fitted another arrow, took careful aim at Andrew, and fired. Andrew ducked under the water as the arrow plunged in with a small splash.

"Andy!" Agnes yelled.

"He's all right," I said, as Andrew surfaced, a few yards closer to the Sidh, who turned away, nearly falling sideways under the surface.

That was all the time it took for Dougie to reach the Sidh.

As Andrew swam forward, Dougie threw himself on the archer, both hands stretching out. The Sidh tried to fit another arrow to his bow, but Dougie was faster, grabbing hold of the creature and pulling him down. Andrew arrived two minutes later, helping subdue the Sidh by holding it under the water.

We watched events unfold, wordless. Agnes had a hand over her mouth while Peter looked eager to jump forward.

Within a few moments, Andrew and Dougie were heading back, with Dougie holding the Sidh's bow and quiver in his hand and the Sidh floating, face-down on the surface of the flood.

"They're all right," Agnes said. She held out a hand for Andrew, who emerged from the deep water looking rather shocked.

"I'm all right," he echoed Agnes's words. "We killed that man."

"It wasn't a man," Dougie said. "It was a Sidh, a thing."

Andrew nodded. "There's no path out, Agnes," he said. "There's nothing underfoot at all. Nothing."

Agnes looked away, biting her lip to hide her disappointment. She nodded. "You tried your best, Andrew. We tried our best."

Dougie held the bow and quiver in his hand. "We killed that thing," he confirmed. "We drowned it."

Peter smiled, hefting his pike. "We watched you," he said. "The Sidh walked on water."

"No." Dougie shook his head. "The Sidh had something on its feet, like a small float that prevented it from sinking."

I nodded. These Sidh seemed less supernatural day-by-day, and more like people who knew how to manipulate the natural environment.

"We can't go any further," Andrew repeated with his right arm wrapped around Agnes. "There's no path and the water is too deep to wade through. Maybe we can make a boat or raft back at the farm."

Agnes gestured to the hills that rose half a mile from us. "Can we not go to the hills and walk over them?"

"Aye, if we could walk on water and the Sidh didn't live there," Andrew said. "We'd be walking right into trouble."

We stood there, with the water lapping at our thighs and the rain falling steadily. Andrew dressed slowly, pulling wet clothes over his gleaming wet body. I did not watch; I did not care about his nudity. I did not care about anybody's nudity.

"We'll have to go back to Kingsinch." Andrew made the only possible decision.

Agnes nodded reluctant agreement, although I could see the tears in her eyes.

We began the return in dejected silence until we reached Chapelinch when the whistling started again.

"The creatures are back," Andrew said. "And what's that? Is it smoke beside the ruin?"

"They're burning the rowan tree," I said. I recognised the smell, and some instinct told me the reason. "The Sidh are scared of it, so they're destroying another of our weapons."

Dougie hefted his pike. "The Sidh are cleverer than I thought," he said.

We moved faster as we passed Chapelinch, pushing through the water in our haste to reach sanctuary.

Agnes was visibly flagging now. "What are they doing to us?" she said, as I took Baby Robert from her arms. "Why don't they leave us alone?"

"They're after the baby," Peter reminded.

"They won't get him," I promised, stupidly.

The steading loomed ahead, an island of grey-stone buildings amidst a sea of leaden water. The Lunans were at the end of the track, watching us, shouting questions that the rising wind whisked away. They looked as forlorn as we felt, a tiny group of beleaguered people in an island of despair.

"I feel sick," Agnes said.

Andrew nodded. "At least we are safe." He took the baby from me. "In a few moments, we'll be sitting beside the fire."

"I'm so cold I don't think I'll ever be warm again," Agnes said.

Smoke from the burning rowan drifted to us, strangely sweet, yet infinitely unpleasant.

"What's wrong?" Mrs Lunan held out her hands for Baby Robert. "Why are you back here?"

Dougie was first to wade out of the water. "The flood's washed away the path," he said. "We only got as far as the marker."

Mr Lunan sighed, helped me onto the island and nodded. "It was the right idea," he said, "and you gave it a good try." He deposited me safely and held out his hand to Agnes.

That is always how I will remember them, with Agnes emerging from the flood with her skirt clinging to her legs and water dripping from her arms. Andrew was a few feet behind, wading through knee-deep water with his hair slicked over his tired face.

They were both weary but smiling, glad to get back to dry land when the Sidh emerged from the water. It was ten feet behind Andrew with an arrow already fitted to its bow, and its eyes narrowed in concentration. A small reed protruded from its mouth.

"Andy!" I yelled, too late.

Andrew turned to look at me, rather than behind him, from where the danger came. I shouted again, just as the Sidh released its arrow. I immediately knew that the missile would hit its target.

The next few seconds seemed to pass in slow motion. I

watched the arrow spin as it arced upward, and then descended, increasing in speed as it neared Andy. At the last moment, Andrew became aware of his danger. He tried to side-step, but the water slowed his movements, and the arrow caught him, lodging in his side.

Agnes screamed, once, and put her hand to her mouth.

Mr Lunan lifted his shotgun from the ground at his feet, slammed it to his shoulder and shouted something incoherent as Agnes stepped towards her husband.

Andrew gasped, more in surprise than pain, and jerked upright, with the arrow a feathered obscenity protruding from his ribs.

I heard the sharp report of Mr Lunan's shotgun even as I sprang forward to catch Andrew, expecting him to fall. By the time I reached him, he had turned around, roaring in rage, and plucking at the arrow. I saw the blood staining Andrew's jacket, rust-coloured rather than red, with his eyes wild with frustration and anger.

"Andy!" Agnes shouted, as a second and then a third of the Sidh emerged from the flood. All held small reeds in their mouths and bows in their hands. Mr Lunan's shot landed in an intense spray around the first bowman, blasting him into a scarlet mush, but the other two Sidh released their arrows, both of which hit Andrew in the chest. He twisted, staggering back as Mr Lunan fired his second barrel, and more of the Sidh bowmen emerged from the water, firing at Andrew, who roared as the small arrows thumped home.

"You bastards!" Dougie shouted, charging into the water with Peter at his side, swinging their pikes.

And then the Sidh were gone, leaving one of their number behind, floating face down in an expanding swirl of his blood. The bothy-boys were waist-deep in water, lashing furiously and pointlessly at nothing.

"Andy," Agnes said for the fourth or fifth time.

Andrew lay on his side, bristling with arrows, with blood seeping from his mouth, but still alive. He groaned as Agnes knelt at one side and me at the other.

"Agnes." Andrew reached for her hand. "Take care of the baby. Don't let the Sidh get him." He looked at me, and his eyes widened in horror; blood spurted from his mouth, he twisted and died.

I knew he was dead; I could sense the life spirit hovering within him, waiting to leave.

I looked at the dead woman with some interest. I did not know how she had died, only that something had killed her. Her spirit remained, though. I could sense it next to me, confused as if it was unsure what to do next.

"You poor woman," I said, kneeling beside her body.

"Did you see what happened?" A gig stopped beside me, with the driver, a bearded, elderly man leaning over to speak to me.

"No," I said.

The driver's wife stepped down from the gig and knelt at my side. "She's dead."

"Yes," I said. "I think something must have hit her, a carriage or a cart."

A heavy vehicle had killed the woman. I saw wheel marks on the road, and a smear of blood, while her body had been crushed, with white bones protruding through her chest and both legs at an acute angle to her smashed pelvis.

"Where are you going? This is a lonely road." The driver's wife took a blanket from the gig to cover the broken body.

"I don't know," I said truthfully. "I am just walking."

"Where do you come from?" the driver's wife asked.

I shrugged. "Elgin," I said, "and Keith."

"That's a long walk." The driver's wife had less interest in

the dead woman and more in me. "Have you a home to go to? A mother? A father?"

I shook my head. The dead woman's spirit was still there, hovering, not sure what to do now her body was broken. I was interested to see what happened now.

The driver looked down from his perch. "The girl's shocked," he gave his opinion. "Come with us, quinie. We'll inform the police about the accident, and then we'll take you home."

I stepped on the gig. I was not shocked, and I had no home. I wondered about that unfortunate woman's spirit for some time, although I knew it would eventually find its way somewhere. When the police gave me a massive mug of hot tea and a cheese sandwich, I answered all their questions about the dead woman. Nobody asked me about the spirit, so I did not mention it.

"Where are you living?" a burly police sergeant asked me, with warmth hidden behind cynical eyes.

"Nowhere," I said. "I was living in a cellar with dogs."

"We can do better than that," he said. "My missus will look after you."

The sergeant's wife was a kindly, no-nonsense woman who insisted I should bath, ensured I was thoroughly clean, checked my hair for nits and lice and found me a whole outfit of clean clothes. "There now." She surveyed her handiwork with a critical eye. "Now you're fit to meet the queen. You're a queer-like creature, aren't you? Has the cat got your tongue?"

"No," I said. I had never heard the expression before.

"That's better," the sergeant's wife said. "I don't know how you got into this state; honestly, I don't. It must have been horrible to see a dead body, but it's all behind you now, eh?"

"Yes," I agreed. I rather liked this bustling, loud woman with the red cheeks and the sad eyes.

The sergeant's wife must have read my thoughts. "I'd have liked a daughter like you," she said.

*I understood the sad eyes. "I'd have liked a mother like you,"
I said, and expected the crushing hug the sergeant's wife gave
me. I knew she needed me.*

*"You poor wee soul." The sergeant's wife said and looked
across to her husband.*

"I don't know," he said.

"Only for a wee while," the sergeant's wife was pleading.

*I slept in a police cell that night, with a mattress under me
and two blankets on top. The sergeant looked in to ensure I was
all right, tucking the blanket under my chin and nodding.*

*In the morning, the sergeant took me back to where the body
had been. The spirit was gone, leaving a hole in the world. I
never found out who killed the woman or who she was.*

*I lived with the sergeant and his wife for some time after
that. The sergeant's wife wanted me to call her "Ma," so I did,
and it pleased her to fuss over me. I responded with all the affection I was capable of, which was not much, but she cried with
every little bit I could show her.*

*People need people, and people need to be wanted. Except
me. I did not need people, for my own company suited me best of
all. Or so my experience of life had taught me.*

*I was with Ma and the sergeant when the whistling began
again. My time with Ma and the sergeant was the happiest I
have ever been if what I knew was happiness. I woke in a
comfortable bed; I was never hungry; I had light duties around
the house and constant companionship with a woman who
enjoyed my company. In return, I called her Ma, learned all she
taught me and hugged her when she least expected it.*

*I think I made Ma happy. I hope so, for she was a good
person, one of the few I had ever met.*

*The whistling came at night-time when a scimitar moon
sliced the sky. I remembered it from my early childhood, and I
remembered the consequences when I mentioned it at the*

orphanage. This time I kept quiet, saying nothing as the whistling sounded outside the small room Ma had made for me.

Night after night, the whistling surrounded me, creeping into my room, entering my head, disturbing my peace.

"Go away!" I buried my head beneath the covers, crying until Ma came into the room, full of love and concern. She held me tight as I shivered, unable to tell her my fears, for I know she would have me locked away again. People fear what they do not understand and do not understand anything different from their normality.

"What is it, sweetie? What's the matter?"

I told her nothing, burrowing into her ample breasts as I fought my tears and tried to block that incessant sound from my head.

Other sounds came with the whistling. I heard the soft scuff of footsteps when there was nobody to see. I listened to the rustle of clothing in an empty room, and I heard quiet breathing in the lobby of Ma's house.

"I think it must be your birthday," Ma tried to cheer me up. "You'll be around fourteen now."

Fourteen. I had been seven when I first heard the whistling with such intensity and ended up in the lunatic cell. Had that been seven years ago? It seemed like yesterday, or tomorrow, for I was never sure how time worked.

"Yes, Ma," I said, as the whistling sounded all around. Somebody was calling me. Somebody was trying to reach me.

"What would you like for your birthday?" Ma was trying everything she could to help me. I wanted to tell her about the whistling; I wanted somebody to understand. Oh, God; how I wanted somebody who would understand. Yet I knew there was nobody who could hear these voices inside my head.

"You," I said. I could not say more. I could not explain that I needed Ma's understanding without telling her what was wrong. *"I want to make you happy, Ma."*

She held me even tighter after that, and I felt her tears hot on me.

I knew then that I must leave, for if I remained in that house, the Whistlers would come for me, and Ma and the sergeant would be in danger. I did not know how I knew, or what form the threat would take. I just knew it would happen.

I left a short note on my bed that night, telling Ma that I loved her, and moved on, crying. The whistling followed me into the dark, and twice I felt the movement of unseen bodies around me. I remembered the spirit of that woman killed on the road and knew the Whistlers were different from humanity.

CHAPTER 17

Agnes stared at her husband as Mr Lunan prised her away from the dead body. "Come on, lass, you can do nothing here."

Andrew's spirit lingered, trying to hold onto Agnes, trying to hell her that he was all right. He could not feel the arrows in his body. He did not know what had happened.

Dougie and Peter returned, shocked to see Andrew lying dead. Dougie put a single hand on Agnes's shoulder.

"Go away," Agnes said, her face white. "Leave me alone."

Peter said nothing; I think Andrew was his first sight of the finality of human death.

"Come on, Agnes," I said, "Let's get you inside."

Agnes looked at me. "This is your fault, Ellen," she said with her voice rising wildly. "You killed Andrew."

"Don't be silly, Agnes. How did Ellen do that?" Mrs Lunan helped prise Agnes from the body of her husband.

"The Sidh want her, not me or Andrew." Agnes looked at me with something like hatred. "This all started when she came here."

"Nonsense." Mr Lunan half-carried, half-dragged Agnes

away from Andrew, with Mr Lunan trying to shield her view of the body. "Come on; we'll take care of Andrew. You think of the baby."

Andrew's spirit still hovered, reaching out for his wife, unable to comprehend the change that had come over his body.

"Go away," I whispered. "This is no longer your place."

"Come along, Ellen!" Mr Lunan growled. "You can do no good out here."

We huddled around the fire, watching the steam rise from our clothes, too numbed by Andrew's death to say anything. The day that had begun with such promise ended in tragedy, and I knew that Agnes was at least partly right.

If I had not been in the farmtoun, the Sidh would not have been so keen to attack. Oh, yes, they might have wanted the unchristened baby, but they had been hunting me all my life, and I had wandered right into their heartland. When I released the captive Sidh, I had vastly increased the danger for all these people and may have led to Andrew's death.

I looked away as guilt swept over me.

"Get changed." Mrs Lunan took charge. "If you stay in these wet clothes, you'll all catch your deaths."

Nobody replied. Most of us stared into the fire, lost in thought, while Agnes was sobbing quietly and uncontrollably, rocking her baby on her lap.

"Men, change ben the room," Mrs Lunan ordered. "Women, stay in the kitchen."

I banked up the kitchen fire, basking in the heat after the bitter cold of the floodwater. I felt wretched, blaming myself for the death of Andrew.

"Come on, girls," Mrs Lunan said. "I'll change the baby. Don't add pneumonia to all our other woes."

Agnes glared at me as I peeled off my sodden clothing and

placed them on the pulley that I lowered from the ceiling. "You killed him," Agnes accused.

"The Sidh killed Andrew, Agnes," Mrs Lunan said. "The Sidh. It was no more Ellen's fault than it was yours, or mine."

Agnes's mouth twisted in a mixture of grief and hatred. "If Ellen wasn't here—" she did not complete her sentence, but I understood. By killing Andrew, the Sidh had terribly wounded Agnes, and now she wanted to hurt somebody in return. As she could not damage the Sidh, she turned her anger and hurt against somebody she could blame, instead. I understood because I shared some of her feelings, but I did not like others to accuse me. I did not like this burden of guilt.

"Cry," Mrs Lunan nearly ordered Agnes. "You need to mourn."

Agnes took a deep breath, saying no more as I towelled myself dry and pulled on my only other set of clothes. I could feel Agnes eyes on me, burning with bitter hatred.

"Now you, Agnes," Mrs Lunan said. "Change out of your wet things." When Agnes continued to glare at me, Mrs Lunan sighed. "I'll change you, then. Ellen! You can help."

We stripped, dried, and dressed Agnes as if she were a baby. After her recent outburst, she was surprisingly supine, alternating between staring into nothing and glowering at me.

"There, that's better," Mrs Lunan said, draping Agnes's wet clothes across the pulley before I hauled it back to the ceiling. "Now we'll talk about things while Ellen makes some tea."

I started at the knock on the kitchen door. "Are you decent in there?" Davie asked.

"Come in," Mrs Lunan invited and the men joined us.

"What do we do now?" Jim asked as we sat around the kitchen table, and I bustled with the kettle, spoons of sugar and an array of mugs.

"Put some whisky in those," Mrs Lunan ordered. "We need

it." She produced a bottle from the walk-in pantry next to the back door, poured a generous portion into a mug and handed it to Agnes. "Here, Agnes. Drink that."

"I was thinking that we could build a boat," Dougie said. "Or a raft, anyway, and float out of here."

"Like Noah in the Flood," Peter said. "We can use planks of wood as oars and push us out." He glanced at Dougie. "It would be quicker than just floating."

Mr Lunan hugged Agnes, holding her tightly for a long minute. "You lads can do that," he said. "Take the women and the bairn with you, but I'm not running."

Mrs Lunan drew in her breath and looked sharply at her husband.

"I'll stay and fight for my farm," Mr Lunan said.

The rest of us remained silent. I was thinking about the Sidh walking on water and rising from the flood.

"Davie," Mrs Lunan began and stopped.

"There are hundreds of them," Peter said. "We all saw them coming out of the water. They can breathe underwater, for God's sake! How can we fight things that breathe underwater?"

I took a sip of my whisky-laced sweet tea and grimaced, although I welcomed the warmth, for I was still shivering. "The Sidh don't breathe underwater," I said. "They had little reed tubes in their mouths; they thrust the end of the tube above water to get air."

"How the hell do you know that?" Dougie asked.

"I watched them," I snapped back. "When you were splashing about in the water, I was watching what was happening!"

"Peter only means they can come any time." Mrs Lunan calmed the tension. "We won't be able to see them in the peaty water."

"I never meant that," Peter said. "I meant they are demons, monsters, and there are too many for us to fight." The boy had become a man and exchanged his false swagger for sense. I reached over and squeezed his hand.

"I'm staying," Mr Lunan said, with no expression in his voice. "These creatures took my first wife and our child; they're not taking my farm as well." He had been sitting with his head bowed, staring into his mug. Now he looked up, fixing us all with an expression that I will never forget. He was daring us to challenge him, with madness in his eyes, and a determination such as I had never seen before.

"They'll kill you," Jim said, "like they killed Andy."

"They might well do," Mr Lunan said, "but they won't see me run."

We were silent at these words, as the fire crackled in the grate, with the occasional hiss as raindrops hissed down the lum to die in the flames.

"Young Peter's right," Mrs Lunan said. "There are too many of the Sidh for us to fight, and, however strong and brave you are, Davie, they will kill you if you stay."

"I'm not running away," Mr Lunan said.

"Then I'll stay with you," Mrs Lunan said, "and you'll be killing me too. Another victory for the Sidh."

I had never heard such an ultimatum before and sipped at my whisky-tea while Mr Lunan continued to stare into his mug. "They stole my wife and bairn and killed my second horseman and all my beasts. I won't run. I'll fight them, and before they kill me, I'll destroy as many of the filthy vermin as I can."

"We'll come back to that," Mrs Lunan said. "I think your idea of an ark is a good idea, Dougie. We'll call it Dougie's Ark as it transports you to safety across the flood." There was dark humour in her smile.

"We'll need wood," Dougie said. "Sufficient to build a platform to hold seven adults and a child."

"Seven?" Mr Lunan said. "Six. I won't be coming."

"Six, then," Dougie said, nodding when Mrs Lunan mouthed "seven" to him. "And shallow draught to go over the dyke-heads."

Even Mr Lunan joined in the discussion as the men worked out how to build the raft; how thick the wood should be, the dimensions, shape and how to navigate it over the tops of the dykes.

"The Sidh will try to stop us," Dougie said. "They'll use their archers, so we need a wall around the raft as protection."

That suggestion provoked more debate, and then Peter added. "We need weapons to fight back as well." He glanced at Mr Lunan. "We won't have the shotgun, so we need something else."

"We have this." Dougie lifted the bow he had captured.

"Let me see that," Mr Lunan held out his hand. He examined the bow for a few moments. "Do you know what this is?"

"A very small bow?" Peter hazarded.

"What's it made from?" Mr Lunan handed it back to Dougie.

"I never looked," Dougie studied the bow again.

"It's a rib-bone," Mr Lunan said quietly. "A human rib-bone."

I think we were in shock for a few moments as we digested the information.

"My God," Mrs Lunan said with one arm around Agnes. "What sort of creatures are these Sidh?"

"That might be Willie Anderson's rib," Mr Lunan said. "You'll remember somebody dug up his corpse and removed the ribs. Now we know why."

Mrs Lunan removed the bow from her table and placed it

on the floor. "I knew Willie," she said, "but I don't want bits of him on the kitchen table; thank you very much."

"We'll make our own bows," Dougie said. "Let's get started with the raft. It's simple enough to make, so we should have it ready in a day or so." He glanced at Agnes. "I wish Andy was here to help."

Agnes stared at me. "He would be if she hadn't come here. I hate you," she said, with venom in her voice. "I hope the Sidh kill you."

I did not reply, for I could understand her feelings. I hated me as much as Agnes did.

~

Men without a purpose tend to mope and complain, while men with a job can work every hour God sends, toiling cheerfully whatever the conditions. The men at Kingsinch were like that, working with a will to dispel their anger at Andrew's death.

"Thirteen," Jim said in a hushed tone. "There were thirteen arrows in Andrew. We took them out."

"I want him buried properly," Agnes said. "In a graveyard in Meigle."

"We'll do that," Mrs Lunan said. "But we can't leave him in the farmhouse, so we'll place him underground here first."

Agnes agreed that was best, and the men dug a shallow grave, lowered Andrew inside and filled it up, with Mr Lunan reading some passages from the Bible as the men placed the largest boulders they could find over the grave.

"We don't want the Sidh digging him back up," Dougie explained with sweat mingling with the rainwater that dripped from him.

Agnes only nodded through her tears as Mrs Lunan hugged

her. "Come on! We can't stand here all day when there's work to be done!"

With Andrew decently interred, the men began work on the raft. They stripped planks of wood from the barns to form the base, sawed them to shape and hammered them together with relentless energy. Mr Lunan recruited me to help, so I fetched and carried nails, held lengths of wood, and gave unwanted advice, to which they listened with quiet patience before ignoring my words and continuing as they were before.

The raft gradually took shape on the edge of the path beside the slowly expanding loch. All the time the men worked, we looked for the Sidh, watching the water for an emerging archer, and scanning the hills for signs of movement.

"Maybe they've gone," Jim said hopefully. "Maybe they'll leave us in peace now."

"They won't go," Mr Lunan said. "They've been here forever, and they'll be here long after Man has left."

As the light faded, the men worked by lantern-light, adding a small wooden fence around the edge of the raft as protection from the archers.

"Lowsing time," Mrs Lunan said sometime around midnight. I thought she was watching Dougie as he bent to bang in the nails. "You can finish it tomorrow. You'll all need your sleep."

I did not argue. It had been a trying day, and a mixture of guilt and horror filled my mind that no amount of physical exhaustion could clear.

"I want somebody on watch all night," Mr Lunan said. "Two hours stints. That includes you, Ellen. Not Agnes; she's had enough today."

Nobody argued. As tired as we were, it was no hardship to remain awake and watch for the Sidh through the gaps in the boarding. We kept the fires alive all night, and peered into the dark, with the swaying lanterns making shadows where there were no Sidh and pooling flickering light around the farmhouse.

As I stared outside, I remembered my vision of Peter lying on a stone slab and shivered. I did not know from where the image it came and hoped it had been a waking nightmare rather than a portent of the future. Despite the exertion and horror of the day, I slept on a kitchen chair, waking stiff and sore next morning to bank up the fire immediately. Outside, the rain continued to patter on the windows.

We started work before dawn, with the men scraping out the last of their brose before they returned to the raft, and Mrs Lunan allowing me to give them extra oatcakes.

"After all," she said, "the Sidh will have all our foodstuffs soon. We don't want to give them a present of oatcakes as well." She glanced at Dougie in his worn and faded corduroy trousers. "Add a skelp of cheese as well, Ellen. Keep the men's strength up."

"Peter," Mr Lunan said. "I don't want you working on the raft today. I want you to make weapons; bows, slingshots and anything else you think of."

Peter nodded with his new maturity shading the innocence in his eyes. "Yes, Mr Lunan."

The final stages took longer than the bothy-boys had imagined, although three times we stopped to investigate supposed sightings of the Sidh. Each occasion proved a false alarm yet slowed us down and stretched our already jumpy nerves.

It was nearly midnight on the second day when the raft was complete. Dougie stood back, wiped the sweat and grime from his forehead. "That's us, lads," he said with satisfaction. "The good ship *Dougie's Ark* is ready to launch."

"We should go now," Agnes said, although she looked sideways at Andrew's grave. "Let's just pile in and get away. It won't be too long to get out of the flood, surely?"

Jim looked upwards, where the rain still descended. "That depends how big it is," he said. "What if this is another great flood, like in the Bible?"

"You mean, the whole world could be underwater?" Dougie said.

"Yes." Jim gestured to the surrounding hills, unseen in the dark. "We've seen no sign of life up there, not old Charlie Fleming or even a wandering shepherd. Maybe they're all drowned, and we're the last survivors."

"Like Noah," Peter said quietly.

"We might float forever, or until we run out of food," I said.

"We'll bring some food with us," Mrs Lunan decided, and touched Agnes on the shoulder. "And dinnae worry; we'll come back for Andrew the first chance we get."

"Watches again, the night." Mr Lunan was surprisingly calm for a man who intended to remain behind in a deserted, besieged farm. "You're first Ellen, with Jim."

"I can go with Ellen," Peter volunteered.

"You and Elizabeth are next," Mr Lunan said, "and Dougie and I'll take the last one."

I nodded, not caring, with the guilt still gnawing at me.

Our watch passed without incident, and I was deep in slumber when I heard the shout. "Fire!"

The word did not penetrate the fog of sleep, so I lay for a few moments, wondering what the fuss was, for the kitchen fire was smouldering and red, sufficient to keep the Sidh from descending the lum.

"Fire!" That was Peter's voice, frantic with panic.

"What's happening, Jim?" Mr Lunan asked.

I closed my eyes again, allowing Mr Lunan to take charge. If anybody needed me, they would wake me.

"Jesus save us! Oh, God, help us!"

Mrs Lunan was not prone to such statements, so the sound of her voice fully woke me. I struggled to sit up, only now aware of the acrid smell of smoke in my nostrils.

"Everyone! Get up!" Mrs Lunan's sharp voice sounded through the house. She shook me roughly. "The barn's alight!"

Throwing my coat over my nightclothes and dragging on my boots, I stumbled to the door. Dougie and Jim were already there. They drew the bolts and dived outside, swearing, only for both to jump back a second later.

"Watch out!" Dougie said as an arrow thrummed past him to thud into the door frame.

Jim ducked, swearing obscenely as another arrow followed the first. "Shut the door!" he yelled. "For God's sake shut the door!"

As they slammed the door, I heard the hollow thud of more arrows hitting the exterior.

"It's an ambush," Peter, our resident expert on all things military said. "They've fired the barn to draw us out so they can shoot us."

"How the hell do you know that?" Jim asked, panting for breath.

"My brother's in the Gordon Highlanders," Peter explained. "He was on the North-West Frontier a couple of years ago and told me how the Paythans fight."

"Well, I wish your brother was here now," Jim said. "He could fight the Sidh for us."

There was a crash, and the window planking shuddered.

"They've fired at the window," Peter explained.

"We're not bloody stupid!" Dougie said. "We ken that!"

"Try the front door," Mr Lunan said, loading his shotgun.

The boys moved to the front of the house, grabbing their weapons.

"What's happening?" Agnes appeared from her bedroom, tousle-headed and with her bare feet making her look very vulnerable.

"You go back to your room," Mrs Lunan said. "I'll stay with you."

The men pushed through to the front door.

"I'll go first," Mr Lunan said, holding an old tweed coat in front of him as protection. He had no sooner opened the door than an arrow thudded into the coat, without penetrating the folds of thick tweed.

I had a glimpse of flames ripping through the barn opposite, with great billows of smoke covering the farmyard. Mr Lunan slammed the door.

"We appear to be trapped," Mr Lunan said.

"Lend me the shotgun, Mr Lunan," Peter said, "And I'll shoot my way out."

"Don't be bloody stupid!" Mr Lunan said. "They'll pick you off in seconds."

"The raft!" Jim had run to an upstairs window for a better view. "The Sidh are burning the raft!"

I could feel the despair in the farmhouse at Jim's words. We had set our hopes on that raft, and the boys had sweated hours in its construction.

"We'll save it," I said. "The Sidh arrows can't penetrate thick clothes, so wear all we can. Throw all your coats and hats and scarves on."

For once, the boys listened to me and dressed as for the Arctic. They stood behind the kitchen door, carrying their weapons and something to douse the flames as they nerved themselves to brave the Sidh archers.

"On the count of three," Mr Lunan said, "I'll open the door, and we'll dash to the raft. Don't stop for anything."

We nodded. I felt sick, yet strangely calm. My death would be retribution for the wrong I had done in freeing the Sidh.

"One, two, three!" Mr Lunan yanked the door open and charged out, with everybody except Agnes and Mrs Lunan following.

Only a single Sidh stood in our way, and Mr Lunan fired his shotgun as soon as he saw the creature. After that, we charged past the madly burning barn to the raft, from which flames leapt for the sky.

"Come on, boys!" Dougie yelled, "rescue the raft!" I had brought a bucket, others had pans and pots, with which they scooped up water from the flood and threw it onto the flames.

The heat drove me back as I tried to rescue the raft. The flames had taken hold, roaring as they consumed the timber despite all we could do.

At last, smoke-smeared, red-eyed, and exhausted, we watched the flames destroy our hope.

"That's that, then," Jim said.

"We can build another," Dougie said.

"What with?" Mr Lunan gestured to the barns, which burned as fiercely as the raft. The smell of burning flesh made me retch as the flames consumed the bodies of our livestock. "All we have is the doors or floorboards in the farmhouse."

"We could use them, then," Dougie sounded desperate.

I said nothing as the flames began to wane, and the timbers of the barn collapsed in a shower of sparks. The smoke and stench were thicker than ever as we made our slow way back to the farmhouse.

Mr Lunan heard the scream first. "That's Lizzie!" he said. "The Sidh must be inside the house!"

CHAPTER 18

WE RAN from the burning raft to the farmhouse, with Mr Lunan as near to panic as I had ever seen him. Despite being at least twenty years older than the rest of us, Mr Lunan was first inside the farmhouse, nearly breaking the door as he barged in, yelling his wife's name.

"Lizzie!"

We followed, with the bothy-boys well in front, gasping as they sought to reach the farmhouse. I was last, sliding on the rain-slicked cobbles with the ululation of the Whistlers soft in my ears.

I did not know what to expect as I ran in the door and pounded upstairs, but what I saw was worse than I had imagined. At least a dozen of the Sidh crammed the bedroom. Most were facing the men, their faces contorted in snarls as they slashed with bronze knives. Others surrounded the bed that Agnes shared with Baby Robert, reaching down with long-fingered hands as Agnes screamed and struggled to defend her child.

One of the Sidh stood in the corner of the room. It was slightly taller than the others, with brown hair on its delicate, handsome face. When I entered, it looked directly at me and smiled, as if to a well-known friend.

The Sidh's gaze fixed on my eyes, so I was unable to move or even to think clearly as I stood in the doorway, enchanted in the worst possible way. I saw its mouth purse slightly, and it whistled, with the undulating sound penetrating the bedlam in that room to reach inside my head. I knew without thought that the Sidh was summoning me; it was trying to draw me to it, for some terrible purpose that I did not understand.

I resisted, trying to step back out of that room as the Sidh continued to whistle. Although I had heard that clear, musical sound all my life, I had never grown used to it. I shook my head, mouthing "no, no," yet without breaking the Sidh's hypnotic stare.

I saw two more of the creatures grab Peter by the arms and haul him to the wide-open window, with the internal planking wrenched from the frames. I saw Dougie throw one of the Sidh to the floor and crash his iron-studded boots on its face, again and again. I saw Mrs Lunan on the rug with blood seeping from her head.

And I saw the Sidh in the corner watching me. It lifted a hand and crooked its finger, beckoning me towards it. The Sidh had the face of a man in early middle-age, marred by what might have been a birthmark. Its' eyes were old and knowing, wise beyond compare, kindly yet commanding.

"Come," the word formed inside my head, softly appealing.

I took a step forward, and then another, with the fighting men seeming to clear away before me. The Sidh beckoned again, nodding its head, yet still with those clear hazel eyes focussed on mine. I could feel its power inside my head and sensed it probing at me, seeking something. It stood beside the younger, whistling man, doubling their influence, yet although I was scared, I also felt a peculiar sense of belonging.

"No," I said. "I won't come!"

I tried to pull away, but the whistling was inside me, reverberating from the bones of my skull, vanquishing all rational thought. I had never felt the whistling so powerful before; it was more than a sound; it was nearly a physical entity.

"No!" I attempted to pull away, feeling my muscles tremble as those kindly hazel eyes summoned me.

"It's all right, Ellen; you have nothing to fear." The words formed inside my head, honey-sweet, laced with sugar, soothing away the anxieties that had plagued me all my life.

I heard Mr Lunan shouting his wife's name, but I could not look in his direction. I was only aware of the hazel eyes, growing ever larger as they drew me closer.

"Ellen; you know me. You have always known us," the words were softly insidious. "We are your friends. You can trust us."

I tried to close my eyes against the hazel that now surrounded me. The Sidh's words, "friends" and "trust" penetrated deep into my psyche. The Sidh had found my soul. Much of me, perhaps most of me, yearned for friends I could trust. I took a step forward, and another, until I was nearly within touching distance of the Sidh.

"Ellen!" The scream cut through the soft whistling, jerking me out of my trance.

I saw the Sidh all around Peter, whistling to one another as they hauled him onto the window ledge, so he was half in and half out of the room. The pointed ears were in evidence and the gash-mouths with rows of sharp teeth.

Peter struggled desperately, kicked with his heavy boots,

and shouted in defiance. I saw him punch one of the Sidh full in the face, and scrape the tackets of his boot down another Sidh's leg.

Once again, I experienced that vision of Peter lying on a stone slab within a rocky chamber, except this time, the picture was more explicit. Although I had only a partial view of Peter, I could see he was bare-chested, and the Sidh were all around him. The men now summoning me stood at Peter's side as I watched from a few yards away.

What am I doing there? I asked myself. The birthmarked Sidh smiled to me across Peter's prone body.

"My baby!" Agnes' agonised cry shattered the image and sliced through all other sounds as one of the Sidh lifted Baby Robert high above its head.

In that second everything seemed to speed up, with the bothy-boys throwing the Sidh aside in their attempt to save the baby. Dougie stretched out his massive hand and gripped the baby-stealing Sidh by the throat, as Mr Lunan shoved a Sidh aside and knelt beside his wife. Peter felled one of the Sidh with a single punch, then concentrated on the creature on his left arm, snarling in a mixture of fury and fear. The falling Sidh passed between the birth-marked man and me, momentarily freeing me from the Sidh's enchantment.

Now I only felt fear as I stood, near petrified and watched the creatures that had been whistling to me all my life. They were savage things with their pointed teeth, yet the bothy-boys were taller and stronger when they came to blows.

Jim jumped to help Dougie, barging into the birth-marked Sidh and utterly breaking the spell. I looked away quickly, gasping for breath. The Sidh were now in full retreat, scrambling to escape through the window with our men in hot pursuit.

As Dougie grappled with the Sidh, Agnes grabbed her baby back and held him tight. Peter landed an old-fashioned kick on the groin of the nearest Sidh and then the affair was over, with Mr Lunan helping his wife to her feet, the men gasping with exertion and not a single Sidh remaining in the room.

"How did they get in?" Mr Lunan asked.

"You let them in." Mrs Lunan had a long gash on her cheek but seemed otherwise unhurt. "When you ran out to fight the fire, you left the back door open."

"It was a double trap then," Mr Lunan said. "They lured us outside with the fire, pretended it was for the archers' ambush, but in reality, it was to keep us occupied while they grabbed the baby."

"Aye, and if you had locked the door, they would never have got in," Mrs Lunan said.

"This is not the time for apportioning blame," Mr Lunan said. "This is the time for being thankful we're still alive."

"We've lost the boat," Jim said. "We're stuck here." He shook his head. "We might never get away, and poor Brenda is out there alone."

"Never mind about poor Brenda," Mrs Lunan said. "You help Dougie to repair that window. I want it blocked, barricaded and secure."

"We've no wood," Peter said.

"Find some!" Mrs Lunan snarled, sitting on the bed with her hand to her bleeding face.

"Ellen! Bring warm water and a cloth! Peter- tear up some floorboards!" Mr Lunan ordered. "Take off the pantry door, anything; use your bloody imagination!"

"Yes, Mr Lunan," Peter said.

While the kitchen floor was stone-flagged, timber planks covered the pantry floor. I reached the kitchen ahead of Peter, for we had the kettle permanently on the range.

"I need to lift the floorboards," Peter said, slightly at a loss until Dougie produced a hammer and chisel from somewhere. The floorboards sat on heavy wooden joists, with space beneath from which chill air blasted out. I left the boys to their work as I carried a basin of warm water to Mrs Lunan.

The bothy-boys worked with a will, sawing the floorboards to fit the window, and nailing them in place. Mrs Lunan supervised, reinforcing her orders with a sharp tongue and an ever-ready hand.

When I saw that Mr Lunan was a clumsy nurse, I replaced him, easing the blood-flow from Mrs Lunan's gashed face, and wrapping a torn sheet around her head.

"I don't need that!" Mrs Lunan said.

"It will stop the blood," I told her, ignoring her protests.

"That should keep out an army." Dougie stepped back to examine his work on the window.

We double-locked both doors, drew the bolts and checked each window before I made food for us all. Then we assembled in the kitchen, the heart of the house, and waited, although the loss of the raft had sent us into a slough of depression.

"What now?" Mrs Lunan asked. "What do we do now?"

"We wait for the rain to stop." Mr Lunan shook his head. "It's all we can do."

I had made strong tea for everybody, which Mr Lunan laced with a stiff dram of whisky. It tasted vile, although the lads didn't mind.

"It might be days, weeks, before the rain stops," Dougie said.

"We have a secure house and sufficient food for weeks," Mrs Lunan said. "You and Ellen bought the flour, remember? And we have oatmeal, cheese, and potatoes, and still a few eggs from the hens. We'll sit it out."

Mrs Lunan's decision may have been correct, but it

depressed us. Mr Lunan shook his head and pointed out the danger we were in, Mrs Lunan raised her voice to her man and Dougie joined in. Within a minute, everybody at the table was giving their point of view in a heated debate. We were so intent in arguing that we did not notice the figure who emerged from the pantry.

I saw the shape from the corner of my eye.

"Watch out!" I yelled, just as the Sidh drew back his bow and fired a single arrow.

I do not know who the intended target was, but the arrow whizzed through the air and landed in Mrs Lunan's open mouth. It penetrated her throat and thrust out, bloody and obscene, from the back of her neck.

"Liz!" Mr Lunan lunged forward with his face twisted in horror. He took hold of his wife as she fell backwards, making horrible choking noises as blood spurted from her mouth.

"Get that thing!" Dougie threw his mug of tea at the Sidh, who was fitting another arrow to his bow. The flying mug was not sufficient to distract the archer, who fired again before Dougie and Peter reached him. The arrow slammed into Mrs Lunan's left cheek, pierced her face, and burst through the other side in a fountain of bright blood.

Jim was a few seconds later than Peter, but the creature vanished.

"Where is it?" Dougie asked. "Where did it go?"

Torn between helping Mrs Lunan and catching the Sidh, I guessed the answer. "Under the ground," I said. "It's under the ground! You lifted the floorboards, remember?"

Leaving the bothy-boys to their hunt, I tried to help Mrs Lunan. She sat with her head back and the two arrows protruding, dripping blood. Mrs Lunan's eyes were wide with shock and pain.

"Liz! We'll get them out," Mr Lunan said.

The arrows were frail, with shafts of reeds attached to the flint head. Mr Lunan snapped the reeds between his finger and thumb and gently drew the shafts through Mrs Lunan's face. The blood spurted out in great scarlet fountains as Mrs Lunan made horrible gurgling noises, putting her hands to her face.

Grabbing a towel, I pressed it against the back of Mrs Lunan's neck, from where the worst of the blood was coming.

"She's choking!" Mr Lunan looked at me in panic. He was right. Despite all we tried, Mrs Lunan choked on her blood at her own table. She took ten minutes to die, and her blood was deep on the stone slabbed floor. I tried my best and failed.

Mr Lunan stared at me as the realisation dawned. "She's dead," he said.

I nodded wordlessly. I did not know what to say.

Mr Lunan let out an inarticulate, strangled roar, grabbed the poker and ran into the pantry, leaving me with the corpse of his wife. I could still feel her spirit in the kitchen, watching me in disapproval.

"Oh, dear God," I said, shaking my head. "Am I responsible for her death, too?"

I have never been afraid of death; if people hurt me in life, then I was not sorry that they were dead, and if they did not hurt me in life, why should they hurt me in death? The dead cannot bite.

"You are dead now, Mrs Lunan," I said to her cooling corpse. "You were a hard woman, but not a bad one, so I hope you have gone to the good place."

I heard the boys moving about in the space beneath the pantry.

"There is nothing more you can do here, Mrs Lunan," I said to her spirit. "This phase of your existence is finished. You'd best be on your way now."

For an instant, so brief time had no word for it, I saw Mrs

Lunan's spirit hover beside me, a grey-white ephemeral mass, and then it vanished.

"God speed," I whispered and began to mop up the blood on the floor, squeezing the cloth over the sink and mopping again as Mrs Lunan's body watched. I could hear her carping voice ordering me to do a good job, or by Jingo, I'd know all about it. After twenty minutes or so, the boys returned, with Mr Lunan in front, his eyes staring.

"Did you get the Sidh?" I asked without ceasing my work.

"No," Dougie whispered. "I only caught a glimpse of it. The Sidh had dug a tunnel to the pantry." He stared at Mrs Lunan.

"Aye," I read his thoughts. "Mrs Lunan's gone."

"Dear God." Mr Lunan sat beside his wife's body. "My Lizzie."

"We'll get revenge," Peter showed his immaturity. I nudged him with my elbow and glared him into silence before I saw the moisture in his eyes.

"Check the other rooms, Peter," I said, roughly, to disguise his tears.

When Mr Lunan began to cry, I shooed the other men out of the kitchen and made him a mug of tea, adding spoonfuls of sugar. "Here," I said. "Drink this." Only then did I realise that he and I were both coated with Mrs Lunan's blood. I washed in warm water from the kettle and suggested he do the same. Mr Lunan obeyed automatically, with his eyes vacant.

I remained with Mr Lunan for the remainder of that night, unable to do anything except offer silent sympathy. In such circumstances, there is nothing one can do to help. Grief must take its unique course and affects everybody in a different way. An hour or so after dawn, Mr Lunan took control of himself.

"Aye," he said. "Lizzie was a braw enough wife, and the farm will miss her. That's another score to settle with the Sidh."

I nodded and patted Mr Lunan's arm. I knew he had locked his emotions inside him, ready for a more suitable time.

"There's no point in wasting time," Mr Lunan called the boys to the kitchen. "We can't leave Liz in the kitchen, and we can exhume her for a proper burial once the flood recedes. Get the spades, lads; we've work to do." Mr Lunan thrust out his chin, with his walrus moustache bristling in the frosty air.

We dug a grave near to Andrew's and lowered Mrs Lunan in that same morning. Agnes did not attend; she was still shaking after the near abduction of her baby.

Mr Lunan said a few words over his wife, the boys piled heavy rocks on the grave, and that was the end of the ceremony. By a hundred words and an awkward silence, they shall remember, you, I thought and stilled my giggle. I recognised the onset of hysteria.

"Well, goodbye, Mrs Lunan," Dougie said awkwardly, and I wondered how deep his affection had been. Had he genuinely liked the woman? Or had he only slaked his animal lust on her? I shrugged; it did not matter now.

Jim looked ready to cry but controlled himself like the man he wanted to be, while Peter was still too young. He dashed away a tear, apologised and retreated hurriedly, in case others should mock his emotions. Men don't, though. Real men understand tears; only the immature and the foolish scoff.

I remained the longest to say good-bye. It felt natural, for I had not disliked the woman although she had always resented me. I did not know why.

I could no longer feel her presence in the steading. Her spirit was free of its confining shell.

Mr Lunan loaded his shotgun. "Today, Dougie and Jim, I want you to check under the house for any more cavities. Fill them in and ensure the creatures can't enter the house." He saw me standing nearby. "Ellen!" he roared. "What are you doing? You've got work to do!"

"Coming, Mr Lunan," I replied, and, for the last time, I felt a twinge of Mrs Lunan as she approved of me returning to work.

CHAPTER 19

"Work!" *Mr Gallacher said. "It's what we all do. We work, or we starve, and those who don't work, don't eat."*

I stood on the quayside with the other gutters, waiting for the boats to come in. It was my first day, and all the others were fishwives, some with years of experience at the job.

Aberdeen quay is open to all the elements that God sends, and some that slipped through when he was not looking. Whichever way the wind blew, it cut through my clothing like a gutting knife.

We saw the boats on the horizon, a cloud of red-brown sails, for the Aberdeen trawlers sought white fish and the sailing vessels hunted the herring, the silver darlings of song and merchants' profit. Mr Gallacher ordered us to get ready, and within half an hour, the boats were scudding into Aberdeen. There were Zulus, Scaffies and Fifies, with their crews of hardy men unloading the fish even before the fishermen secured the cables to the quayside, and the fish merchants could calculate their profit by the number of crans each boat landed.

The women were there to gut, salt and pack, with the fish-

wives working at an astonishing speed. I was slow and clumsy in comparison, wielding my knife with much less dexterity. Like the others, I had strips of linen around my fingers to protect them from the sharp blade, but still, I had half a dozen nicks before the first hour was done.

We gutted and packed into barrels, with the herring tight together and a layer of salt on top. Mr Gallacher supervised, ignoring the older women who knew the job better than he did and concentrating on the youngsters, such as me.

"Pack these fish more tightly!" Mr Gallacher roared at a girl who could not have been more than fourteen.

The quinie tried, nearly panicking until an older woman showed her the technique.

We worked on from dawn to dusk and well into the night, with great oil-lanterns giving us light and bawdy humour helping to stem the weariness.

Only when the last fish was gutted and packed did the work halt. We retired to our quarters, a bothy much like farm-labourers used, with basic facilities, yet a camaraderie unique to a team who works together. They were swank, well-made women, each with a to-name, for the fisher-families were close-knit, with a limited number of surnames.

"So, you're Ellen, are you?" The speaker was a large woman with rough hands and a stern voice. I knew her as Bessie Spinks from Arbroath; the others called her Drudger's Bess.

"I said, are you called Ellen?" Bessie said and tapped my head with a rolled-up newspaper.

"Yes," I said.

"What brought you to the herring trade?"

I shrugged. "It's work," I said.

"It's damned hard work unless you're born and bred to it."

Two other women joined Bessie as she questioned me, empha-

sising her words with sharp jabs with her newspaper. "What did you have to do to get the job?"

"I don't understand," I said.

"Aye, you do," Bessie said. "What favour did you grant Sandy Gallacher?"

The other women laughed, not pleasantly.

I stiffened as I realised what Bessie meant. "Nothing," I said shortly.

"You don't belong here," Bessie said bluntly, prod-prod-prodding with the newspaper. "You're neither born to the fishing nor married into it."

I agreed. I did not belong there, yet I was loath to leave without a parting shot. "No," I said, "and it seems that the only other way is by sleeping with the boss." I looked Bessie up and down, slowly. "Well, it's as well you're a fishwife then, for no man in his right mind would want you."

I slipped Bessie's furious punch, pushed her as I passed, lifted her newspaper, whacked it hard across her ample backside, shoved a gutting knife up my sleeve and left the hut at a run. That was the shortest-lasting job I ever had. As I huddled in the cold streets of Aberdeen, I decided that the nautical life was not for me, lifted my bag onto my shoulder, and headed for the south country.

"Did you hear her?" Jim stepped over me as I awakened from sleep and headed for the back door. "That was Brenda." He looked ludicrous with heavy boots pulled over his white underwear and a long coat flapping around his ankles.

I sat up, automatically checking that the fire was still alive. "This is a queer time for Brenda to call! Are you sure? I didn't hear anything."

"It was Brenda." Jim still favoured his injured leg. "She's come to see me." Jim's smile could not have been broader. His eyes danced with the joy of meeting his girl again. For a minute, I envied him the complex pleasure of love, and then the implications hit me.

"Wait, Jim." I rose, ensured that I was decently covered, and put a hand on Jim's arm. "Wait. Are you sure that it's Brenda?"

"Yes, I'm sure." Jim drew back the bolts on the back door and fumbled for the key on its hook. "I know her voice; she's my lass."

I fought off the shackles of sleep to try and reason. "How did she get here? If we can't get out, how did Brenda get in?" I tried to prevent Jim from unlocking the door.

"I don't know. Maybe Brenda has a boat." Jim turned the key in the lock. The click seemed to echo like church bells on a November Sunday evening. "Maybe she found out that we're trapped, and she's come to rescue us." Jim looked at me over his shoulder. "I'll ask her." When he pulled the door open, a blast of rain-laced cold air surged inside. Jim stepped outside, "Brenda! Where are you?"

I hurried after Jim, closing the door behind me, and only now aware of the undulating whistle reverberating inside my head. The woman stood fifty yards from the farmhouse on the very edge of our slowly diminishing island. She seemed to glow, as if from some inner force, or perhaps with light from the earth below.

I am no judge of what men consider attractive in a woman, but Brenda was undoubtedly striking. She was about three inches taller than me, with red-gold hair that flowed over her shoulders and a smile that could charm the birds from the trees.

"Is that Brenda, Jim?" I asked.

Brenda was shapely, too, with swelling hips and breasts that would hold a man's attention, as she undoubtedly had with Jim.

"Yes, that's my lass!"

"No, it's not," I said. "How could Brenda get here, Jim?" I took hold of Jim's sleeve in an attempt to hold him back. I may as well have tried to halt the progress of the moon as influence a love-struck young man.

Jim stepped towards her with both hands outstretched, a young horseman with a future of incessant labouring limping towards the woman of his dreams. The whistling was louder now, although I could see nobody except Jim and Brenda, as though their love created a bubble that excluded the outside world.

"Jim!" I stepped forward, wincing as the whistling became so intense it was painful.

"What's happening? Why is the door unlocked?" Mr Lunan joined us outside, bleary-eyed with lack of sleep. "What's that young fool doing? Jim! Get back inside the house!"

The whistling was needle-sharp, stabbing at my brain, so I cringed, closing my eyes. "Stop!" I said. "Go away!"

"Jim! You bloody idiot!" Mr Lunan strode forward. "Get back here, for God's sake!"

At Mr Lunan's words, the bubble burst; the scales fell from my eyes, and I saw Brenda for what she was, not for what she wished us to see. Her height dropped, her hair colour darkened, and her body shape altered, so she was stocky rather than statuesque. Even her face changed shape, sharpening, and the slightly pointed ears became the best indication that the woman was a Sidh. For an instant, I thought of the wooden figure at the horseman's initiation, with its almond-shaped eyes and slightly pointed ears: a Sidh of the Sidh.

"Jim!" I shouted. "That's not Brenda!"

Mr Lunan was more direct. Leaving the door gaping open, he ran, long-striding, to where the Sidh stood. Without wasting time on words, Mr Lunan grabbed Jim by the shoulder, threw him aside and pushed the Sidh onto her back.

The whistling continued, louder and louder, as though more than one of the Sidh was probing my mind. I could sense their presence within my head; I could see them, standing in the shadows of my subconscious, watching me as they had done all my life. The woman I had rescued stood in front, with a smile on her face and one finger beckoning me forward.

"Get away," I screamed, holding both hands to my head. "Leave me alone!"

Jim staggered and recovered. "What was that for?" Ignoring Mr Lunan, he stepped forward to help the Sidh woman to her feet.

"Come away from her, Jim, you fool! That's one of the Sidh!"

"This is Brenda!" Jim said, holding onto the Sidh's hand.

"Then Brenda is a Sidh." Mr Lunan pulled Jim violently away. "It's another trick, Jim; a deception."

With the whistling still echoing in my head, I ran towards Jim. The Sidh called Brenda greeted me with the same sweet smile as the male Sidh had the previous day. I stopped, frowning, for the whistling now formed a pattern inside my head. It was not quite a tune, but neither was it formless. I stood, static, trying to work out what the message was in the pattern of sound. And not only sound, I realised. There was colour there, too, as if the whistling created soft-pastel shades in my mind. The beauty entranced me as the tune formed music unlike any I had heard yet was vaguely familiar.

The Brenda Sidh smiled at me, with her eyes an invitation to a happiness I had never experienced in my life. I saw a place of greenery and laughter, with music as a constant backdrop and a whole host of friends. I had always yearned for true friends, for I was always different, and always on the move.

I saw myself as in a dark mirror. I was the orphan, the stranger, the girl from the lunatic asylum. I was the wanderer, the loner, the stoorie-foot, the teuchter, the lunatic girl who heard things; I was the one who did not belong. The music transported me to a place where I felt comfortable, a place that welcomed me for myself, where people understood my past and accepted me despite my frailties and failings. I felt that if I remained here, I would never be alone again; I would never be the unwanted, barely tolerated stranger.

No! I shook off the music, forcing myself to see the truth beyond the image.

Somehow, and I did not understand how the Sidh had entered my mind. It had discovered my deepest pain and manipulated my feelings so I would accept its poison within me.

"No!" I said. "You are not my friend. You are not here to help me. You are a deceiver, fooling me by offering what I most want in life."

Something hit me then, knocking me to the ground. The impact jarred my teeth, causing me to bite my tongue, with the sharp pain jolting me back to reality.

I rolled on the ground for an instant, tasting salt blood in my mouth yet with my mind working.

That must be how the Sidh operated. They were tricksters who found out what you desired and offered you a better life. They knew Jim was desperate for a sweetheart, so created an image of his perfect girl. They discovered that I had always sought to belong, so showed me a place of friendship.

"Ellen! Get up!" Mr Lunan dragged me to my feet. "Get back to the house!"

I obeyed, as Mr Lunan hustled Jim through the door. Dougie was already there, holding the shotgun in both hands.

"You're a pair of bloody fools!" Dougie said. "You know how dangerous these creatures are!"

The clock struck the hour; it was three in the morning.

"How long was I away for?" I asked.

"Away?" Mr Lunan repeated. "Away where?"

"When the Sidh put her spell on me," I said. "How long was I away for?"

Mr Lunan stared at me as if I was stupid. "You were not away at all."

I closed my mouth. In my head, the Sidh music had transported me to that beautiful, almost magical, place of friendship and colour. In reality, I had never left this grey farmtoun of rain and stark stone buildings. I remembered the old stories of men who entered the underground dwellings of the Sidh for a single night of dancing and festivity, to emerge a hundred years later. I had scoffed at such ideas as pure fiction. Now I wondered. If the Sidh could manipulate one's perceptions, why could they not also alter time? Or one's perception of time?

I closed my eyes, and for a moment, I was back in that place of beauty, with smiling faces around me and a feeling of serenity and peace. These were indeed the People of Peace.

"Ellen?" Mr Lunan leaned close to me. "Are you all right? You looked far away for a while there."

I glanced at the time. We had come back at three o'clock. Now the clock read five, yet I knew I had not been two hours inside the house. I had barely stepped in the door. I knew then that the Sidh were still inside my head, twisting reality with their music. Perhaps they always had been there.

"I am all right, thank you." I forced a smile and, in a gesture that was quite alien to me, reached over and squeezed Mr Lunan's arm. "Thank you for asking."

Once again, we all sat around the kitchen table after a massive scare by the Sidh.

"What next?" Jim looked stunned. "We've lost Andrew; we've Mrs Lunan; we've lost the raft, and we nearly lost the baby." He shook his head. "I thought that was Brenda," he said. "I could have sworn that it was Brenda. It looked like her; it sounded like her, and it even smelled like her." He looked away, shaking his head. "That was Brenda! I know it was!"

"The Sidh play with our perceptions," I revealed my hard-acquired knowledge. "They enter our heads and make us believe things that are not there."

The fire hissed and crackled in the background as everybody pondered my words. "How do you know that?" Agnes asked, narrowing her eyes in suspicion.

"They were inside my head," I explained. "Outside there, I felt them, and they seemed to be offering me what I want."

"What's that?" Agnes held the baby tighter.

"Happiness," I said. I felt no need to explain any further.

"Whatever we try, the Sidh counter," Dougie said. "Maybe Ellen is right. Maybe they are inside all our heads, searching for our weaknesses."

Once again, I heard the music creep within my head. "Be careful." I tore myself away from the beauty. "When they were in my head, I didn't know the difference between the truth and what they wanted me to believe."

Jim sat slumped in his chair with his once-cheerful face downcast. "That Sidh looked exactly like Brenda," he said.

"Maybe that Sidh was Brenda," I said quietly, trying to think and speak simultaneously. "Maybe the girl you thought was Brenda was a Sidh."

"I don't think so," Jim objected.

"Where did you meet her?" Dougie joined the conversation. "At the Pictish House, wasn't it?"

"At the Pictish House," Jim confirmed.

"The Sidh have always infested that place," Agnes said bitterly. "Where did this Brenda come from? Where does she live?"

"I don't know." Jim was becoming angry. "She's not a Sidh though; I know that."

"How?" Agnes pushed for an answer. "How do you know that? You don't know anything! All you wanted was a woman's body, and you never thought beyond that! Men!" She looked away in disgust. "For all we know that Sidh followed you here and brought all the rest of the clan."

"Easy, Agnes," Mr Lunan said. "We're all in this together here."

"We're getting nowhere." Dougie fiddled with his pipe. "What are we going to do next? Are we going to sit here and wait for the next attack? We've lost Andy and Liz - Mrs Lunan; the night before last the Sidh nearly took the bairn and last night they tried for Jim. What's next?"

Agnes pulled the baby close to her chest. "They might come back for my baby." She looked at me with a mixture of fear and loathing. "And if it's not Jim's fault, it's hers."

"We've been through this before," Mr Lunan said. "It's not Ellen's fault."

Dougie leaned back in his chair, pressing his hands together as he looked at me. "I can see Agnes's point," he said. "We think the Sidh are after two things. They want the bairn, and they want a virgin as a sacrifice."

When Dougie put things so bluntly, I shivered. It sounded like a Gothic novel, or like something from the Middle Ages. Human sacrifice belonged in the distant past, not in nineteenth-century Scotland.

"That's what we think," Mr Lunan said.

Dougie kept his gaze on me as he spoke. "Well, we're not

giving away the baby, but if we halve their interest in us, they might go elsewhere."

"How?" I challenged him.

"There are two ways," Dougie said without taking his eyes off me. "The first is to hand Ellen over to them. We just have to open the door and push her outside."

Agnes nodded eagerly. "If we do that, they might leave us alone, and my baby would be safe."

I shifted uncomfortably in my seat, wondering about these people I had considered friends calmly discussing handing me over for the Sidh to sacrifice. I should not have been surprised; I had always been the outsider. Yet part of me was willing to go, partly to atone for having released the captive Sidh, and partly because of a desire to return to that place of peace where I belonged.

"I don't like that idea," Mr Lunan said coldly. "I don't agree with murder, so what's the other choice?"

Dougie placed his stubby pipe on the table and began to stuff tobacco into the bowl. He gave me a lowering look, like a young bullock wondering whether to charge or not "Do we all agree that the Sidh are after a virgin?"

"We believe so," Mr Lunan said.

Dougie nodded. "If Ellen loses her virginity, then the Sidh will have less reason to attack us." He gave me an elaborate wink. "I could take her to the bedroom and do the deed here and now."

"No." I kept my voice cold, eyeing the poker. The gutting knife pressed cold against my forearm.

"I'd be doing you a favour." Dougie did not hide his smile. "And probably save your life. You might even enjoy it; most women do - with me."

"No," I repeated, holding Dougie's gaze.

"Oh, come on, Ellen. It's going to happen sometime, and I'm good."

"No," I said for the third time, fighting the panic that threatened to engulf me. I could have that poker in my hand in one second and land a powerful blow on Dougie's head.

"Dougie's right," Jim tried to persuade me. "You're putting all our lives in danger, Ellen. You're very selfish. If you don't want Dougie, I could do it." He looked over to Dougie. "We might have to force her."

"Ellen said no." Peter lifted the pike that rarely left his side. "I'll kill the first man to touch her. Ellen's my girl."

I said nothing to that as I edged closer to the poker.

Mr Lunan had been quiet for the past few moments. "We've discussed this nonsense before. There will be no killing and no rape. And you sit down, Peter, and put that thing down. We're all getting heated now."

"What are we going to do, then?" Dougie asked, still allowing his eyes to roam across my upper body. "Do we wait here for the Sidh to kill us, one by one, and then take the baby? And carry off innocent little Ellen here?"

I jumped when somebody knocked at the door, the double rap that I had once used.

CHAPTER 20

I DID NOT LIKE BEGGING, *the demeaning reality of knocking at doors or sitting on the street asking strangers for help. Yet that is what I did when I left Ma's house. I ran as far and as fast as I could, knowing Ma would be upset and the sergeant would mobilise all his constables to search for me. I spent a day or a week begging for food, rapping at doors, and accepting the insults or the scraps of waste with equal gratitude and humiliation.*

When the policeman threatened me with the jail, I ran again. I ran until grey dawn revealed a countryside I did not know, with bare, wind-scoured hills that rose, rounded and bleak, to the silver-streak of the horizon.

Out here in this wasteland, there would be little to forage, even although I was an expert at finding food in hedgerows and the edges of fields. Bitter experience had taught me which mushrooms were edible and which were not, when to harvest fruit and how to guddle a fish behind the keeper's back.

The hills provided heather, and if grouse could live on young heather, then so could I. there would be lizards in the coarse grass, and maybe mice or other creatures. I did not like to kill, but I was a child of nature and needs must when hunger drives.

The hills can be lonely places, or companionable when one's mood is ready to receive the embrace of granite and the stern kiss of the wind. I found a snug neuk beside a gabbling burn and fashioned a nest for myself, with a basket to catch leaping fish and snares for unfortunate animals. There were brambles in season, blueberries under a copse of elder trees, and sufficient firewood to keep me warm when the air nipped, and white frost crept across the heather.

I was there for a year or two, perhaps more, perhaps less, before somebody discovered me. I had been checking my heather-root basket in which I caught the odd trout when I heard a plaintive bleating.

"Where are you, sheep?" I asked for sheep were plentiful on my hills. They were less friendly than cattle, but hardier when the weather turned coarse.

The ewe had fallen beside my little den, and now she was trapped, upside down and kicking her legs.

"You silly sheep," I said, soothing her, for sheep panic when they cannot find their feet. "Come on." Grabbing hold of her wool, I was in the process of hauling her upright when a woman shouted down to me.

"What are you doing to my sheep?"

It was so long since I had heard a human voice that I found it hard to reply. "Saving her life," I said, eventually. "She's taken a tumble."

The woman was about forty, at a guess, bundled up in a battered old coat against the weather and with bright eyes in a weather-browned face. The long crook in her hand told me she was a shepherd.

"I'll come down," the woman said, scrambling down the

steep slope to my side. Between us, we righted the ewe and half-dragged, half pushed her back to the braeside.

"I don't know you," the shepherd said.

"No," I agreed, wishing she would go away. Living alone had made me even more suspicious of human company.

"Who are you?"

"Ellen Luath." I gave the minimum of information.

The shepherd nodded, with her eyes appraising me. "Do you know what day it is?"

I thought the question strange. Every day was important, with only the seasons dividing them. I had nearly forgotten the artificial concept of diving time into named days and months. "No," I said.

"It's Christmas Day," the woman said and held out her hand. "I am Jemima."

Jemima's hand was as hard as mine.

"We rescued a young sheep on Christmas Day," Jemima said. "Where do you live?"

"On the hills," I said, without showing my den.

"You'll be cold," Jemima said. "You are welcome to come to my home."

I wondered how to get away. After so long alone, I found human companionship difficult. Yet something inside me yearned to belong, to have a friend, to be normal.

"Thank you," I said.

Jemima lived in a small cottage at the head of a glen a bare handful of miles away, with the scent of a peat fire sweet in the air. Her two dogs lay on the ground with their heads on their paws, watching me without movement.

"Come away in and tell me about yourself." Jemima divested herself of her coat. "My man is around somewhere."

The cottage had two rooms, one of which was a bedroom, the other used for all other purposes. The warmth was welcome, and

I sank gratefully into one of the home-made chairs which some-body had padded with a soft cushion. It felt strange being inside a house after so long. I looked around at the furniture and the pictures on the wall.

"Where are you from?" Jemima asked, sitting at the table while the kettle boiled on the fire.

"Elgin," I said. "A long time ago." I was bewildered by the profusion of luxuries.

"And where do you live now?"

"On the hills," I said.

"Alone?" Jemima asked, busy cutting bread from a white loaf.

"Alone," I agreed.

"Where are your parents? Your sister or brother? You look too young to have a husband yet."

"I've no parents, or anybody else," I said. "And no husband."

Jemima shook her head. "Well, you are welcome here." She glanced at the door. "My man will be here soon." She added a generous hunk of cheese and passed it over to me. "You look hungry."

I had not eaten bread or cheese for so long that I nibbled delicately before I took a bite. I was chewing mightily when the door opened.

"Here's my man now," Jemima said.

Jemima's man was about sixty, with hungry eyes. He was undoubtedly the tallest man I had ever seen, with hair that descended to his shoulders and a grey beard that he might have combed sometime, but not that day or that week.

"I've brought you a guest," Jemima's voice changed as she spoke. "Ellen is all alone in the world."

The man gave the ugliest grin I had ever seen. "She has us now."

"She's yours, husband," Jemima said. "My Christmas present to you."

The words gave me all the warning I needed. Whatever hospitality that house offered came at a price that I was not willing to pay. Without taking a second bite at the bread, I ran for the door, ducked under the man's outstretched arm, and ran outside. I had suspected something was wrong when the dogs did not greet me, so I was prepared to run.

The hills welcomed me with their cool dark as I ran. I never returned to my little neuk beside the nameless burn but headed south into the wilderness of heather and rough grass.

Loneliness appealed more than unpleasant company, but if even the hills had their predators, then maybe it was time to return to civilisation.

The memories fled through my head before the echo of the knock had faded from the kitchen.

"What in the name..?" Mr Lunan looked at us as we sat in sudden silence. "There's nobody out there except the Sidh."

"Brenda?" Jim said with new hope in his face. "I'm telling you, that was Brenda out there!"

"Maybe somebody has brought a boat to rescue us?" Agnes said.

The knock sounded again, more urgent than before. "Are you there, Mr Lunan?"

"That's Heather Jock," I recognised the voice.

"Let him in," Mr Lunan said, and I drew the bolts and opened the door.

Jock stumbled in, looked around and grinned. As ragged as any tramp, he smelled of damp earth, while his hair was tangled across his eyes. I could have sliced the silence with a blunt kitchen knife as everybody stared at Jock as if he were some apparition from the moss.

"You lot look as if you were expecting a monster," Jock said.

"Maybe we were," Mr Lunan said. "I thought we got rid of you."

"I've come back," Jock said. "I think you'll need some help." He sat himself down at the table. "This used to be a hospitable farm," he said, looking at me. "Don't you even offer tea to your guests?"

I poured him a mug from the teapot that sat on the range, added a generous spoonful of sugar, and stirred the mixture together.

"Thank you, Ellen." Jock grinned at me and looked around the strained faces around the table. "Where's the lady of the house?"

"Dead," Mr Lunan said shortly.

"I'm sorry to hear that." Jock waved away my offer of milk and sugar and sipped at the steaming hot contents of his mug. "How?"

"The Sidh." Mr Lunan spoke without emotion, although I could see the dark shadows in his eyes. That man was suffering, I knew.

"They don't normally kill people," Jock said. "You've had a fire as well. Was that also the Sidh?"

"Yes," Dougie said.

"Bad times, then." Jock finished his tea and held out his mug for a refill. "You need my help."

"What can you do?" Agnes asked as I refilled Jock's mug.

"I know the Sidh better than anybody," Jock said.

"Did you bring them into the house?" Mr Lunan asked the question that was in all our minds.

"Did they only come when I was here?" Jock asked.

"No," I was first to reply.

Jock shrugged. "There's your answer. You are allowing your fear to control you."

Dougie nodded. "Are you part Sidh?"

Jock shrugged again. "I don't know. Are you? Do any of us know who we really are? There have been tales of humans mating with these creatures for centuries."

Mr Lunan grunted and told Jock what had happened since he was last in Kingsinch, with the death of the livestock, Mrs Lunan and Andrew and the attempt to abduct Baby Robert.

"I see." Jock sipped his second mug of tea more slowly. "What do you plan next?"

"We'll take the fight to the Sidh," Mr Lunan said. "We've had enough waiting for them to come to us.

That image returned to me, of Peter lying on a stone slab with a crowd of the Sidh gathered around. I could not make out their faces, only their shapes, and I knew I was at the periphery of the group, watching, waiting for something. I could taste Peter's fear.

"Do you know where they are?" Jock asked, half smiling.

"Everywhere," Agnes said. "The Sidh are everywhere."

Mr Lunan held out his mug towards me for more tea. "I was thinking of the Pictish House," he said. "People have seen them in that area."

"It has a sinister reputation," Jock said, drinking his tea with more delicacy than I would expect. "That's where I would start."

"We have to get there first," Mr Lunan said. "Across the floodwater."

"There is a way," Jock said, "a way that was old even before the Sidh arrived."

I listened intently, for I thought that the Sidh were here first. I thought the Sidh knew everything about this part of the world.

"How?" Jim asked, rubbing at his injured leg. I was glad that nobody suggested deflowering me again.

"Mr Lunan keeps one of his buildings locked up," Jock said.

235

Mr Lunan nodded. "It's not safe," he said. "Someday I'm going to demolish it and build something useful." He snorted. "Or I was, rather. I cannae see me doing that, now."

Jock finished his tea, placed the mug on the table and leaned back in his chair. I could smell the heather on him, and the dark aroma of peat. "Have you ever been inside that building?"

"Once," Mr Lunan said. "I nearly fell through the floor and closed the place up. I will go inside someday."

"Tomorrow could be that day," Jock said. "First, you have to plan your strategy. The Sidh are dangerous."

"We find them," Dougie said, "and we kill them."

We were silent at Dougie's words. Peter ran his hands along the shaft of his pike. Agnes nodded vigorously, mouthing "kill them all," without a sound crossing her lips. Mr Lunan stared at his hands on the table in front of him, and Jim sighed. I opened my mouth to say something, but stopped, unsure if I should speak.

"You need more than that," Jock said. "Do you know how many there are?"

"No," I said.

"Dozens," Dougie said. "Dozens of them attacked this house."

"And you are, how many? Three men and a boy?" Jock raised his eyebrows.

"Three men, a boy and a woman," I said. "I'm coming, too. These things have been hunting me all my life. I want to fight back."

Jock nodded at me. "Three men, a boy and a woman," he said.

"I'm coming too," Agnes said stoutly. "You're not leaving me behind on my own."

"You'll be safer here in Kingsinch," Mr Lunan said. "You'll be carrying the baby into the heart of the Sidh territory."

"Everywhere is the Sidh territory," Agnes said. She held Baby Robert closer. "If the Sidh try to take my baby, I'll kill them," she lowered her voice. "And I'll kill him too, rather than allow them to make him one of them."

When I looked at Agnes, I experienced another image, of her lifting a jagged rock and crashing it down on the baby's head, while in the background a host of the Sidh extended long, taloned hands. I sensed the desperation in Agnes and the desire of the Sidh. I shook myself free of the picture. What was happening to me? Was that image a vision of the future as I did not wish it to be, or had I conjured it from Agnes's words? Even worse, were the Sidh creating these terrible pictures inside my head? I knew of the Highlanders curse of second sight, but I did not know if I had Highland blood in me, or if I was the seventh daughter of a seventh daughter. I remembered Mhairi from Skye and shivered; she had been fey if anybody had.

"Ellen?" Peter had a hard hand on my arm. "Are you all right? You looked all queer there for a moment."

"Yes," I said. "I'm all right. I just want this to be over, that's all."

"Are you all sure about trying to beard the Sidh in their den?" Jock asked.

We nodded one-by-one. I was last to agree, for the prospect of entering the domain of the Sidh terrified me.

"Well then, you'll need weapons, and protection," Jock said. "And you'll need a better plan than merely killing every Sidh you see because they'll just melt into the landscape and become invisible."

"What do you suggest?" Dougie asked.

"The Sidh are a matriarchal society, headed by a queen,"

Jock said quietly. "Every group, or clan of them has its female leader. Capture her, and the rest will leave you alone."

"Was that a queen you held in the old Church, Mr Lunan?" Dougie asked.

Mr Lunan nodded. "Yes; I think so. Now we have to get her back. The Sidh were always here, but lately, they've been more active, as we know."

I opened my mouth again until Jock threw me a warning glare. "Then that's what we'll do," he said.

"They'll still want my baby," Agnes said.

"And they want Ellen," Peter stood behind me, a teenage boy who had already experienced more than most men twice or three times his age.

"If that is true," Jock addressed me. "You'll be walking into danger as well."

I nodded. "I know," I said. "I've been running from these things all my life. I want to live like a normal person."

Was that possible? Could I be like everybody else? Could I settle down in one place, make friends, maybe even find a man, and have children? I shivered, for the possibility had always seemed so remote in my life of running, hiding and running again.

"Look." Jock showed us a small cross he wore around his neck. "I made this cross from rowan wood and tied a red cord around it."

"The Sidh got past our rowan," Agnes said.

Jock frowned and thought for a moment. I saw the intelligence behind his eyes. They were dark brown, I noticed, flecked with hazel. "The only way the Sidh can get past rowan is if one of you invited a Sidh into the house," Jock said at length. "That would negate the rowan's power. Did you ever get any beggars, tinkers or gypsies at Kingsinch?"

"We had a small family at the beginning of autumn, just

after the hearst – the harvest," Mr Lunan said. "Liz fed and watered them in this very room and bought some of their wares."

I remembered the gypsy family I had passed when I first arrived at Kingsinch.

"Aye," Jock nodded. "I'd wager they were Sidh, preparing the way. How long after that did the Sidh appear?"

"Not long at all," Mr Lunan said.

"That'll be it, then," Jock said. "We'll need rowan wood and red thread."

Peter cut lengths of rowan from the tree beside the ruinous barn, while Agnes unearthed a ball of red twine from deep in Mrs Lunan's cupboards. After the men cut the twigs into suitable lengths, we fashioned little crosses from rowan and tied lengths of the red twine around the crossbar.

"Wait." Mr Lunan produced a Bible from somewhere and put all the crossed between the pages for a moment. "It might not help," he said, "but it can't do any harm."

We nodded, and Mr Lunan handed us our crosses, one by one.

"Make sure the loop is long enough to go around your neck," I advised.

The men laughed at me, and then Peter swore as his cord was too short. I removed his cross, lengthened the line and slipped it over his head.

"There you go, Pete," I said.

He grinned at me. "I hoped you would do that."

Wearing their crosses, the boys fetched their pikes and sharpened them on the circular grinding stone that stood in the courtyard.

"What weapon are you carrying, Ellen?" Jock asked me.

I fetched the largest knife from the kitchen, without mentioning my gutting knife. "The pikes are too heavy for me."

Jock nodded. "As you wish."

"I'll look after you, Ellen," Peter told me.

"I know you will, Peter," I said.

"We'll go tomorrow, early," Mr Lunan decided. "They seem to be stronger at night."

With the crosses and pikes ready, we were nearly ready. "We'd better eat well tonight," I said. "We might need all our strength tomorrow."

I made them brose, boiled as many eggs as we could find, and added oatcakes and cheese.

"This is a feast," Peter said, looking at the spread on the table.

"The last meal of the condemned man," Jock murmured, looked at me, winked and looked away.

"Let's hope not," Mr Lunan said as Jim tested the edge of his pike before sitting down to his meal.

"If any of you are religious," Jock said. "Now is the time to pray."

The orphanage insisted that we attend the parish church every Sunday, so we marched there in a long crocodile, two-by-two. The good people of Elgin watched us with sanctimonious nods, and more than one commented that she hoped we were grateful that the orphanage cared for us so well.

Miss Deas wore her best, all prim and proper. I think Sunday church was the only time she was without her belt, while Mr Snodgrass looked benevolent as he brought up the rear. I hated the hypocrisy of those trips. Once I foolishly told a church elder what Mr Snodgrass did to me, and that earned me another visit to his study, where Miss Deas demonstrated her skill in subduing a cringing child.

"The Lord has a reason for all things," the Kirk minister told us in his sermon, and I looked sideways at Mr Snodgrass and

wondered what the Lord's reason was for allowing Mr Snodgrass to hurt me.

"Are you going to pray, Ellen?" Jock was looking at me through his tangle of hair.

I shook my head. "No."

Jock grunted, with his eyes narrow. "As you wish. Just don't confuse Man's corruption with the reality of God."

I said nothing to that. Mr Snodgrass's face came before me, and Miss Anderson's huge blue eyes.

"May God help us all," Jim said.

"I didn't know you were religious, Jim," Dougie said.

"I wasn't until all this nonsense started."

I kept my thoughts and memories to myself. Life had repeatedly taught me not to share my experiences. I noticed Mr Lunan flicked through his Bible before placing it on the kitchen table. He filled his pockets with shotgun cartridges.

"Trust in God and keep your powder dry," Mr Lunan said. "I don't know who said that."

"Oliver Cromwell," Jock murmured, "or so somebody claimed."

The Sidh were quiet that night, with only a few whistles around the steading and no attacks on the house. I listened to the murmur of voices as Jock stayed with the men, taking his turn on watch. Twice I heard somebody in the kitchen, but both times it was Peter, checking up on me as I lay curled up beside the fire. For some reason I remembered Mrs Lunan here, dying with two Sidh arrows in her mouth. I lay where her blood had been. It did not matter; blood is as natural as the air we breathe, and as necessary.

I woke well before dawn and had the breakfast ready to feed the men. Again, I made brose with oatcakes and thick skelps of cheese. We sat in tense silence around the table, listening to the ticking of the clock as the fire sent out its heat. I wondered what would happen before I heard that clock again or saw the intricately scrolled numbers around the face. I would be older, the earth would have moved tens of thousands of miles, many babies would have been born, other babies created, and men and women would have died. Nature continued, whatever I did or did not do.

"Come on then," Mr Lunan said, hefting his shotgun. He glanced at me. "You can leave the dishes until we get back, Ellen."

I nodded, unsure if he was joking or not.

We left the farmhouse, four men, one boy, two women and a baby, to try and capture the queen of the Sidh.

CHAPTER 21

Jock had a key that fitted the padlocks, and he dragged back the bolts without any hesitation. We stepped inside the old stone building, with the atmosphere immediately oppressive. I could feel the evil, seeping from the walls. It was a malevolence that a previous inhabitant had left, an essence of himself that had soaked into the stones.

"A hangman lived here in the olden days," Jock told us, pretending nonchalance. "The place has been empty ever since."

"Who was that?" Peter asked.

"Old Hangie," Jock said with a curious little laugh that betrayed his stretched nerves.

The interior was in worse condition than I expected with loose masonry in the roof, and the floor crumbling beneath our feet. Jock knew the place, leading us to the furthest corner. "Walk where I walk," Jock said, "and be careful." He lifted a slab. "Down here," and indicated a dark hole.

Jock scratched life into a match and applied it to the wick of a lantern that hung from a rusted nail. Soft light pooled over the top step of a flight of stone stairs that descended into the black. I looked downwards, wondering what was down there, and if we could trust Heather Jock. I knew he was different from the bothy-boys, and from all other men I had met. His curious, hazel-flecked eyes hid a dark secret, a hurt that recognised the pain within me.

"Come on!" Jock moved without waiting, and we followed, one by one on the narrow, worn steps. I was second last, with only Peter behind me.

"I'll look after you, Ellen," Peter said yet again.

"I know you will, Peter." I treated him to a smile.

I felt Peter's eyes on me as I took a deep breath. I was unsure why he felt attached to me. Should I trust him? I thought of Old Hangie in this building, fancied I heard his raucous laughter and shook away the thought. Peter's hand brushed against my backside, either on purpose or inadvertently. I said nothing; it was a natural action for a teenage boy and did not matter.

With Jock's lantern-light bouncing in front of us, we descended the stairs, one-by-one, deeper and deeper into the bones of the earth. For the first few minutes, dressed masonry surrounded us, and then rough stonework, and then it was raw rock, dark and so smooth it was almost like ice.

"How deep are we going?" I asked, for I am not happy in confined spaces. When I was in the lunatic asylum, the keepers held me in a small room, nearly a cell, and ever since, I have dreaded the feeling of being trapped. I felt cold sweat course down my back.

"We're going all the way to the centre of the earth, I think," Peter said with our voices echoing from the shining-black walls. He touched my shoulder. "Don't be scared, Ellen."

The stairs ended in a long, smooth-floored passage that

thrust downward at a steep angle, with Jock's light still bobbing in front.

I started and looked down when something scuttled across my feet.

"It's only a rat," Peter soothed me.

Other creatures were also here; multi-eyed spiders that watched us from the shelter of silver-white webs, and strange, many-legged horrors whose very appearance made me shudder. I imagined I could hear these things; I could hear the scuff of their feet and the click of their jaws as they devoured each other. Down here, every sound seemed magnified, so that I was aware of everybody's breathing, and even the beating of Peter's heart as he watched and occasionally brushed against me.

"Don't straggle." Jock's voice came from in front, and although it echoed, I heard it with such clarity that the words were nearly written on the smooth walls. "You don't want to get lost down here."

A few minutes later, I understood what Jock meant as the passageway split, and then split again, with dark corridors branching out in different directions. I shivered, wondering what lay down these passageways, and if anybody had ever been there, or ever would. I fancied I could hear breathing as if the earth itself was alive, and the resounding thumping in my head was an echo of the heartbeat of the world. Were we all connected, humankind and the earth? Were we all part of one gigantic whole, an entity with uncountable lives, separate yet together?

I shuddered as the strange thoughts cascaded through my head and wondered if the doctors at the lunatic asylum had been right to lock me away. Perhaps I was indeed insane, to harbour such thoughts.

"Push on." Peter sounded nervous for the first time since I

had met him. "Keep up with the others, Ellen. Jock's right; I'd hate to get lost down here."

"We can't get lost here," I said. "We'll just follow the sound of their voices."

"There are too many echoes," Peter said, "and anyway, they're not talking."

"If they're not talking," I said. "How can I hear their voices?"

Peter gave me a gentle shove in the back. "There's nothing to hear," he said.

I shook my head, for the voices were as clear as sunlight in summer. Jock was concerned in case he lost us, Dougie was talking about the Sidh as the enemy and wondering about some female, Mr Lunan was mourning his first wife and daughter far more than he grieved for poor Liz, while Agnes spoke only of her baby. Jim was confused, speaking of Brenda.

I shivered again when Peter spoke, for his mouth had not moved, and surely, he had not meant me to hear his words as his eyes followed the curves of my body. I was about to express my disapproval when I realised Peter had not voiced his pubescent thoughts, and therefore, neither had the others.

Had I heard their thoughts? Or was I imagining things, down here in the terrible dark? I pushed the ideas away, trying to concentrate on other matters. I wondered who created these tunnels, why, and when, as we continued to walk along the amazingly smooth floor.

"Wait!" That was Mr Lunan's voice, and this time Peter heard him, too.

We stopped for a few minutes with the lantern-glow highlighting the line of our jaws, glinting from cheekbones, and transforming our eyes into deep pools.

"Are we all still here?" Mr Lunan asked quietly and counted us. "How are you bearing up, Agnes?"

"I'm fine, thank you," Agnes replied.

"Who made these tunnels, Jock?" Mr Lunan echoed my earlier thoughts, or perhaps we had read each other's minds.

Jock grinned; he was again quite relaxed. "I don't think anybody created these tunnels. Nature, or God, made them. Man only added the stairs."

Jock led us on, with the tunnel now inclining upwards, getting steeper with every few yards.

"We're nearly there," Jack called over his shoulder. "It might be safer for Agnes and Ellen to remain in the tunnels than come to the surface."

"I'm coming," Agnes lifted her chin. "You're not leaving me down here."

"I'm coming as well," I said. I could not hear the whistling now, and the voices inside my head were silent. I did not know if they had been my imagination or my companions' thoughts, but I welcomed their absence.

Jock said no more but led us up another flight of stairs to what looked like a substantial chunk of rock. I did not see the rudimentary handle until we were close.

"Stand back," Jock said, twisted the handle and pulled, so the rock swivelled and eased open. I felt cool rain and then we were stumbling into a small copse of wind-twisted trees set in a bowl of the hills. I had seen the tops of these trees before, near the Pictish House.

"If we had known about that passage," Agnes said, "we could have escaped days ago."

"Without Jock to guide us," Dougie said, "we could have wandered down there forever."

I examined our surroundings. The trees were all rowans, with winter having stripped them of both leaves and berries, so bare branches dripped water onto the already saturated ground. A small burn churned through the centre of the grove, bubbling over stones, and lapping around the gnarled trunks of the trees.

"Rowans." Jock noticed the direction of my gaze. "That's why the Sidh did not discover the passageways."

Nodding, I climbed to the lip of the grove and peered over the rain-slicked hills. Grey-green grass mingled with patches of brown heather, with an occasional outcrop of rock for variety. Far below, half-hidden by the grey rain, I saw the loch lapping around Kingsinch, dull brown water surrounding what was unmistakably an island of austere buildings. The steading looked very vulnerable from here, with the heights overlooking from three sides.

"It feels like God is weeping on us," Jim said.

"Oh, very poetic," Agnes shielded her baby from the incessant rain. "Is there anywhere I can shelter, Jock?"

"Aye." Jock gave her a sidelong look. "There's Kingsinch farmhouse, or back in the tunnels."

"Is that not Fleming's cottage there?" Agnes pointed to a lonely stone building that hugged a fold of the hill, a quarter of a mile away.

"Yes," Jock said, "but you'd be daft to go there with all the Sidh wandering free."

"I can't see any Sidh," Agnes said.

"I can," Jock told her. "And if you're ever stupid enough to leave these rowans, they will see you."

"It's wet." Agnes tried to shield her baby.

"Then get back inside the tunnel, if the rain bothers you," Jock said.

We lay down on the lip of that bowl in the hills. The rain was cold on our backs, and the wind rustled the bleak branches above our heads. Although I was aware of the subdued whistling in my head, I could not see any Sidh.

"Over there." Jock pointed to one irregularly shaped rock. "Watch that stone."

I watched, wondering if the rock was going to move. Nothing happened for a few moments, and then it altered shape, seeming to grow.

"Can you see it?" Jock asked.

"Yes, but I don't understand."

"What you see is a Sidh standing beside the rock. He's dressed in a mottled grey cloak, so he looks just like his background."

"Dear Lord," I said.

"Aye, that too."

"If we can see them, can they see us?"

"Not if we stay among the rowans," Jock said. "They won't look this way, and with the wind blowing from them to us, they can't hear us either."

Now aware what to look for, I stared at the hillslope. The Sidh were gathering. They came in ones and twos and small groups. The harder I concentrated, the more Sidh I saw, small patches of grass that moved against the wind, tufts of purple heather in a bed of brown, rocks that altered position; all were the Sidh sliding across the hillside. The spoke in low whistles that merged with the wind's gentle whisper, and the rustle of the branches. Their speech reverberated through my head, echoing, insidious, so that I could hear them without understanding.

I fought to control my thoughts, to concentrate on our task rather than listen to the sibilant whistling.

"I had never heard of the Sidh before I came here," I said, "and now there are hundreds of them."

"There used to be thousands," Jock told me. "Maybe tens of thousands, spread all over this land, from Caithness to the Eildons." He spoke without moving, and all the time, he scrutinised the slope of the hills around. "People believed that a mountain called Schiehallion was their headquarters. People were wrong; these hills, the Sidlaw Hills, was their main home in Scotland."

"Is that why they are gathering?" I asked. I was aware of the humans behind us, yet ignored them, with their clumsy movements and guttural voices. Compared to the Sidh, they were large, lumbering things, slow of thought and action.

They were? I meant we were. I shook away the ideas that the constant whistling formed within my head.

Jock was looking sideways at me through his tangle of hair. "No, Ellen. The Sidh are gathering to meet their queen."

"The one we are going to capture?"

Jock nodded. "Each of the Sidh communities, or clans if you prefer, owes allegiance to a queen. The Sidlaw clan has the most important queen of all, the High Queen. If she gives an order to leave the Lunans in peace and let Agnes's child alone, then the Sidh will obey."

"Can we persuade her? What is she like?" I conjured up an image of a queen sitting on a shining throne, rather like Queen Victoria, an unsmiling, regal woman with immense dignity and power.

"I have never seen her," Jock said, "or if I have, I didn't know." He gave me a brief smile. "We can only try, Ellen, if we even recognise her."

I nodded, fighting hard to block out the sounds that filled my head, and I wondered if the others shared my experience.

"Can you hear that whistling?" I asked.

Jock nodded. "It's a constant companion," he said. "I have to block it all the time." He drew in his breath sharply and swore.

"What's wrong?" I asked.

"The Sidh have got Agnes," Jock said.

CHAPTER 22

I STARED at Jock in incomprehension. "What do you mean? How could they?"

"She must have slipped away to Fleming's cottage."

"But we warned her not to!" I said.

I had to claw through the whistling to enable me to hear Agnes. She was screaming for help as the Sidh hustled her away, with half a dozen of the creatures surrounding her. I saw the Sidh clearly now, with their pointed ears and gashed mouths, they were the living embodiment of that thing in the Muckle Barn, an ancient evil I did not understand.

"You're not getting my baby!" Agnes yelled. "Dougie! Mr Lunan! Help!"

Dougie was first out of the trees, bounding down the hill like a young stag. Peter was only a few steps behind, holding his pike in both hands and roaring a challenge. Jim gasped as the wound in his leg re-opened, but limped down manfully, with Mr Lunan in the rear.

Jock pushed me back when I rose. "Stay, Ellen," he said. "You are no fighter."

"Are you not going to help?" I asked.

Jock gave me a twisted grin that lacked any humour. "I might be a liability," he said and sighed as he rose. "Stay in the trees, Ellen."

Before Dougie reached Agnes, the Sidh pushed her to the ground, wrestled the baby away and vanished.

"Where did they go?" Peter halted on the apparently empty hillside beside the near-hysterical Agnes. "Where are they, Agnes?"

Dougie slashed all around with his pike, challenging the Sidh to come out and fight. "Come on! Show yourself, you ugly bastards! Come out and face me!"

"What happened?" Mr Lunan asked. "Where are they?"

"Everywhere." Jock had reached them. "The Sidh are all around you."

"I can't see them, either," I shouted from the trees.

"They've gone to ground," Jock spoke with infinite patience. "Look again."

I frowned, concentrating on the hillside, looking for anything out of place. At first, I saw nothing, although the whistling was overpowering. The Sidh were there, communicating with each other and disturbing my thoughts.

"Pick up Agnes!" Mr Lunan ordered, and Jim limped forward, leaking blood from his leg.

I saw a patch of heather move against the breeze. "There's one," I pointed to the place, "and there's another!" I saw a tuft of grass remain still amidst a clump that the wind blasted hither and yon. The Sidh swarmed over the entire hillside. Some were wearing cloaks of woven heather; others plaited grass or a mixture of both. They all moved towards a slight mound in the hillside.

"I can see them," I shouted, "but now I've lost Mr Lunan and the bothy- boys!"

"They're still there," Jock said. "You need to look with a different part of your brain. Humans and the Sidh co-exist; we are side-by-side all the time and have been for thousands of years."

"Why have I not seen them before?" I asked.

"Because you have not looked with the right part of your brain," Jock told me.

At that time, I felt an outsider again. I knew Agnes was distraught from with the loss of her child, I could sense Mr Lunan's grief, Dougie's anger, Peter's desire to prove himself and Jim's confusion, but I was not part of them. I was outside their group, looking in, as through a bottle-glass window, observing without taking part. I shook my head; that was the epitome of my life, being outside the mainstream.

"Where are the Sidh going?" I asked. "I thought they would head for the Pictish House."

"Watch," Jock advised. "Do you want to rescue the baby?"

"Yes," I said.

"Even if it means putting yourself in danger?"

I paused at Jock's words. I knew I could walk away from this hillside, the Sidh, Mr Lunan and the bothy-boys. Since I came to Kingsinch, I had discovered some of the secrets that had plagued me from early childhood, but I wanted to know more. I needed to understand why the Sidh pursued me and why they wanted me as a sacrifice. I had to know, even if the knowledge killed me.

"Yes," I said.

Jock looked at me for a long thirty seconds. "If you are sure, we will follow the Sidh."

"All of us?" I indicated Mr Lunan and the others. Already, I felt the gulf widening between them and us. By us, I meant Jock and me, and by them, I meant all the others here.

I looked sideways at Jock, with his tangle of dark hair, his saturnine expression, his scent of earth and grass and that laconic attitude that concealed hidden knowledge. What was the connection between us?

Jock and I were both outsiders. Neither of us fitted into modern, nineteenth-century society, and we both had some strange connection to the Sidh.

"All of us," Jock said.

"Look!" Jim's roar broke my concentration again. Jim was close to Agnes yet was pointing fifty yards away to Charlie Fleming's cottage. "They've got Brenda!"

Jim was correct. I heard a female scream and saw a lone woman struggling with a group of Sidh. The woman must have emerged from Charlie's cottage, and the Sidh had pounced.

"Jim!" I heard her shrieking as the evil creatures dragged her towards the grassy mound. "Help me, Jim! Don't let them take me away!"

"Brenda!" Forgetting his injured leg, Jim ran forward, staggered, recovered, and moved on, yelling as he wielded his pike. "I'm coming, Brenda!"

I looked to Jock, who shook his head. "No. No, Jim! That's not Brenda!"

To me, the woman looked like Brenda. She was the same beautiful blonde I had seen outside Kingsinch farmhouse and looked to be in terrible distress. Jim staggered as his weak leg failed him, swore mightily, and threw himself forward.

Jock was faster, racing light-footed across the rough grass. I had never seen a man run so fast, or so gracefully.

"Jim!" Jock said. "That's not Brenda!"

"Get away!" Jim was as strong as a lifetime of physical labour could make him. He threw Jock aside and powered into the Sidh, knocking them back without apparent effort.

The Sidh pulled back, leaving Brenda lying on the ground. Jim scooped her up, one-handed, and then the blade of his pike caught the red cord of his rowan cross. The thin line parted at once, with the cross falling, spiralling end over end.

Immediately the cross struck the ground, the Sidh turned on Jim, more and more of them rising from the grass and heather. They piled on top of him, so quickly that even Jock seemed to move slowly, and when they withdrew, they left him a bloody pile. The Sidh had ripped open Jim's chest and torn out his ribs.

The thing I had thought was Brenda stood, smiling at me, and then her face altered, with the hair darkening, the ears becoming more pointed and the mouth changing shape.

"Ellen!" Jock dragged me away, back to the rowans, while the Sidh vanished from my sight.

"Jim." I looked over my shoulder.

"Jim's gone," Jock said. "You can't help him now."

I stared at the scene. Everything had happened so quickly, yet I remembered every detail, every expression on the men's faces, every sound and sensation. The incident was imprinted on my memory as if etched there by one of those shadowy tattoo artists who operate in Aberdeen's docklands.

Mr Lunan and the bothy-boys looked around them, unable to see the Sidh, who trickled back inside the mound. I watched, knowing I was privileged, or perhaps cursed, in that I could see both the humans and the Sidh.

"Are the Sidh ghosts?" I asked.

Jock shrugged. "Perhaps. Maybe when people think they see ghosts, they see the Sidh. That would make sense; the half glimpse of something they know should not be there, the feeling of unease, and then the cold shiver."

I nodded, understanding the logic. I wondered if any of us know who we really are, or from where we originate. Mr Lunan and the bothy-boys continued to scour the hillside, unable to see the Sidh who crawled past them, unseen. If the bothy-boys could not see the Sidh, I wondered if the Sidh saw us or lived on the same ground but somehow in different places. When I tried to work out the concept, I knew I lacked the vocabulary and knowledge.

I only knew the Sidh wanted me, for some reason of their own. The idea was terrifying, and I wanted to flee but knew I could not. To where could I escape when these things were everywhere, even inside my head? I had run all my life, and still, they found me or perhaps had merely been waiting, knowing I would arrive at their Sidlaw Hills.

Swearing in their frustration, the bothy-boys abandoned their search as Mr Lunan escorted a frantic Agnes back to the rowan copse.

"Why didn't you help?" Agnes screamed at me through her tears. "You just lay here and watched the Sidh steal my baby!"

"Why did you leave the safety of the rowans?" Jock countered with his voice calm. "We warned you not to."

Agnes balled her fists and ran at Jock, punching at him. Jock did not resist, allowing Agnes to vent her fear on him until Mr Lunan wrapped his arms around her.

"Come away, lassie; it's not Jock's fault."

Jock waited until Agnes calmed down, then returned to my side. "There's the entrance," he pointed to the mound. "Can you see it?"

I saw nothing for a few moments.

"Halfway down the slope," Jock said and added something I could not hear.

I had managed to control the whistling inside my head, but now it intensified, becoming louder until it blocked out all other sounds. Although I was aware of Jock's mouth moving, I could not understand his words. As before, the different whistling combined into a unified whole, to form enchanting music. In turn, the music solidified into a kaleidoscope of iridescence, myriad patterns that surrounded me, whirling, always altering, and unfailingly resplendent.

"It's so beautiful," I said, momentarily lost in the ever-changing designs within my head.

"Be careful!" Jock's voice cut through the colours. I could not see him, although I knew he was somewhere inside my head, a blurred figure within the patterns of sound. "Don't let them control you!"

I closed my eyes to blank out the colours and the music, only for both to increase.

"Fight them!" Jock said. "Think of something else! Think of something powerful!"

I thought of the sea, breaking on the rough cliffs beneath Findlater Castle, heaving, rising, and splintering on the rocks at the castle base. I thought until I could taste the salt spray and hear the raucous screams of the seagulls, so different from the alluring siren-call of the Sidh.

The great grey surges of the sea rose before me in long rollers that had been born in the distant Arctic. I watched them power in and hurl themselves to extinction on the unyielding cliffs with the spindrift rising, hovering on the eternal wind, and then falling with a rapid patter on the haunted beach below. The hammer of the waves forced back the music, one element combating another.

"That's better." Jock was clear now, watching me through his deep eyes, with the hazel flecks more prominent than before.

"How did you know?" I asked.

"I've been there," Jock said. "Many years ago. Far too many years ago." When he smiled, I saw the wisdom of age in his eyes, although he did not look any older than thirty. "If you want to escape, you have to fight, as you did."

"I thought of the sea," I said.

"Nobody can control the sea," Jock said. "Not even the Sidh." He was fading away, his voice faint and his figure merging with the rejuvenated colours.

Suddenly, I did not wish to expel the music. I wanted to remain here forever and lose myself in the beauty. I could see shapes in the colours and hear words in the music. I could see movement; I could hear the grass growing and feel every single drop of rain that fell on the earth. The wind had a voice, the hills had a soul, and the trees were bending closer to whisper their secrets.

"Ellen!" The voice was harsh as it crashed into the beauty. "Ellen!"

The kaleidoscope cracked, with a thousand colours cascading around me. The voice splintered the music, sending the notes into jarring disharmony. The beauty faded as the colours altered into the bleak hues of winter.

Cold reality broke the dream, and a spatter of rain washed my face.

"Ellen!" Jock stood in front of me, his long, saturnine face concerned. "They nearly took you, then."

I nodded, listening to the branches of the rowan above my head. "Nearly," I said. "It was so beautiful that I wanted to remain there forever."

"They are deceivers," Jock said. "They trick you. They'll promise you the earth and give you a handful of dirt, show you rich food and feed you dry leaves and heather, smile and steal your soul."

"How do you know?" I asked.

"I've been there, remember?" Jock shook me roughly.

"How long was I away for?"

Jock shook his head. "You can't think of time. Their concept of time is not the same as ours; it's not linear; it does not move in straight lines as we do."

I shook my head. "I don't understand."

"I'm not sure I do, either," Jock said. "The Sidh seem to live faster than us, so one of their days is a hundred years to us, yet they don't age as we do." He shrugged. "I might be wrong in all these things; I only say what I have worked out from observing them."

I shuddered. "Time is time," I said. "It can't jump around."

"Have you read Jules Verne's *Time Machine*?" Jock asked.

"No," I said. "I've not read a book since..." I was about to say, "since I left the orphanage," but I never mentioned that part of my life. "I've not read a book for a long time."

Jock noticed my hesitation. "The others are here," he said quietly.

I nodded. By that time, I knew that Jock understood a lot about me. Perhaps he understood me better than I understood myself.

"Let's get moving," I said. Jim's sudden death shook me, but less than it affected the others. Death holds less fear for people whose lives have been a constant struggle.

If Jock had not been watching so closely, we would never have located the entrance to the Sidh's domain. It was not a doorway, but a turf-covered opening in the hillside. Lying full length on the ground, Jock thrust his hand into a depression in the grass.

"I saw the Sidh do this," he said and did not explain more when Mr Lunan pressed him for details.

I heard a slight click, hardly more than the turning of a key in a household lock.

"Everybody," Jock said, rising to his feet. "Push at this small ridge."

We hardly saw the ridge until Jock pointed it out. Then we crouched and shoved, feeling rather stupid until a section of the hill rolled up, revealing a hole from which a greenish light shone.

I heard the music and shivered, while Jock stepped back, suddenly pale under his weather-beaten appearance.

"I can't go any further," he said, shaking visibly.

I stepped to his side, realising that Jock's previous experiences had caught up with him, rather like a man rescued from drowning going back into the water.

"You can't leave us now," Dougie said. "You know more about the Sidh than all of us together."

I felt the clammy sweat on Jock and knew he was reliving old memories. "You go home if you wish, Jock," I said. "You don't have to come."

"But my baby," Agnes said. "How will we get him back without Jock?"

The music was louder, enticing me inside the Sidh's den. "Can anybody else hear the music?" I asked.

"There's no music," Dougie said. "You're talking nonsense."

"It must be the wind," I backtracked quickly. The music retreated to the back of my mind and quavered there, stropping its claws.

Mr Lunan entered the green hole first, stepping gingerly inside the hill with his shotgun in his hand and his rowan cross prominent on his chest. We followed, with Jock, always so calm, now the most nervous of us all. I was surprised that the interior was not dark and stuffy but instead glowed with light from the walls, which seemed to recede as we stepped further inside.

"Where is this place?" Dougie looked troubled. "I feel that I know it."

"Is my baby in here?" Ellen opened her mouth to shout until Jock clapped a hard hand over her mouth.

"Keep quiet. If you value your soul, don't make a noise."

I had imagined the place would be full of the Sidh, but I did not see any although I sensed their presence. They were here, somewhere.

We moved on, walking on ground that was soft as sponge under our feet, while the walls were of luminescent green. I could not see a source of the light, nor could I see where we were.

"I think we should get out of here," Dougie said. The man who had boasted about joining the Black Watch was losing his nerve.

"I must save my baby." Ellen shook Dougie's arm. "Please help, Dougie."

"Where are we, Jock?" I asked. "Do you know?"

Jock was shaking. "The old folk called it Elfhame, for want of a better name. I was here once, for a day that lasted a lifetime."

We walked on, and now the music surrounded us, although without form or colour. I looked around for the Sidh, with the rowan cross seeming to burn a hole on my breast and my gutting knife a comforting presence up my sleeve. I had dropped the kitchen knife somewhere.

"How far is it?" Mr Lunan asked.

Jock forced a smile. "How long is a piece of string?" he replied with nervousness making his voice harsh. "Maybe better to ask, when is it?"

I do not know how long we walked. Time did not matter; only the opaque green glow around us and the soft whistling inside my head. I could feel the music behind the whistling, although it had not yet formed colours.

"Fight it," Jock knew what I could hear. "Don't let them control you."

Beads of sweat rolled down Jock's face to drip from the

point of his half-shaven jaw. I could feel his tension increase with every step we took in this unearthly place. I wanted to hold him, to tell Jock that everything would be all right, that what happened was meant to happen.

Instead, I touched Jock's arm. "We'll be all right," I said softly.

Jock started at my touch. He looked at me as if for the first time. "Oh, dear God, Ellen," he said. "I hope you are correct."

The green glow increased as we progressed until Dougie pushed in front, pointing his pike before him. "Come on," he said. "Let's get this done."

Agnes followed, and Mr Lunan looked around him. He had lost something since Elizabeth had died; the light had gone from his eyes, and his tread was heavier, less confident. I suspected he only lived to avenge his women.

The alteration came gradually, with the corridor slowly widening until we stood at the entrance of a chamber, so large that I could not see the far side. The same green light was here, with the ground so soft we seemed to be walking on the finest Axminster carpet.

"Where are we?" I asked. "Are we under the Sidlaw Hills?"

"Time and place are different here," Jock's voice trembled. "I wish I had not returned. I should have stayed out of this nightmare."

"Why did you come back?" I asked.

Jock took a deep breath. "I had to return," he said at length. "Like a murderer returning to the scene of his crime, or a soldier to a bloody battlefield."

I could understand that. After I left the orphanage, I used to stand outside, stare at the walls and relive the horrors I had endured. Now I looked into the green light and wondered at the soft music that sweetened my ears.

"It's beautiful," I said.

"It's an image," Jock reminded. "The Sidh are manipulating your mind. What you see is unreal. Don't forget that."

I nodded assent, yet when I touched the wall, it felt real, like the softest sponge, and the music drifted around us, without a visible source. I felt the most remarkable sensation of peace overcome me as if I belonged here.

Perhaps I did belong? The words slipped, unbidden, into my head. Maybe the Sidh were trying to rescue me from my life of unending drudgery and rejection and transport me to this beauty.

"Fight it!" Jock warned. "For the sake of your soul, fight it!"

The Sidh had appeared all around us, smiling, holding out bowls of fruit and gourds of wine. Dressed in green, yellow, and red, they spoke in musical whistles that formed words I understood.

"Welcome, Ellen Luath," a man said with his teeth white behind red lips and what looked like a birthmark covering half his face. I blinked, for I had met him in the farmhouse.

"Welcome, Ellen Luath," a woman greeted me, holding out her arms in an embrace.

"Do you know me?" I asked, gazing at a circle of smiling, open faces.

"We have known you since before you were born," the Sidh woman said. Although I could not tell where I had seen her before, there was something familiar about her features.

I had seen her near the Pictish house and Charlie Fleming's pendicle, yet that was not it. I had an older memory, something from further back in my life.

"I know you," I said.

When the old woman looked directly at me, I remembered her face. I had been lying wrapped in a green blanket, and she had been holding me. "Are you my mother?"

From where had that thought or that memory come? Was it genuine? Or had the Sidh planted it in my mind.

The woman drifted away, although I did not see her legs move.

When Mr Lunan lifted his shotgun, I shook my head and pushed down the barrel. "No, Mr Lunan; we don't need that here."

Mr Lunan was staring at the Sidh, with his mouth open and his eyes glazed. I knew he could not see what I saw. The Sidh were inside his head, altering his thoughts.

"Welcome back, Jock!" A group of Sidh held out plates of fruit for him. "We missed you."

I felt as if I were in a dream. "Where are we?" I asked.

"Jock already answered that question," the man with the marked face said. His eyes were kindly, bright with wisdom. "Elfhame."

A woman joined him, smiling as she reached out to touch me.

"I know you," I said.

"You released me from confinement," the Sidh said, and only then did I see her through different eyes. This was the woman that Mr Lunan had imprisoned under the ancient chapel. She was brighter of face, cleaner of person and fully clothed, but undoubtedly the same woman.

"Are you the leader of the Sidh?" I asked. "Are you the queen?"

The woman's smile was as gentle as anything I have ever seen. "Would you like me to be a queen?" She lifted her hand. "What shall I do with your companions, Ellen Luath?"

Dougie and Peter stood as if in a trance, staring into space as the Sidh gently removed their weapons. They did not resist.

"Don't hurt them," I said. "They are trying to help Agnes."

"They want to rescue Agnes Shaw's baby." The elderly

Sidh spoke without moving her lips. I had never felt such warmth and kindness in my life.

"So do I." I found myself speaking the truth to these so-called deceivers who were inside my head. "We planned to capture the queen to persuade her to hand back the baby and leave Mr Lunan in peace. Can I ask you to leave Mr Luath and the others in peace? The Sidh have already done much damage to them."

The middle-aged Sidh man. "Perhaps you should have asked Davie Lunan to leave the Sidh in peace."

The image of Mr Lunan patrolling the steading returned to me, with his shotgun ready loaded and his three black mastiffs at his heels. I remembered him up at the Pictish House, hunting for Sidh as if they had been rabbits, or vermin to be exterminated.

"The Sidh stole Mr Lunan's first wife," I said, "and his baby."

"Let me show you," the Sidh female said and touched my face.

Within a second, I was in an unfamiliar farmhouse kitchen with a much younger Davie Lunan and an auburn-haired woman I thought I knew. The woman was cringing, trying to protect herself from Mr Lunan, who was alternatively slapping and kicking her.

"Leave me, Davie!" the woman screamed. "I couldn't help it! Please! It just happened."

Mr Lunan aimed a final kick that sent the woman sprawling, and then left the house. "You'd better get the thing out of my house before I return, you little hoor!"

I was aware of others in the kitchen, three Sidh, watching unhappily as the woman, presumably Davie Lunan's first wife, picked herself from the ground, wincing at her hurts.

Only then did I hear a female baby crying from an upstairs room. Mrs Lunan left the kitchen, lifted the baby, wrapped her in a green shawl, and ran out of the house, sobbing.

I accompanied the first Mrs Lunan as she ran along an unmade road, with the wind plucking at her clothes and tangling her hair around her head. After a mile, she stopped, held her baby tight and looked around her.

"Where shall I go? Oh, God, where can I go with this little mite?"

I heard her thoughts and read the panic in her eyes as the coldness of night closed on her.

"Can I help?" I asked, but nobody heard me. I was a witness to another time; I was a woman who was not there; I was the shadow one senses at the fringe of one's mind. I held out helpless hands, for I could feel Mrs Lunan's distress as if it were my own.

The music was ever-present, a backdrop to the drama, like a play in a theatre, for in the beginning was the Word, the Word was beauty and beauty is good. Now it took form, and the Sidh emerged from a stone-built earth house on the south side of the road.

"Come, little one," the Sidh said, talking to Mrs Lunan. They were gentle, smiling creatures as they drifted her inside the earth-house. I was with them, watching without taking part.

The Sidh gentled Mrs Lunan, with one Sidh female taking her baby away.

"No," Mrs Lunan said. "You can't have my baby!"

The Sidh female handed it back at once. "Then you must return to Davie Lunan," she said softly, "and within the year, he will kill you and the baby."

"What can I do?" Mrs Lunan asked, speaking through her tears.

"We shall take care of the child," the Sidh said, "She is our baby, too. We will look after her from this side. Davie Lunan shall not get her. You will follow in a day."

I watched as the female Sidh drifted away with the baby in her green shawl. She had no sooner left the earth-house than Davie Lunan saw them. He shouted at once, and charged forward, swearing.

"Davie!" Mrs Lunan said. "Don't hit me!"

"You little hoor!" Mr Lunan lifted his shotgun and fired, *killing his wife outright. She fell backwards with the shotgun blast having shredded her upper body.*

The Sidh melted away so Mr Lunan could not see them in the near-dark. Only the female Sidh remained, holding the child in its green shawl.

"Your baby!" The Sidh held the child out. "Your wife gave her life!"

"Damn the wee bastard," Mr Lunan said, *hastily reloading his shotgun.* "Damn it to a life of hell!"

I saw the Sidh hold the baby tight, smiling down on her, a smile I recognised, and then she placed it on Mr Lunan's dogcart and melted away.

"Damn all of you!" Mr Lunan *fired his shotgun.*

I watched him glare at the body of his wife, then tip her into the earth house door and throw in rocks until he covered her body. Only then did he look at the baby girl, who was crying in the soft rain.

"Right, you little bastard," Mr Lunan said, "you're no blood of mine." *He jumped in the cart and drove to the orphanage in Elgin. Hastily scribbling a name, he scribbled out the Lunan and left the child at the orphanage door before whipping his horse furiously and driving away.*

I stared at the Sidh. "Oh, dear God," I said. "Was that what happened?"

"You saw it happen," the Sidh said.

"You were that Sidh," I said, "and the baby, was that me?"

The Sidh nodded. "That was you. We have been trying to

help you ever since, but you heard your father put a curse on you. A father's curse is a powerful thing that we could not break through until you returned to us of your own free will."

I was unsure of what to say. In common with most, if not all, orphans, I yearned to know who my parents might be. Now I knew that Mr Lunan was my father. Or did I? He had called the child – me – a bastard, and said it was no blood of his. Did that mean that Mrs Lunan had a lover?

"Were the Lunans my parents?" I asked.

The Sidh's smile was the gentlest thing I have ever seen. "Oh, Ellen, my dear, sweet, confused child. You still don't understand, do you?"

I shook my head. I felt I could trust this woman who had known me, albeit briefly, as a baby, and who had tried to help me.

The Sidh put out her hand. "Come with me, Ellen, and meet somebody who will explain everything."

I did not feel myself move, yet I was in a smaller chamber, with softly luminescent walls and a carpet of rose petals. The Sidh woman sat on a tall bronze chair, with a man seated at either side of her. All three smiled at me while music played in the background.

I addressed the woman in the centre, asking her the same question. "Are you the queen of the Sidh?"

"No," the woman replied without moving her lips. I heard her words within my head. "You are."

CHAPTER 23

"You are." The words tumbled through my brain for a long time before I understood the significance.

"I am?" I repeated as the kindly faces smiled at me.

"You are," the central woman repeated.

"How can I be?" I asked. "I am an orphan; I am a nobody; the orphanage gave me my name. They could not make out all my surname, so they called me Luath, after Robert Burn's dog – the orphanage named me after a dog, for God's sake."

"Luath was Ossian's dog before he belonged to Robert Burns," the old woman said. "A most famous dog with a noble past."

I fought through the fog of words. "I am not the queen of the Sidh."

"You are the queen of the Sidh," the old woman said. "Your mother was a human; your father was a Sidh prince, born of human and Sidh stock."

I struggled with this new concept in a day of illuminations. "Was Mr Lunan not my father?"

The old woman smiled, shaking her head. "He was not.

Did you not wonder at your differences? You are like us in stature, and have the gifts of sensing atmosphere, befriending animals, and listening to thoughts."

"I have only become aware of these gifts recently," I said.

"And you can hear us talking, which other humans cannot." The woman continued as I tried to understand my new position. "Your mother's husband cursed you when you were young, so we could not accept you. We placed you with the humans, to live as they live. You grew up among them to know their ways and test them. Were you happy there?"

As the woman spoke, I saw my life in a series of images. I saw the green shawl as I lay outside the door of the orphanage in Elgin. I saw a circle of faces as the officials examined me. I saw Miss Deas magnified eyes as she leaned over me, shrieking abuse, and I saw the worn, ink-stained surface of the desk as I bent over it to receive the belt.

I saw the jeering faces of my fellow orphans when I told them about the whistling inside my head, and the sharp eyes of the doctor as he declared my insanity. I remembered the loneliness of my asylum cell, and my desperation to belong.

I saw me return to the orphanage and the turned shoulders of my companions. The years rolled, and I walked out into a world of loneliness as I tried to hide the madness of the whistles and escape by moving from one poorly paid position to another.

"I was not happy," I answered truthfully.

"Did they welcome you among them?"

I remembered the long hours when I was alone and unwanted, rejected as the loner, the girl who did not fit in, the person outside any of the closed peer-groups. I remembered the treatment of outsiders, from single strangers in town, to the official shunning of gypsies, tinkers, and those with lifestyles outside the accepted.

"No." I shook my head. "I knew loneliness. People are only accepted if they conform to certain attitudes and looks."

"Are the humans peaceful people?"

Again, the images returned. I saw the childhood squabbles when boys traded punches within a cheering ring of their friends with the chant of "Fight" Fight!" Echoing around the playground. From those petty encounters, I recalled the brawls outside public houses when drunken men and sometimes women swung at each other, and I remembered the march of the Black Watch through Coupar Angus.

"No," I said. "There are fights, disputes and wars between them."

I felt the horror as the Sidh exchanged their thoughts.

"You are home now," The old woman said. "Back where you belong." Her smile wrapped around my heart, the warmest and most loving emotion I had ever experienced.

Home. I toyed with the concept of belonging somewhere, of being with people who cared for me. I could not prevent the tears that formed in my eyes and rolled, hot and salt, down my cheeks.

"We've been trying to contact you all your life," the old woman said. "And you have heard us talking as we tried to help you."

"I did not understand," I said. "I was frightened."

The three Sidh nodded solemnly. "The outside world taught you fear. We understand that. We tried to send our thoughts to you wherever you were."

"I heard the whistling," I said. "I did not understand it."

The love was stronger now, holding me secure. It encased me in a cocoon of warmth, friendship, and security.

"Come with us," the three Sidh said.

I obeyed, drifting with them from that small room into a large chamber filled with Sidh, who welcomed me with smiles and soft touches, who surrounded me with a sense of wellbeing and belonging.

"We are all equal here, under our queen," the three Sidh said. "There is no striving, no worry, no hatred, no money, no wars or disputes."

I looked around this paradise, listening to the most beautiful music I had ever heard.

"Join us," the Sidh repeated again and again. "You are welcome. Eat and drink with us, become part of our community, re-join your family, my queen."

The Sidh had piled food on three long tables. Used to the never-ending brose and oatcakes of the farmtoun, I stared at the feast. There was every variety of fruit on display, including some fruits I did not recognise, with bowls of vegetables, potatoes, tomatoes, and crisp leaves of lettuce. Among the food, bottles and gourds of wine waited, with jugs brimming with ale and sparkling clear water.

"I've never seen such a banquet," I said.

"You'll see it every day," the Sidh said. "We always feast in this manner."

The music became louder, with couples dancing, sometimes men and women, at other times women together or men together, laughing with the sheer joy of existence.

Two of the younger Sidh came beside me, smiling as they took my hands to lead me in a gentle dance that became more active as the music altered. I found myself leaping and dancing with them, singing to the music, responding to the Sidh's smiles with smiles of my own.

"We feast and dance and sing all day," the Sidh told me.

"And at night?" I asked, wondering why I was not breathless after so much frantic activity.

The Sidh laughed again. "You are the queen," they told me. "You may have your bed to yourself or share it with anyone you wish. It is better than to curl up on a stone slab beside the embers of the kitchen fire."

I pictured my bed in Kingsinch, with its worn blankets on the ground and me lying like an unwanted dog, with the fire baking one side of me and a draught from the door chilling the other. I did not have to glance around the chamber to know that many Sidh men were well-made and handsome. I shook my head, reminding myself that I did not like men. I had no interest in the physical side of a relationship.

The music was wilder, with one handsome Sidh, with high cheekbones and the body of a Greek God, advancing towards me with his lips curved in a smile and his arms extended in invitation.

"Oh my goodness," I said, as something inside me stirred. "Oh!" I looked again, unable to help my mounting desire.

"Later," my Sidh woman read my emotions. "Come this way." All three of my Sidh were back, easing me into the most luxurious bedroom I have ever seen, with silk sheets and feather pillows on a four-poster bed, gold-framed mirrors on the walls and rose-petals strewn on the floor.

"Do you like it?" the Sidh asked, suddenly anxious. "Is it to your taste, your Majesty? We can change anything you say."

"It's perfect." I had envisioned such a room when I was a child in the stark chill of the orphanage dormitory when the bullies waited until the lights were out before they began their nightly torments. I had imagined myself as a queen then, without realising that I would ever touch the reality.

My tears were back, tasting salty on my face. Something else was there too, a nagging voice at the edge of my consciousness. I listened to the subliminal warning, allowing my innermost fears to surface.

"How about Mr Lunan," I said, tearing myself away from the opulence the Sidh presented to me. "Mr Lunan, Dougie,

Jock, Agnes and her baby, and young Peter. What will happen to them?"

"What do you want to happen to them, your Majesty?"

I tried to concentrate, wondering what was best for each. "Allow Mr Lunan to live his life in peace," I said.

"We will if Mr Lunan stops hunting the Sidh with dogs." The words were soft but edged with bitterness.

"Does Mr Lunan remember shooting the first Mrs Lunan?" I knew something about the vagaries of the human mind. "Or does he honestly believe that the Sidh stole his first wife? I know the Sidh killed Elizabeth."

The three Sidh shook their heads. "Mr Lunan murdered his first wife, and his second wife attacked us. He is aware of what he did."

The words and colours in my head wavered. I tried to concentrate, bring sense out of confusion, and find reality from a fog of deception.

"Does Mr Lunan believe that the Sidh stole the baby? Does he remember that he abandoned it – that he abandoned me?"

"He hides his guilt," the three Sidh said.

I struggled with that answer. "Does Mr Lunan hide his guilt from himself?" I asked.

The nagging voice was stronger in my head, intruding on the music of the Sidh. I felt a burning pain in my temple as if somebody was pressing a red-hot poker against me.

"I don't understand," I said. "If Mr Lunan is not my father, then who is? Who is this Sidh prince of whom you speak?"

"We tried everything to bring you home," the three Sidh did not give me a direct reply. "We had to use the baby to entice you in. Now we have you safe where you belong."

I could sense the Sidh's satisfaction. "And all the others?" I asked as the pain in my temple increased.

"If they wish to stay, they may stay," the three Sidh told me. "If they wish to leave, they can leave."

The pain was acute now. I pressed my hand to the place without alleviating the agony in the slightest. "Somebody told me that the Sidh sacrifice a virgin every seven years. Is that correct?" I tried to recall the image, where Peter lay on a stone tablet with the Sidh crowded around.

"Did you think we would sacrifice our queen?" The Sidh read my thoughts.

"Why would you sacrifice anybody?" I cringed as the pain increased. "Where is Peter? Take me to Peter."

With that question, I was in another chamber. Peter lay on a soft bed, with two Sidh women looking after him. He was smiling, evidently happy, and without even a suggestion of a sacrificial knife. As I looked, Peter sat up and reached for one of the women.

"He seems content," I said. "Paradise for Peter!"

"The cross!" The harsh words grated through the music as the three Sidh faded slightly. "Touch your cross!"

"My cross?" I repeated the words, as the music increased and the three Sidh returned.

"Ellen. Now, do you believe us?" Something had altered with the three Sidh. I could sense some new anxiety as if they had a limited time to convince me of their truth.

The pain in my temple was excruciating. I doubled up, with one hand to my head, and in doing so, the rowan cross around my neck swung free on its red cord. The edge of the cross touched my hand, and everything changed.

CHAPTER 24

I STOOD with Mr Lunan and the others in that same chamber, with Peter missing and the others staring into space, transfixed, as if in a trance. Jock was beside me, pressing the edge of his rowan cross against my forehead.

"You're back!" Jock sounded tense.

I started, relieved to be free of the awful pain. Jock removed his cross from my temple. "I lost you there," he said.

"What happened?"

"The Sidh get inside your head," Jock reminded me. "They read our thoughts and use them to control us. What did they promise you?"

I remembered the tables of food, perfect for a woman who had been hungry most of her life, and the luxurious bed. When I was young, I had dreamed of a bedroom like that and had dreamed of being a queen. My dream-bedroom had been exact in every detail, down to the rose-petals on the ground. "They promised me everything I always wanted," I said. "They told me that I was the queen of the Sidh, and Mr Lunan had murdered his first wife."

"Lies and deception," Jock said. "They did the same to me, the first time I was here. You already know that the Sidh find out what you fear and what you want most and use the knowledge to manipulate you."

"Mr Lunan shot his first wife," I said.

"No." Jock shook his head.

"And the first Mrs Lunan was my mother."

"Lies and deception." Jock shook me, but gently. "Mr Lunan has always farmed around the Sidlaw Hills, and you are from Elgin, a hundred and fifty miles further north. The Sidh are manipulating you, Ellen. Don't believe anything they say."

I nodded, more scared than I cared to admit. I looked over the others. Mr Lunan, Agnes, and Dougie were all staring into nothingness. "Where's Peter?" I asked. "Everybody's present, except Peter and Baby Robert."

Jock started. "The Sidh must have taken him away."

"They're going to sacrifice him." I heard the terror in my voice. "The old stories say the Sidh sacrifice somebody every seven years."

"They sacrifice a virgin," Jock said. "You may be in danger."

"Peter's a virgin," I said. "Not all virgins are female."

Jock gave me a sidelong look as if the idea had not occurred to him. "You may be right."

"You know this place, Jock. Where would the Sidh hold Peter?"

Jock pondered for a moment. "I might know the place. We'll free the others first."

"We haven't got time," I said. "The Sidh will kill Peter! I've seen him, Jock!" I explained about the stone table, and the Sidh gathered around. Jock listened without ridiculing me.

"All right," Jock said. "Peter comes first, but we'll give the rest a fighting chance." Without another word, Jock hurried to Mr Lunan and ripped open his jacket. "Come on, Ellen, bring out Agnes's cross!" Jock placed Mr Lunan's cross in the farmer's hand, and then Dougie's. I did the same with Agnes.

"That might help them recover," Jock said. "Come on, Ellen; let's find Peter."

Jock led the way, striding from that chamber along another corridor that looked exactly like the last. I followed, trusting in this strange man with the tangled hair and scent of damp soil. For some reason, I watched his legs and hips, shook my head at the images that ran through my brain and nearly smiled. Underground was no place for erotic thoughts; or had the Sidh planted these ideas? Since Mr Snodgrass had raped me as a child, I had kept men at a distance. Why was I changing now?

"Keep your cross handy," Jock said. "Hold it in your hand, if you can."

Immediately I grasped the rowan cross, the glow around us faded and the walls altered. Rather than soft glowing green, the walls hardened into solid rock, laced with old tree roots and deep fissures. We were deep underground, not in some magical place of colour and light. The Sidh had placed the false images in my head. I looked at Jock again and started. He was no different, a ragged man of above medium height with tangled hair, yet my feelings for him had not changed after I held the rowan cross. I smiled; if ever we got free from this place, I had plans for Heather Jock. If ever; my life seemed to be composed of many "if evers."

I was unsure where we were as Jock led us from one tunnel to another, so I felt like we were moles, burrowing into the damp ground. Did the feared Sidh live here all the time, as frightened of humanity as we were of them?

"Here!"

Jock had led us through a bewildering series of tunnels to a long chamber, carved out of solid rock and with a delicate light. I could neither see the farther end of the room, nor the source of the illumination. I could hear the music, soft in the background, rising and falling like the humming of ten thousand bees. It was strangely soporific, lulling me to a state of security as if everything that happened was meant to happen.

I stood still, momentarily feeling that all was right with the world. A feeling of absolute well-being swept over me.

"Ellen!" The voice intruded on my feelings.

"Ellen!" Jock pointed to the rowan cross, which had slipped from my grasp. I took hold of it, realising I was in the midst of a battle between two forces. My mind was the battlefield and my person, perhaps my soul, was the prize.

I looked ahead. Four Sidh surrounded Peter, who lay supine on a stone slab. As I watched, the Sidh were stripping off his clothes, whistling among themselves and taking their time. They made a show of the procedure, removing each item with care, folding it, and placing it carefully on a second, smaller slab a few steps to the left. Peter's jacket, boots, socks, and pike already lay there.

Peter lay inert, unmoving, staring upwards at the rocky ceiling. I wondered what dreams the Sidh had put into his head.

"No!" I screamed. All my guilt returned, my horror at having freed the Sidh woman. "Not Peter! Sacrifice me instead! The Kirk hasn't christened me either!"

I could feel the Sidh probing inside my head. I was back in Mr Snodgrass's study with his body pressing onto mine.

You are not suitable. You are not entire.

The Sidh had found the memory I held most secret. I tried to push forward, to save Peter.

"Wait!" Jock hissed; he pointed to the shadows, where a score of Sidh waited. Unlike any Sidh I had seen before, these were wiry men in shining bronze chain armour, carrying the small, human-rib bows and short, leaf-shaped bronze swords.

I froze. I had never seen a Sidh warrior before. I thought they were the People of Peace?

"We can't do anything yet." Jock held my arm. "Wait until the time is right."

"When will that be?" I asked, squirming with anxiety.

"When the ceremony is at its height," Jock said. "We can try then when everybody is distracted. Wait, watch and pray."

I prayed. I prayed harder than I had prayed since I was an abused little girl in the orphanage. I prayed for Peter, and I prayed for myself. I also prayed for Jock, who stood at my side with his hard hand gentle on my shoulder.

"Oh, dear God," I said as I watched the Sidh, the so-called People of Peace, at work around their sacrificial table.

Two of the Sidh lifted Peter's hips while the others unfastened his belt and slipped his trousers down over his legs. They paused for a moment to examine his long white underwear, then folded up his trousers and added them to the growing pile on the other slab.

"I can't move!" I whispered to Jock. "I can't get closer even if the guards were not there!"

"The Sidh have erected a barrier in your mind," Jock replied. "Concentrate! We'll move it together."

I tried, focussing my thoughts on entering that sinister chamber of rock. I could see the barrier in my mind, a shimmering, translucent curtain, impervious to human apprehension. Very well, if the Sidh told me I was partly of their heritage, then I would use that against them.

Tapping into a source I did not understand, I began to ease the barrier away, although I was aware that others were intruding inside my mind, reading my desires. Two of the warriors stirred as my thoughts reached them.

"Careful, Ellen," Jock said. "They can sense us."

The Sidh bent over Peter again as they slowly unfastened

his shirt, one button at a time. Even on the opposite side of the invisible barrier, I felt the Sidh's sudden fear when they exposed Peter's chest, and the rowan cross dangled free on the end of its red cord. The Sidh dropped poor Peter like a sack of seed and stepped back, whistling to each other in consternation.

"The rowan cross is the best protection," Jock murmured.

I barely heard Jock as I focussed my mind on that barrier, so intent on penetrating it that I had no fear of the warriors.

I knew the Sidh's thoughts. The words were not coherent; they only arrived in sensations. I felt them order Peter to tear off his cross and throw it away.

"No, Peter!" I said and saw the warriors jerk their heads towards me. Again, I tried to step forward, to intervene and help Peter until that barrier blocked me. I could only watch, helpless, as the Sidh approached him again.

"You must fight them inside your head," Jock said. "Ready? Try again, you and me together!"

I nodded, gasping as Jock faded away. Four of the Sidh warriors faced me across that barrier, then five, then six, all staring into my face, focussing their power directly at me. Their eyes enlarged until they filled my vision; at first hazel-coloured, the Sidh's eyes darkened by shadows that merged into a black pit that sucked me in. I fell, deeper and deeper into nothingness, unable to resist, unable to even scream.

I fell forever, with time folding, so that Kingsinch, Mr Lunan and Heather Jock were only memories. My existence consisted of falling into that sucking darkness. There was nothing else, no substance and no time in that place of only space and movement.

Who was I?

I tried to stop my descent by asking myself questions.

Where was I?

I was Ellen Luath, orphan, of Elgin in Scotland. I held onto my name as something concrete in this broken world. I told myself that I had not always fallen. I have walked, run, and wandered over the hills. I bit my lip, feeling the sting, tasting the salt blood in my mouth.

"I am Ellen Luath. I am not falling. The Sidh are inside my head, deceiving me. I am standing beside Heather Jock, with young Peter Kinnaird nearby. Peter is lying on a stone slab and needs my help. The Sidh are manipulating my mind."

I heard my words without believing them. I was not me; I was the little sobbing orphan with no hope. I was the ragged wanderer huddling in a shop doorway as the winter sleet bounced off the pavement. I was everybody I had ever met, for we take a small piece of everyone with us and carry it inside our mind.

I am Ellen Luath.

I am Ellen Luath, and all else is an illusion. The dark hole is chimerical; the barrier is an illusion.

Dear God, help me separate reality from the contrived.

Despite my words and prayers, I continued to fall. Something was bouncing at my neck, touching my chin. I looked down in irritation and saw the rowan cross, glowing faintly in the dark.

"Go away." I brushed it out of my way, and the touch was like a shock, spinning me end over end in that never-ceasing tunnel. The cross returned, and I grasped it firmly.

The descent ended abruptly, leaving me gasping for breath and shaking with my rowan cross in my hand and the Sidh warriors standing in a line, arrows ready and eyes as unrelenting as any Black Watch soldier in the Boer War.

Jock was cringing on the ground, shivering like a whipped puppy, and whimpering. I knew the Sidh were infesting his mind. I thrust my cross against his forehead, still very aware that the Sidh were staring at me.

"Jock!" I screamed, knowing how deadly the Sidh arrows could be. "Jock! Come back!" His cross lay beside him, just beyond his fingers.

More Sidh arrived. Glittering bronze warriors, they extended into a line, which became a horseshoe of Sidh that moved towards me. Gripping my cross, I continued to press it against Jock's temple, fighting the images the Sidh forced into my head.

I was back in that royal bedroom with all the luxuries a woman could desire at my fingertips. I knew it was false; I forced myself free, feeling the Sidh try to drag me back to that place of false peace and tasteless feasting.

"Jock!" I shouted. "Come back to me! Please! I need you."

I did not know if I saw the real faces of the Sidh, or if they distorted my vision. They had seemed so friendly earlier, but now the Sidh were ferocious, their faces triangular, snarling, with rows of sharp teeth, pointing inward like the sharks I had seen in a picture.

That was it; I was dredging that image from my mind. Or rather, the Sidh were hauling it out and imposing it on my present consciousness as their advance continued to the invisible barrier, where they halted.

"Jock!" I pushed my cross against his forehead. I smelled burning flesh and saw smoke rising from Jock's skin.

"Oh, dear God!" I removed the cross and Jock screamed, falling flat on the ground. There was no mark on his forehead.

"You deceived me!" I shouted to the Sidh and thrust my cross in the very centre of Jock's head, between his eyes, and I began to pray.

I have never been good at prayers. Miss Deas taught us the Lord's Prayer, with her belt always waiting for those of us who forgot a word, or who did not pray hard enough or prayed too hard. After that, there was the obligatory Sunday service when the respectable people reminded us how fortunate we were and drummed home how grateful we should be for our benefactors in the orphanage. That version of Christianity left me with a gaping hole in my soul, unable to reconcile the Biblical God of Love with the smug faces of churchgoers.

Now I realised the reality was much different. There was a constant struggle between Good and Evil, with the Word the most potent weapon one could wield. In my opinion, the Church establishment corrupted the Word, rather than enhancing the Bible's message.

I prayed harder than I had ever prayed in my life, and although the Sidh tried to interfere by pushing images inside my head, I found the words. They were simple.

"Oh, Lord," I said. "Help me to help this man. Use the cross as a conduit of your Word."

I felt the surge in the rowan cross, and saw Jock start, as though some new energy had entered his body.

"Ellen?" Jock lay on the ground, drenched with sweat and his eyes dazed. "How long?" He looked around him.

"Not long." I prodded him with the toe of my boot. "Get up, Jock. Look!"

Jock pushed himself upright, still swaying. "Is that Peter?"

The Sidh had stripped Peter stark naked and spread-eagled him face up on the stone slab. Half a dozen female Sidh stood around him, chanting something I could not understand.

"Peter!" I shrieked.

"He can't hear you," Jock said. "He's away in another place."

I prayed again, and this time the barrier wavered. It appeared like semi-opaque glass, rainbow-striped in bands of green, yellow, and gold. I pushed forward, stepping into the false glass, feeling it give before me.

The chanting increased, and we were inside the stone cavern, with Peter in the centre on his table, and the Sidh gathered around, rank after rank of them, a sea of watching faces and moving mouths.

I could not move. The Sidh's words transfixed me so I could only watch. I do not know why the Sidh sacrificed Peter, and I do not know the name or nature of the god he died to placate. I only know the Sidh killed him slowly, carving him up piece by piece as the crowd chanted and we watched, unable to interfere.

It took a long time for Peter to die. I think a little piece of me died with him, and when the last of the blood had flowed from the stone table, the Sidh, the so-called People of Peace gradually moved away to return to whatever underground homes they inhabited. Only then did I see two of them holding Agnes's baby in their arms.

CHAPTER 25

THE ROAR CAME from behind me. I had all but forgotten Mr
Lunan, Dougie, and Agnes in the few minutes, or was it a few
hours – since we had left them. I do not know how they found
their way through the nightmare of passages to reach us.

"The rowan crosses woke them," Jock said.

Now Mr Lunan led a mad, suicidal charge against the gathered Sidh. Mr Lunan fired his shotgun, blasting two of the Sidh
into a mass of blood and bone, fired the second barrel and ran
forward. Dougie was at his side, brandishing his pike like a hero
of old.

"Agnes! No!" I shouted as Agnes followed, screaming, and
waving her arms in the air.

The Sidh warriors gave way, stepping back, and then the
arrows began. Each one was small, too light to kill a man
through his clothing, but there were so many that the cumula-
tive effect was deadly.

I saw Dougie slash sideways with his pike, felling two of the
Sidh, and then an arrow slammed into his groin. I winced at the

expression on Dougie's face as he clutched at himself. A second arrow joined the first, pinning Dougie's hand to his inner thigh. He fell to his knees, gagging, the handsome first horseman who could never pleasure a woman again. The Sidh warriors took their time, aiming their light arrows where they pleased as they killed Dougie slowly, aiming at his groin, his eyes, and his mouth.

Eventually, after terrible suffering, Dougie died. I think he would have been glad to die.

While the Sidh killed Dougie, Mr Lunan had stopped his crazy charge, with Agnes at his side.

"They've got back inside his head," Jock said as Mr Lunan stood there, eyes staring at nothing.

"Oh, dear Lord," I whispered as two Sidh stepped up to Mr Lunan. "What are they going to do to him?"

Jock touched my hand "Don't move," he said.

I could not move. I could only watch as the Sidh stepped beside Mr Lunan, with one taking hold of each arm. Mr Lunan's expression altered as he smiled. I could feel his pleasure, and then I was inside his head.

Mr Lunan held out his hands to the woman I had seen as his first wife. Both were smiling as the first Mrs Lunan held a baby. There was no violence, nothing but love between wife and husband.

"The Sidh have reunited the family," I said.

"Aye, they have," Jock said.

"It's all Mr Lunan wanted," I said, "to have his wife and child back. Will he know that he's down here?"

Jock shook his head, wordless.

I could sense the happiness as Mr Lunan walked away with his family, and then only Agnes remained, staring into the abyss.

The Sidh woman I had rescued stepped up to Agnes,

holding Baby Robert in her hand. As I watched, she placed the baby in Agnes's arms.

"Are they trapped here, in Elfhame?" I asked.

"Trapped, yet happy," Jock said. "Mr Lunan has his first wife and daughter back. He only lost his second wife, a carping woman who cheated on him, and a lifetime of toil. Is that such a bad exchange? And what would Agnes's life have been like in the upper world, our world?"

For an instant, I saw Agnes's future. I saw Andrew in a khaki uniform, dying in a maelstrom of horror at a place called Ypres. I saw an aftermath of poverty and depression, with two ragged, barefoot children in some urban slum. Yet I remembered Peter's hideous death down here, and the cruelty beneath the deceit.

As I foresaw Agnes's potential future, the Sidh surrounded us, keeping at a distance.

"I think it's our turn next," I said.

"They sacrifice virgins." Jock gave a twisted smile. "That leaves me out. Are you a virgin?"

I remembered the orphanage in Elgin, and the brutal, probing fingers. I had tried to block that memory from my mind, with the even more brutal aftermath as Mr Snodgrass forced himself inside me. Now I remembered every last hideous, sordid detail.

"No," I said, sickened by the thought that any man could do such a thing to a child. "And the Sidh already found that out."

Jock gave me a small, knowing smile. "The Sidh won't sacrifice us." He sighed, holding his cross tightly. "How was your life before Kingsinch?"

I frowned. "It might have been better," I said.

"Bad?" Jock asked.

"Bad," I agreed.

"If you allow the Sidh into your mind," Jock said, "there will be no more bad times."

I thought of the music, dancing, and friendship the Sidh offered and the hardship and loneliness of reality.

"It's false though," I said.

"You won't realise that it's false." Jock reminded.

I wondered if Jock had decided to remain in Elfhame. "I intend returning to reality," I said, "but I don't want to leave Agnes and Baby Robert here."

Jock scraped his foot along the ground. "Have you read the newspapers recently? Have you heard of a place called Magersfontein?"

"There was a battle there." I did not know the details.

"There was," Jock said. "Hundreds of men were killed or maimed. That was one battle in a war between Great Britain and two small republics in South Africa. There will be other battles, and hundreds of thousands more men will be killed and maimed. That's human sacrifice for the worship of money or a flag. Do you want Agnes's baby to grow up in such a world?"

"The war will be over before Baby Robert is old enough to fight."

"There will be another, and another after that," Jock said. "What's better for the baby, living with these Sidh? Or marching to war for the benefit of men who despise him?"

The stark reality of Jock's words stung me. I had never met a man with such a point of view. I remembered my life of hardship, pain, deceit, and fear, and thought of the vision the Sidh had shared with me. Which was better? Dear God, what was wrong with this world if I preferred a false image to reality?

"How about Agnes?"

"The Sidh will accept her if she wishes to remain with her baby, which she will," Jock said.

I knew that was true. Agnes would remain with the Sidh, who looked after their own.

"The question is," Jock asked urgently as the Sidh slid closer. "What do we want to do? Remain here? Or return to the surface?"

I thought of the struggle of life on the surface, and how easy it would be to remain with the Sidh and accept the semi-dream state in which they seemed to exist. A lifetime of parties, of music and laughter and friendship, beckoned.

"We? What do we want to do?"

Jock nodded. "After what we've been through, Ellen, I think we should stick together."

My heart rate began to increase. With a true friend by my side, I could cope with the surface. I remembered the sergeant and his loving wife, the old soldier and his dog, and Cathy and the farm gang. They were as much part of the surface as Miss Deas, Mr Snodgrass, and the shepherd woman.

"Together?" I sought confirmation.

"Together." Jock looked at me through his tangle of hair. His eyes were dark brown, flecked with the hazel of the Sidh, and filled with some emotion I could barely recognise. I started; Ma had the same look.

"How do we get back to reality?"

"Hold your cross in your right hand and follow me." Jock took hold of my left hand.

I did as Jock said, feeling the warmth of his lean, muscular body as we marched towards the Sidh with our rowan crosses held firmly in our hands.

When we got close, I saw the smiling Sidh man with the birthmark on his face, and on one side was Agnes, holding her baby and looking serenely happy. On the other side, Mhairi from Skye lifted a small hand in greeting and the matriarchal

Sidh woman held out her hands in supplication, pleading for me to remain.

"Wait," I said, "I've changed my mind," but it was too late.

One moment we were walking in that underground corridor, and the next we were in the open, with terrible wheeled monsters roaring past us and a smell as sickening as anything I had ever experienced before.

"Oh, dear God in heaven!" I shouted. "Where are we?"

CHAPTER 26

"THEY'RE COMPLETELY MAD, of course; both of them."

I heard the voices from the room next door as we huddled over our mugs of hot, sweet tea. I looked at Jock, who sat opposite, holding a grey blanket over his shoulders.

"I mean," the voice continued, "wandering along the road in ragged old clothes mumbling about something called the Shee and talking about a farm called Kingsinch."

I sipped my tea, finding it insipid, lacking flavour, far too weak. Strange furniture filled the room, and the light above was very bright, from some artificial source more outlandish than anything the Sidh had produced. Garish posters covered the wall, with pictures of clean-faced men and women in smart blue uniforms.

"Are you all right, Jock?"

Jock nodded, "Aye, I'm all right." He smiled to me from under his tangle of dark brown hair. "It's best not to tell them too much," he said. "We don't know when we are, or what's happened since we were..." He paused, "down there."

The voices sounded from next door again, a man and a

woman talking together. The woman laughed deep throated. "The woman said her name was Ellen Luath, and she had been with the Shee for days. Did you see the clothes she was wearing? And she nearly had a fit when we took her into the patrol car."

The man's voice was more resonant. "It was if she's never seen a car before."

"Or anything else," the woman said. "She said she lived at Kingsinch. That place was abandoned over a hundred years ago after a big flood. All the people drowned trying to cross the Kings Moss."

"Weirdos," the man said. "We'll get the doctor to look at them and let them go."

I tried to hear more, but some mechanical jangle interrupted me. Instead, I looked around the room. "There's a calendar on the wall," I said.

Jock put down his mug and stepped across. "It's 2021," he said. "We were 122 years down there." He shrugged off the blanket. "It was 100 years last time I was in Elfhame."

I stared at him. "Everything will be changed." I shuddered, unable to comprehend the passage of time. "How old are you, Jock?"

Jock smiled. "I was born in 1750, I think. Come on, let's go. I'm sure we can poach in this century as well as we could in the nineteenth, or eighteenth."

I nodded and followed Jock. Whatever the future held, I had somebody I could trust. Maybe in this century, I could discover who I was, or why I was here. As I watched Jock stride in front of me, I smiled; suddenly, my antecedents were less important than my future.

GLOSSARY

A'body – everybody
Auld – old
Ayeways - always
Bannock – a round, flat cake, often flavoured with raisins.
Bairn - child
Biggin or bigging – building
Bogle – ghosts; things that go bump in the night
Bothy – a small building, in the context of the book, a building in which the unmarried farm workers live
Bothy-lads – the men and boys who live in the bothy
Brae, braes – hills, hillsides
Braw – good, fine
Brose – oatmeal mixed with boiling water, occasionally with salt or butter added.
Byre – barn in which cattle are kept
Cannae – can nae – can not
Canny – cautious, careful; to be not canny could also mean to be a bit silly, or strange
Couldnae- could not

Corbie – crow – a bird of ill omen

Dinnae – do not

Douce – sedate, respectable

Doup – the buttocks

Dreich - dreary

Drystane dyke – wall built of loose stones, often taken from the field when reclaiming the field from wasteland

Dub – a pool of water

Eildit - elderly

Fail dyke – wall of turf alongside fields

Farm toun – literally, farm town, but usually meaning the farm house and surrounding buildings.

Feared - scared

Frae - from

Gey – very, extremely

Guddle – catch fish with one's hands

Hairst - harvest

Halflin – lowest man in the bothy-boys, often a young boy learning to be a man.

Hindmost – the furthest behind, the last.

Hoor – whore, prostitute

Horseman – ploughman

Howe – a depression in the ground

Inch – island

Ken – know, often used as a suffix. The word is from Kenow, the same Anglo-Saxon root as know.

Kent – knew

Kirk – the Church of Scotland; Free Kirk is the Free Church of Scotland (not established)

Kye – cattle

Larick – larch tree

Loon – young man

Lowsed – finished work for the day

Moss – area of wet moorland

Muckle – large

Paythan – ill educated pronunciation of the Pashtun people of North West Pakistan

Pict, Pictish – people who inhabited much of Scotland in the Dark Ages and before. They left a legacy of beautiful carved stonework.

Puir – poor

Quine- woman

Quinie – girl

Rickle – heap, pile, or an old ramshackle building

Rowan – mountain ash; supposed to give protection against supernatural agencies.

Saft - soft

Sidh – pronounced Shee – the fairies

Skelp – could mean a slap, or a section or piece

Soughin – the shush of the wind

Steading – farm

Stoorey-foot – country person, an outsider to the community, an incomer or traveller

Swank – agile, lithe, strong

Strathmore – the shallow valley between the Sidlaw Hills and the Grampian mountains in eastern Scotland

The morn – tomorrow morning

Thigging - begging

Tryst – arranged meeting

Teuchter – somebody from the north, a disparaging term for a highlander or country person

Whaup – curlew

Wasnae- was not

Yett – gate, but in the context of the book, also a road or route

NOTES

I only know of one Suicide's Graveyard in Scotland, although there may well be others. The one with which I am familiar is near Ardoch Fort in Perthshire, on the parish boundary with Muthill. It is a small area of unhallowed ground, for the church would not bury suicides in consecrated ground.

The Sidh, or People of Peace, or fairies, seem to have existed in folklore and mythology for centuries. There are hundreds of fairy stories the length and breadth of Scotland and many theories about their origin.

One of the most plausible theories suggests that the Sidh might be the people who inhabited Scotland before the Celts arrived, a pre-iron-age culture who the Celts pushed to the marginal lands. From there, the Sidh would raid the Celtic invaders, kill their cattle, and perhaps steal their babies. The Sidh would have become masters of guerrilla warfare and camouflage, so might be thought to appear and disappear at will.

The Sidlaw Hills are a low range to the north of Dundee. By Scottish standards, they are not spectacular, but they do boast many legends of the Sidh. Some of the stories, including one set at Carlungie earth-house near an old Pictish site, include the abduction of a wife. Other Sidh sites include the Eildon Hills in the Borders, Calton hill in Edinburgh, Tomnahurich in Inverness, the Fairy Bridge in Skye, and Schiehallion in Perthshire.

Glen Lyon in Perthshire has one interesting twist to the legends, for here is the Sithean Tom na Cloin, or the Children's Fairy Hill. According to Archie McKerracher in his *Perthshire in History and Legend*, unbaptised children were buried here, "for the fairies to take away."

There are many glens called Glen Shee (of various spellings) in Scotland. I camped in one such glen in the Island of Arran, near to an ancient Standing Stone – but I neither heard nor saw anything supernatural. The midges were savage, however, and could have scared away anything.

I took the idea of the Sidh using human ribs for bows from one of their sites on the Island of Skye. After a clan battle in Harta Corrie, near Loch Coruisk, the victorious MacDonalds buried the corpses of the defeated MacLeods at a place called the Bloody Stone. The Skye Sidh were said to use the ribs of the MacLeods for their bows, or perhaps their arrows. It seemed too gruesome a story not to use. (I found that little piece in Jack Strange's *More Strange Scotland*.)

When people in old Scotland found flint arrowheads from the Stone Age, they believed they were from the Sidh and called them elsfshot, or elf-bolt. In Gaelic, they were *saighead shith,* and anyone finding them was assured of good luck. My great-grandfather, who collected historical curiosities, kept a couple in an old Victorian snuffbox, but sadly, somebody stole them.

Two books about Meigle, *Our Meigle Book* and *Meigle, Past and Present*, both mention the Sidh. The former states that

Meigle people believed that the fairies would carry babies and young girls to "their caverns or underground houses". The latter book claimed that "men in this district have cohabited with females of the fairy race." It may be significant that Meigle, in Perthshire, was also a Pictish centre, with a fascinating museum of Pictish carved stones, and the reputed grave of Guinevere, King Arthur's unfaithful wife. There are other Arthurian tales in the area.

The slightly-off-putting idea of dogs being reared on Sidh milk to help them hunt the Sidh, I adapted from an old legend that the Campbells of Persie had a pack of black hounds that had been reared on milk from MacGregor women to help hunt the Children of the Mist.

Heather Jock is a reasonably well-kent character in Scottish folklore and seems to be a name given to any wild young man on society's fringes. There is at least one ballad that describes one such lad:

"*Heather Jock was stark and grim,*

Faught wi aa wad fecht wi him; (fought with all who'd fight with him)

Swank and supple, sharp and thin,

Fine for gaun agin the win'." (Going against the wind – breaking the law.)

Elfhame was the Lowland Scots name for the supposed home of the Sidh, fairyland if the reader prefers.

The use of rowan wood against dark forces is well-known in Scotland. Rowan trees are often found growing near ancient settlements, and once women would wear necklaces of rowan berries as protection. The old folk used twigs of rowan or iron horseshoes to fend off the Sidh, and farmers placed them above the doors of barns and byres. In one house I lived in, up in Moray, the previous occupant had placed horseshoes over the front door, back door and garden shed, with a rowan tree prominent in the garden. Was that merely tradition? Or a folk memory of an earlier time when people shut their door against the dark and hoped not to hear the whistling voices of the Sidh.

If the Scottish Sidh are of interest, I would recommend Robert Kirk's classic *The Secret Commonwealth of Elves, Fauns and Fairies*, particularly as Kirk allegedly entered the realm of the Sidh and may still be there. It was a passage in this book that gave me the idea for the whistling: "They speak but little and that by way of whistling, clear, not rough." Kirk also said, "They live much longer than we," which ties in with the stories of mortals spending one night in their company yet ageing a hundred years in our time. Kirk's book also says the Sidh's "bodies be so pliable through the subtlety of the spirits ... that they can make them appear or disappear at pleasure," which is a power I adapted to suit my story.

Marian McNeill's *The Silver Bough* also has a comprehensive chapter on the same subject, and it from her writing that I gleaned the idea of the human sacrifice every seven years.

Helen Susan Swift.

Dundee, looking out to the Sidlaw Hills,

January 2021

Dear reader,

We hope you enjoyed reading *Whistlers of the Dark*. Please take a moment to leave a review, even if it's a short one. Your opinion is important to us.

Discover more books by Helen Susan Swift at
https://www.nextchapter.pub/authors/helen-susan-swift

Want to know when one of our books is free or discounted? Join the newsletter at
http://eepurl.com/bqqB3H

Best regards,

Helen Susan Swift and the Next Chapter Team

Printed in Great Britain
by Amazon